TWO TOES

Two Toes

The Coyote Legend of Green River

▲ ▲ ▲

The Black Rock Press
University of Nevada, Reno
1998

▲ ▲ ▲

by Preston Q. Hale

Illustrations by Pam McAdoo

Printed in the United States of America

ISBN 1-891033-13-1

The Black Rock Press
University Library/322
University of Nevada, Reno
Reno, NV 89557-0044

Cover illustration by Pam McAdoo

The publication of this book was supported
by a grant from the John Ben Snow Trust

This book is dedicated to our son, Robert Q., who was my hunting and fishing partner from the time he was five years old. He was an advocate for preservation of our wildlife and a serious student of Western Americana. We had many discussions on the problems of the development of theWest and the clashes over the treatment and survival of our wildlife populations. He was a true sportsman.

CONTENTS

▲   ▲   ▲

AUTHOR'S NOTE

▲ ▲ ▲

OVER THE YEARS, friends and associates have often asked me questions about wildlife, knowing I once was a biologist with the U.S. Fish & Wildlife Service. The most frequent questions, especially from those who knew I had been involved in trapping predators, have been about coyotes. And whenever this has led to any kind of deep discussion, I've always told about the coyote we called Two Toes.

The response has usually been the same: I ought to write a book about him. This suggestion has come not only around campfires on fishing or hunting trips, but in boardrooms or after business meetings. I even had three directors on our bank board tell me so at lunch one day. I guess I understand why.

The coyote, *Canis latrans*, is a very popular animal in the United States. People in cities and rural areas across the West know what a coyote is and are interested in him. The coyote was revered in the American Indian world, lore about him passed down by the tribes for centuries, and a great deal of mystique continues to surround the species. He is wholly entwined in the history of the American West. Farmers, ranchers—anyone who's worked or slept outdoors outside the cities and towns of the West—has likely heard the coyote's howl at night. It stirs the imagination—which can run wild.

So it was with Two Toes.

It was in 1939 through 1941 that sheep ranchers in northeastern Utah were beset by the wily depredations of the coyote they came to call by this name, because of the telltale imprint of his right-front paw missing its middle two toes.

In 1939, I was working in a Civilian Conservation Corps camp in Vernal, Utah, supervising crews poisoning prairie dogs, kangaroo rats and jackrabbits, when the district agent for Utah asked me to take the civil-service examinations for the U.S. Biological Survey—a predecessor of the U.S. Fish & Wildlife Service. I passed the exams, and in 1940, I was made a junior biological aide. The job meant controlling rodents and predators that attacked crops and livestock in the state of Utah, and it included trapping coyotes. Until 1951, that's what I did, first in Utah, then in Wyoming and finally Nevada.

The year I became a junior biological aide, I was transferred to Salt Lake City, the district headquarters. My boss immediately put me out with some of the top government trappers to learn all I could about trapping and denning coyotes and taking bobcats, mountain lions and bears. Over the years I spent in the wild, I came to realize that the coyote is the smartest creature on four legs. Sheepmen still think this today. The coyote is the only predator whose territory has actually increased with the encroachment of man.

The coyote was hunted unmercifully in the 20th century, especially during World War II when food and fiber were vital to the war effort and the nation's welfare. Like the wolf, his larger cousin, the coyote constitutes a stalwart obstacle to man's efforts at livestocking. But unlike the wolf, now an endangered species in the lower 48, the coyote has proved fiercely resilient. In spite of continued efforts through the ensuing decades to control him through trapping, unrestricted hunting, poisoning and even shooting him from airplanes, the coyote is more numerous today than a century ago.

It was in 1941 and 1942 that I worked with one of my government trappers in trying to get Two Toes.

I can think of many individual coyotes I've dealt with in my life, but Two Toes topped them all.

ACKNOWLEDGMENTS

▲ ▲ ▲

I am deeply indebted to Mike Sion, who helped to edit this book. He brought order to my manuscript which was filled with too much description and repetition, hopefully making *Toe Toes* a straightforward story of the conflict between the live-stock man and the predatgor, the coyote.

I am also deeply indebted to Bob Laxalt, one of Nevada's truly great writers. As a boy, he worked with his father, a noted sheepman in western Nevada, helping to handle the family sheep business. When I told him about the book I was writing, he said, "No one really understands the serious conflict between the sheepman and the coyote—you've got to write that book." He was constantly checking my progress and giving me invaluable suggestions. After he read the manuscript, he remarked, "Don't make too big a hero out of Toe Toes—remember, he killed sheep."

Sessions S. "Buck" Wheeler, Nevada writer and longtime director of the Nevada Fish and Game Commission said, "This is one of the best descriptions of the life of a coyote I've ever read—it pulls no punches.

I also want to thank Nevadans Bill Bliss, Roger Newton, Rollan Melton, and the late Mark Curtis for their encouragement, comments and support.

Pam McAdoo's cover painting and drawings are a tremendous asset to the book. This talented artist worked long and hard to make sure the illustrations reflected true accuracy and aesthetic value.

Thanks to Paul Starrs, professor of Geography at the University of Nevada, Reno for his outstanding maps of northeastern Utah and the country where the story takes place.

Final thanks goes to the John Ben Snow Trust and its Nevada board member, Rollan Melton, for granting funds to the Black Rock Press to make the publication of this book possible.

INTRODUCTION

▲ ▲ ▲

THE HIGH UINTAH MOUNTAINS, the longest east-west chain in North America, cut across northern Utah like a granite spine. Starting east of Salt Lake City, they run deep into Colorado, their snow-capped peaks rising close to 14,000 feet. Through them, severing the chain in two, the Green River flows, rushing through the vast Flaming Gorge Canyon its waters have carved since the end of the Ice Age.

The Green River raises in the Wind River Mountains of Wyoming and flows across the sagebrush-strewn Red Desert. It hits the foothills at the Wyoming line, then turns east to bore through the High Uintahs. Then it turns south again, passing the dinosaur skeletons preserved in the silt over centuries that have washed the granite ledges away.

The Green River leaves the range near where the Yampa River enters the basin from Colorado, joining it. Farther south, the Uintah and the Duchesne empty into the Green from the west as does the White from the east. Then the Green enters high desert again. Its next impediment is the Book Cliff Mountains, which are not nearly so high as the Uintahs, then Green River continues on through the most desolate territory in the United States—canyon-riddled badlands. Above Moab, Utah, it is met by what was called in my day the Grand River but is now referred to as the Colorado, and the two become the Colorado, which runs on through Desolation and Marble canyons, down through the Grand Canyon to Boulder Dam.

For most of its life, the Green River has flowed when the continent west of the Mississippi was a vast expanse of unexplored

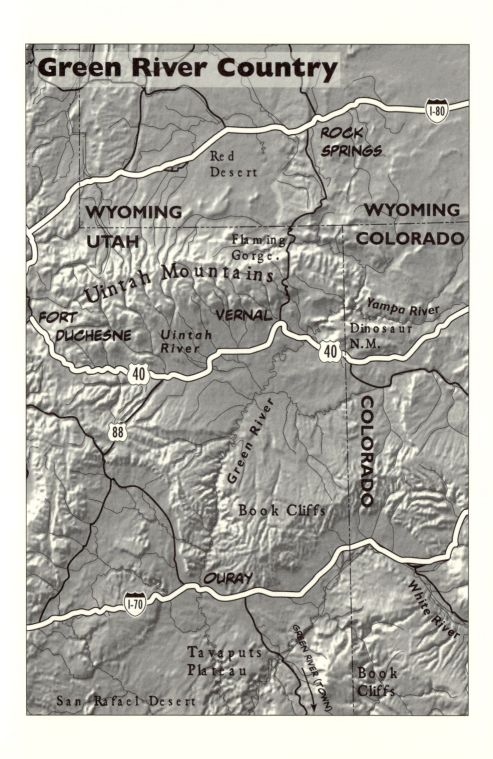

Green River Country

land, a breathtaking virgin continent of seemingly endless prairies, some that were seas of grass for the thundering buffalo herds. It flowed when mountains were covered with forests of pine, fir, cedar, juniper and aspen; when valleys were lush with grazing grasses; and when lakes, rivers and streams were alive with ducks, geese, swan and trout. It flowed when buffalo, antelope, prairie chicken and sagehen roamed the prairies in vast numbers; when deer, elk, moose and grouse filled the woods; when grizzly and black bear, bobcat and mountain lion, wolf, coyote and fox preyed on the abundant game.

The Green River and its tributaries flowed when Lewis & Clark returned from their 1804-5 exploration of the Louisiana Territory full of reports of an astoundingly rich and plentiful land. It flowed when tales of mountain men and trappers whetted the lust of easterners to go west. It flowed when the flood gates for Manifest Destiny opened after the Mormon exodus to Utah in 1847 and the California Gold Rush of '49. It flowed when settlements, villages and towns linked a chain along the Pacific Coast, and when mining begat more outposts of civilization that grew into towns and cities across the West, marking the spots where millions of tons of ore were hauled from the Earth.

The Green River flowed as placer and hydraulic mining contaminated rivers and streams with arsenic, mercury and a host of other toxic minerals and chemicals. It flowed as forests were clear-cut of timber until mountainsides were bare of trees; as the West was "won" in a spirit of take what you want, the resources seemingly inexhaustible. It flowed as the U.S. Army and Cavalry cut down the American Indian, overwhelmed him with numbers on the battlefield and let disease and starvation do the rest, until his tribes dwindled and way of life was forever destroyed. It flowed as the buffalo was hunted to near-extermination for his meat and hides, and because it was a way to starve the Indian into final submission.

The lands around it changed, but the ancient river ran on.

The Green River flowed as the railroads laid tracks across the vast terrain to connect a continent, and as the great cattle drives began from Texas through the wide-open range up to shipping points in Kansas. It flowed as year after year the cattlemen and sheepmen let their flocks and herds devour what they would on the range, with little thought of preserving grasses and browse for another year, in what seemed a never-ending Eden.

The Green River flowed as little herds of cows and small bands of sheep were loaded on Union Pacific Railroad cars by farmers in Iowa and Missouri and shipped off in spring in the care of hardy herders to remote rail points in Wyoming—to footholds in the wilderness that were old Indian villages or mountain men trading posts. There, the livestock would graze from one camp to another on the prairie until late summer, when they would be driven back to the loading point and returned to their Midwest farms. It flowed as the flocks multiplied, until great herds and bands were returning each year to the grass-rich prairies of the West.

The Green River flowed as good land grew scarce in the face of the livestock invasion, as overgrazing killed off lush feed, cheat grass and foxtail choked out the high-protein grasses that sheep and cattle need, and more toxic weeds, the hardy Russian halogeton whose juice is fatal to sheep and the loco weed that drives horses crazy spread on the unmanaged range. It flowed as spring snow runoff and heavy rains and flash floods eroded topsoil on millions of acres of land, filling rivers and lakes with mud and silt.

The Green River flowed as the century turned into the 20th and sheepmen and cattlemen, now entrenched on the range, zealously guarded their herds against nature's predators, posting bounties and using guns, traps, snares and strychnine-poisoned baits. It flowed as the mighty grizzly was decimated, and the proud wolf, standing his ground in the face of the human onslaught, was nearly exterminated in the West.

The Green River flowed as the federal government took charge of preserving the wilderness for ranching following World War I. It flowed as the U.S. Biological Survey took over control of rodents and predators and made hunters and trappers full-time employees. It flowed as they poisoned prairie dogs, ground squirrels, marmots and jackrabbits because they competed with grazing animals for the precious green feed. It flowed as the government hunters used cyanide guns and the synthetic poison 1080 against bobcats and coyotes because they preyed on the sheep and cattle of the large ranching concerns that now grazed the deserts in the winter and the mountain meadows in the summer with livestock driven on well-worn trails.

The Green River flowed on as the Uintah Basin in northeastern Utah and northwestern Colorado became great ranching country, home to thousands of cattle and hundreds of thousands of sheep. It flowed past the heart of the basin, Ashley Valley, named for the fur trader and mountain man William Ashley, whose exploits helped open the region to the white man.

And it is there, near Ashley Valley, beneath the snow-capped High Uintahs, where our story begins.

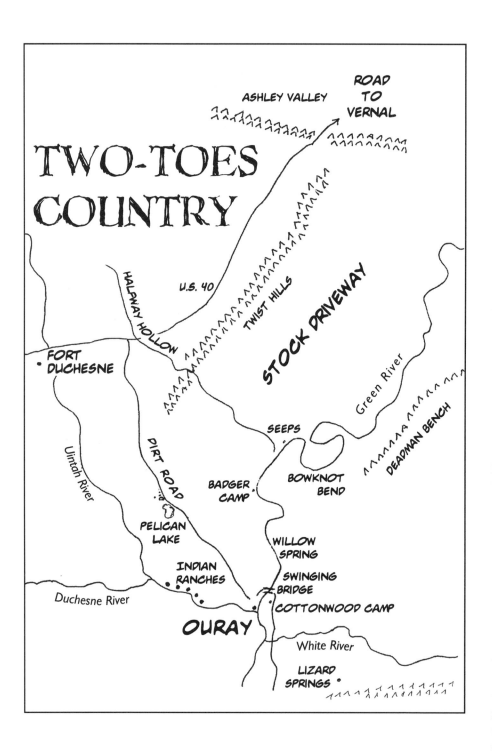

TWO-TOES COUNTRY

ROAD TO VERNAL

ASHLEY VALLEY

U.S. 40

HALFWAY HOLLOW

TWIST HILLS

STOCK DRIVEWAY

FORT DUCHESNE

Green River

DEADMAN BENCH

SEEPS

Uintah River

PIRT ROAD

BADGER CAMP

BOWKNOT BEND

PELICAN LAKE

WILLOW SPRING

INDIAN RANCHES

SWINGING BRIDGE

Duchesne River

COTTONWOOD CAMP

OURAY

White River

LIZARD SPRINGS

▲ ▲ ▲

ONE

Billy Butts

BILLY BUTTS woke before dawn from an old dream of confinement, one he'd not suffered in months and months, then was immediately reassured by his surroundings. The wool blankets were pulled up to his chin, and as he lay in bed the square outlines of the Dutch door slowly emerged, its top and bottom panels shut fast against the mid-March chill.

The sheepherder threw the covers back from the bed, swung his legs over the side and dropped down in his longjohns to the cold linoleum floor of the sheep wagon. He pushed open the top of the door and peered into the black. He could see nothing, but could smell the grassy valley air and hear faint stirrings of sheep on the bed ground in the deathly silence. Somewhere, a ewe coughed from cheat grass stuck in her throat, and another bleated. The two shelty sheep dogs, instantly awake and alert under the wagon, remained undisturbed.

For two weeks, Billy Butts had been driving the herd of more than 800 bred ewes north, coming off the winter range on the vast Uintah Desert toward the lambing grounds near the home ranch in Ashley Valley. It was a late spring, and the Green River would be low and clear. The big snow-melt runoff from the high peaks of the Uintahs would not come for nearly a month. Even half-awake, Billy Butts felt the urgency.

The grama, fescue, buffalo and curly grasses would be scanty for the sheep once they crossed the swinging bridge near Ouray and grazed up the posted stock driveway along the foot of the Twist

Hills that lay to the west. Billy Butts wanted to be one of the first to cross the river. There were other herds on the move, and this year most had started trailing for home about the same time. The feed would be nearly gone when the seventh or eighth outfit made it over the swinging bridge.

The rule of the trail was constant motion. Billy Butts would move camp every five to ten days, always pushing a few miles farther north and closer to home. He knew every hill, cliff, ledge and spring running toward the river. He knew every campsite— carefully selected for water for the sheep, wood supply and a good high and dry bed ground for the herd at night.

At each new camp Billy Butts would move the sheep off the bed ground in the early morning, grazing them out a little farther each day until it took sunup to dark to get them back. He knew from experience when to tell the camp tender to return. The tender would come with his pickup full of supplies—firewood, cans of tomatoes, fruit and milk, sugar and salt, coffee and flour, bacon and eggs, mail, magazines and newspapers—hitch up the sheep wagon and they'd move to the next site.

Billy Butts shut the Dutch door against the biting chill. Fully awake now, he lit a fire in the wood stove and hoisted the bucket of water to fill the coffee pot and kettle. Then, with the routine of ritual, he laid out a straight-edge razor, bar of soap and towel. As the water boiled, he made his coffee, then poured warm water in the wash pan on the bench. He washed his hands and face and lathered his deeply tanned cheeks and chin to shave.

At 45, Billy Butts' brown hair was flecked with gray, his frame just shy of six feet was wiry and slender. But in one way he didn't resemble most sheepherders. He kept himself clean and clean-shaven. His speech, too, set him apart. Billy Butts' habits and manners were holdovers from a previous life. He'd come from a good family, no doubt. He had been educated. These facts had been readily discerned by rancher Ty Bingham when he hired him.

William Butterman came to Bingham's ranch in 1930, looking for a job. Sitting in the ranch house office, he said he'd been working on a sheep ranch in Texas but hankered to settle in the Rocky Mountain country. Bingham noted the stranger's neatness, correct grammar and clean, if well-worn, clothes. He was dubious.

Ty Bingham was a sheepman and the son of a sheepman. Every herder he'd ever seen was pretty rough. Not many could stand the long days and lonely nights in total solitude, going weeks on end never seeing another human save for the camp tender. It was hard dirty work caring for hundreds of sheep from daylight to dark, and on top of that sheepherders did their own cooking and washing and mended their own clothes.

Bingham asked if Butterman was used to being alone for long periods. The stranger openly smiled.

"If I wasn't I wouldn't be herding sheep," he said.

Bingham knew full well that many sheepherders were crude, callous losers and loners. They couldn't do anything else so they herded sheep. Most had run from something—a marriage, a crime, a battle—and many were drunkards, which was why they weren't allowed any whiskey while out herding sheep. They largely minded this rule, too. They understood if they messed up they'd be kicked back to civilization, where they were failures. Even so, Bingham from time to time had to dig a herder out of the whorehouse or bar the employee had roosted in on the two weeks off a year, hoist him into the pickup and sober him up on the way back to the herd.

In the West, one didn't pry into a stranger's past. But the more he talked to William Butterman, the more Ty Bingham realized this man knew sheep. He began to suspect that Butterman might be the exception to his trade—the sheepherder you met maybe once in a lifetime.

"On the desert in the winter, sometimes we tend to camp only every two weeks," Bingham said. "If we get heavy snows, it could be longer. We keep you supplied with three to four weeks of food in case of emergency."

"I can always eat mutton," Butterman replied, smiling again. "What do you pay and what goes with it?"

"We pay $30 a month, furnish all your food, equipment, your own sheep wagon, horses, sheep dogs, rifle and ammunition. We buy your Levi's, shoes, shirts, socks and underwear. All your work clothes. You buy your own dress clothes and personal belongings. If you get hurt or ill on the job, we pay your doctor bills. If you're off the job or drunk, you're on your own."

Bingham paused, then added, "As long as you do your job well, we'll stand behind you. I won't tolerate laziness, carelessness, lying or drinking. Any of those and you're on your way to town."

"Sounds like an outfit I'd be glad to work for," drawled William Butterman, who neither drank nor smoke.

"Take your bedroll and gear and put them in that sheep wagon by the corral," Bingham said. "You are on the payroll starting now."

That was 11 years ago.

Billy Butts—as his boss christened William Butterman—did his job well. He liked his work. He loved the long days and the solitude. He felt in harmony with nature, a part of its great seasonal cycle.

In the summer the sheep moved to the mountain ranges where the grasses and browse provided strong, nutritious feed. In early September, the herd would be driven back down near the home ranch, where the bucks would be turned in with the ewes. After the fall shipping, new herds would be made up and moved out to the winter range in the deserts and prairies where they would stay in the often bitterly freezing cold until spring, when they would be brought to the home ranch again. That's when the ewes would be dropping their lambs, and would be sheared and branded at the ranch, while the lambs were "docked"—castrated and short-tailed, and, sometimes, ear-marked. Then the herds would be made up again to start for the summer range.

Billy Butts' life moved according to well-worn habits. Before he dressed this day, he flicked on his portable Zenith radio tuned to a Salt Lake City or Denver station for the early news. He'd built a railing of 2-by-4s attached to the posts that held up the curved canvas roof and his clothes hung there from nails. He pulled his jeans and plaid shirt on and his flannel-lined Levi's jacket over that and put on his Stetson. He laced up his boots that had lain by the Winchester carbine that was leaning against the railing at the foot of the bed, where his dog-eared copy of "Call of the Wild" was tucked into the canvas cover.

It was daybreak as he stepped down out of the sheep wagon. A few rosy rays were glinting over the jagged tops of the eastern hills. Billy Butts surveyed the bed ground. It was a sea of white. The rambouillets had a year's coat of wool on them, four to six inches thick. But the heavy pelt of wool couldn't hide the full bellies that held lambs. Butts knew they'd be dropping soon.

If lambs began dropping on the trail, he would be hard-pressed. Newborns slowed the herd down. They were too young to keep up and the ewe wouldn't leave them, so Billy Butts would have to put such a lamb across his saddle. As soon as the herd got back to the bed ground he would get the lamb back to its mother, but sometimes a young ewe wouldn't take it. Then the herder would tie the ewe to a sagebrush so she'd have to let the lamb suck. Often when a ewe dropped twins, she would run one of them off and Butts would go through the same routine for the "bummer" lamb.

If too many ewes started dropping early it would mean 18- to 20-hour days. It would also mean more losses to the coyotes who always followed, though seldom seen, waiting for the ewes or lambs to be separated from the herd.

From his cover of brush, wary of the sheepherder on his horse and his dogs, a coyote would stalk a ewe until he saw his chance. Then he'd run alongside and grab her behind the ears, pinching down to bite the spinal cord or brain, riding her until she fell. When she went down, he'd rip her open and start to feed, sometimes with the ewe still kicking.

A ewe, ready to drop her lamb, standing splay-legged waiting for it to slide out before turning around to nose it to its feet, is easy prey for a coyote. So is an eight-pound lamb, drying off before getting to its feet—so easily bit in two at the vertebrae. And then its remains would lie—head, feet, paunch, guts—for the magpies, crows and hawks, eagles and badgers to feast on until all that was left was a slick, greasy spot with scattered bones and wool. A sheepherder takes note of a flock of crows, magpies or hawks circling low in the morning and alighting at the edge of a wash or on a ledge of rocks. It usually meant a dead sheep.

Billy Butts hoped the ewes would not be dropping too soon this year. They were rising to their feet now. He climbed on his horse and called the shelties, which quickly came.

"Get 'em movin'," Butts said to his dogs. They barked, rousing the flock. Immediately, the woolly, heavy ewes rose and started to move out.

"Turn 'em!" the herder called out, motioning with his hands. The dogs turned the sheep. Butts followed on his horse for a half-hour until the herd slowed to feed on fresh grazing ground. Then he turned back toward the sheep wagon for breakfast.

He paused to gaze for a moment across the river to the horizon. The Twist Hills, rough and rocky and full of gullies, loomed 10 miles away, sandstone knobs dropping to a series of ledges like stairs.

Butts knew as he pushed the sheep along the river in coming weeks that the ledges above would be yellow and crimson, the sandstone and clay covered with scattered cedars and pale green buffalo brush. Beyond the ledges, the plateaus would be painted with the short green-blue grama grass and the shadscale brush, the low-growing green button sage and the prickly pear cactus.

As he rode back to the sheep wagon, the herder heard a distant caw. A flock of crows, their wings wide, had started up from the river. But their images soon faded from his sight and mind.

The coal-black birds flew across the river and toward the Twist Hills, rising past a strange outcropping of rocks above a sandstone ledge. Under it, in the warming sun, lay a large coyote, his senses primed to everything that moved below.

His ears pricked up to hear the crows caw.

TWO

▲ ▲ ▲

Two Toes

T HE DOG COYOTE lay, head resting between forepaws, feeling the sun warm the chill from his matted, winter's fur that was half-shed.

The night before, he'd dug his sleeping spot in the sand on the east side of a giant red and yellow sandstone boulder in an outcropping that centuries before had fallen away from the cliffs and rolled to the head of a plateau. Now, the nest he had curled up in was in the dawn's emerging rays. On nearby brush, the insects were rapidly drying out from their heavy night wet. Soon the silent buffalo gnats, pinpoints of black, swarmed, searching for flesh for their sharp bites. The coyote's cocked ears twitched as a faint cloud of gnats neared his head.

He pawed against his right ear with his right-front foot to scatter the gnats. This was the foot that had given him his name. The two middle toes—pads, nails and all—were missing, torn off in a steel trap before he was a year old.

Like all predators, Two Toes' internal clock was set to sunup and sundown. Presently, the pert prairie dogs would be popping from their holes; the grayish jackrabbits, plump sagehens and beady-eyed, big-whiskered kangaroo rats would be up feeding on grasses from their night security spots. In good time, the coyote would be out hunting them. For now, he lay facing down toward the river, his big ears cocked, now forward, now back, catching every sound.

The language of the hawks, crows and magpies spoke volumes. Two Toes' ears pricked up at the long, loud caws of crows coming across the river from their roosts in cottonwoods down on the bank. They were calls to hunt.

Two Toes' mate was in her den nearby, heavy with pups. The day before, for the first time, she hadn't come out at daybreak to hunt. He'd left his shelter beneath the big boulder and hunted by himself. He'd found a sand hill with fresh kangaroo rat sign and easily dug out a nest. After he'd eaten his kill, he'd hunted for food for his mate. He'd crossed a prairie dog town on the plateau below the boulders and caught a large white-tailed dog that had strayed too far from its hole. Two Toes had brought the prairie dog back and the bitch had come out to eat. Then she'd crawled back in the den and curled up. Her pups were due soon.

Two Toes and the bitch had been running together since late January. He had come into his yearly heat in December, following his nose for the scent of female. He had chased the bitch for several days, until she was fully in heat and stopped fighting him off. Once bred, she immediately took charge. She led Two Toes out hunting, guiding him gradually several miles away toward the denning country where she had been born three years before. Eventually, she found a narrow hole dug a previous season by another bitch in a clay bank a couple feet above a wash. Two Toes' mate had cleaned it out further, making it 10 feet deep so she could easily turn around after having her pups. A mound of dirt now lay outside.

Both coyotes' coats, in transition from winter to summer, resembled worn-out quilts in shades of pale and dark tan, hair hanging in clumps. The bitch's tits were swollen now. Two Toes would continue feeding her after the pups were born until she could again join him after four or five days, teaming up to bring food to the young ones as they weaned. While the pups were weaning, the dog and bitch coyotes would return from the hunt and vomit up food, the pups fighting over it and wolfing it down. They would be ready to stray out of the den after three or four weeks. Then the bitch would begin to teach them to avoid danger and to hunt.

Two Toes, however, would largely ignore the pups. As they grew, they'd nudge and crawl on him as he'd nap but he would growl and snap until they'd leave him alone. He would continue hunting with the bitch until June or July, when the pups would be ready to hunt with her. Soon after, the dog coyote would leave them and go off on his own.

Two Toes knew the terrain of the Twist Hills like he knew his own den. He was from a litter of six pups born to a bitch coyote who had denned only a few miles away and raised her young in this same wild country on the west side of Green River. He knew every hilltop point and saddle, every prominent rocky ledge, every one of the many coyote pissing posts for miles, including across the river where three cow carcasses had lain for more than a year in a field of sagebrush, where the ground was light sand and heavy clay. Two Toes would scratch and piss on the bones to stake his claim; and because he was large and strong, few other coyotes would fight him for the rights should they meet him there.

In this entire territory, Two Toes had no larger member of the wild kingdom to fear. There were no bears or mountain lions, and few bobcats. The only smells that truly spooked him were those of horse and man. Coyotes will fight fiercely among themselves, but otherwise, timidity in the face of a threat is inbred. A coyote will escape harm's way at every opportunity. He relies on his nose, eyes, ears and legs to protect him. So it was with Two Toes.

Like all full-grown coyotes, he was equipped with God-given abilities to endure the struggles of the wild. His black nose could detect the scent of rabbit or deer or a lathered horse's smell carried hundreds of yards on the wind. His gold-flecked eyes with pupils slit crossways could spot movement three miles away. His cocked ears could hear a bird's call even farther. His reflexes were lightning-quick. And he could run full out on the desert flat as fast as a greyhound, fleeing danger full speed.

But like all animals born in the wild, Two Toes had needed more than natural abilities to survive. First, he'd had the great good fortune of being whelped in a den that had escaped the attention of trappers hired to control the coyote population. Second, having survived birth, he'd been given the chance to steadily absorb the lessons of the wild. Both parents were good providers. Coyotes, in fact, are the most efficient parenting mates in the animal kingdom. And neither his dog coyote father nor his bitch coyote mother were killed by the government men.

A few days after her litter was born, Two Toes' mother went out again with her mate to find food. The pair were skilled, deadly hunters. They'd leave the den going in a different direction each day, crisscrossing the flat plateaus and maintaining a good distance from each other to cover more ground. They'd check each bush, rock pile, dirt bank, sand hill and hole, working as a team. If one dug out a kangaroo rat or ground squirrel, the other would wait while its mate ate. If one flushed a white-tailed jackrabbit, it would be a life and death race with the coyote yipping to alert its partner. The second coyote would follow the pursuer and the pursued, cutting across to intercept as the rabbit circled. As one coyote tired, the other would pick up the chase. They'd trade off—and very seldom would the rabbit escape. Then, prey in jaws, the coyotes would head back for the den.

When the pups were newly born, their baby blue eyes not yet opened and before they would begin to venture beyond the crease of light at the front of the den, their parents ate their prey where it was killed. Back at the den, they vomited it up partially digested for their young. After a few weeks, when the pups had developed teeth, the adult coyotes began leaving their kills at the mouth of the den.

The young coyotes soon learned to strip the meat from bone and hide. As they grew older, they roamed farther and farther from the den while the adults were out hunting, and also developed their pecking order from most dominant—the largest pup— down to the most cowering. At times the bitch moved her young to another den some distance away and closer to a new hunting area with more plentiful prey. This also allowed the coyotes to get away from the litter of bones, feathers and fur, wool and their own droppings that attracted fleas, flies and gnats.

When the pups were big enough, they joined their parents in the hunts. They often watched the pair of adults team up and catch a jackrabbit. Soon, they learned how to hunt themselves, which smells meant food, how to dig out mice and squirrels. At about this point, the dog coyote left the litter. But the pups still ran with their mother. The bitch taught them to avoid danger, whipping them away from a porcupine feeding off a succulent clover patch on a wet bank of the river. She showed them to be wary of horse smell and to fear man smell.

One day, the bitch smelled out a sprung trap that had been set for coyotes. She let the pups smell the trap and the scent used by the trapper, then growled and ran the pups off. They learned to flee from the sound of a truck and knew man was an enemy. One day, they were cutting a deer trail when a great, strange, two-headed animal—a smaller animal atop a larger animal—came suddenly out of a deep draw. It was a trapper. He piled off his horse, grabbed his rifle from its scabbard and killed one of the litter and wounded another.

Two Toes never forgot the thunder of the gun and the dying howls of the coyote, the one who had been the dominant pup. Thereafter, he associated the smell of horse and man with great fear.

The bitch and remaining pups continued to hunt together, and might have been mistaken for a pack. By September, the pups were as large as the 35-pound bitch. By October, with winter approaching, their coats were in prime. Two Toes was first to leave the litter and set out on his own. It was shortly after that he learned a bitter lesson and earned his name.

The full-grown pup was cutting around the point of a hill in high brush when he caught a scent he did not recognize. Slowly, he circled the smell until he was fully downwind, then cautiously approached its source. Alongside a clump of creosote brush was a bare spot next to the point of rocks. Under one bush lay sheep bones and hide. The young coyote came forward slowly, his nose picking up the curious odor. It smelled as if other coyotes had been there, pissing and scratching up the ground.

He came closer still and realized the smell was coming from a rotted piece of sheep hide at the foot of the bush. Still careful, sniffing the breeze, the coyote drew up to the piece of sheep hide. He took one step too many. He felt the dirt give under his right-front foot and leaped up. Too late. The jaws of the trap snapped at his foot and clamped tight on his paw.

Only the coyote's caution had kept him from getting his whole foot in the trap. But his first tug at the trap slid the jaws firm and tight behind the pads of his middle two toes. The trap was on a chain eight feet long and fastened to a steel peg driven a foot into the ground. The coyote ran in panic—only to hit the end of the chain and be jerked flat on his back.

Several more times he ran to the end of the chain only to be slapped backward onto the ground. Finally, he lay there panting, pain burning in his right front leg. His foot started to swell and the pain got worse. The young coyote started to circle out at the full length of the chain. At the end, he would claw at the dirt, trying to rid himself of the trap and its terrible pressure. The pain grew so intense that he chewed on the creosote brush. Later, as his foot numbed with the nerves and blood supply closing off, he gnawed on his two toes sticking out from the trap's jaws.

Finally, thirsty and nearly spent, the coyote lay under the shade of the creosote brush, his tongue lolling out the side of his mouth. Several more times he chewed at his toes—only to quit when the fiery pain shot up his leg. The hours passed and his struggles ceased. He realized he was caught, escape was impossible, pain was horrible.

Suddenly, he froze. His ears pricked up at a sound of movement that came from the other side of the rocky point. The sound came closer, then stopped. A little breeze blowing past brought the smell of horse and man. Instantly, the coyote was wild with panic. He could hear the leather squeaking as the man stepped out of the saddle to the ground. Then footsteps were coming his way from around the point.

When the man came in view, the coyote bolted out from under the creosote bush on a dead run, crazed with fear. He hit the end of the trap chain at full speed. The jaws tore off his two middle toes as if cutting them with a knife. Before he'd taken three more jumps, he was gone in the brush, running on three legs.

Two Toes could not touch his right-front foot to the ground for several days; it was too sore. Soon, he was nearly starved. A coyote with only one good front leg cannot catch rabbits or dig out ground squirrels. Two Toes' only food in four days was a young prairie dog that ran right up to him because the coyote was standing beside his hole and the frightened dog, in a panic, ran for it.

Two Toes was weak from hunting continuously, his empty stomach driving him on. Now he was hobbling along an old deer and sheep trail on the river bottom. The trail led through heavy willow patches toward the mouth of a gully that emptied into the river. As he was about to break out of the willows, he suddenly stopped. His keen nose lifted high, sniffing the breeze. A blood smell came from around a large boulder that had fallen from the bank of the wash and lay in his path.

Gingerly, the coyote began to round the boulder. Then he stopped dead still. There, at the foot of the rock, a raven was picking a freshly killed rabbit. The jack had been caught in a coyote trap and, exhausted, proved an easy kill for the carrion bird. Catching sight of Two Toes, the raven issued a hoarse cry and flared into the air with the heavy flapping of black wings.

Two Toes, recognizing the trap scent, was unwilling to approach. But the smell of the fresh rabbit became too much. In a moment he was ripping the fur off. He completely devoured the rabbit—bones and all—and then limped down to the river's edge and lapped up a long drink.

Under an overhanging ledge, in the shade and away from the gnats and flies, the coyote curled up and slept.

▲ ▲ ▲

It was three years later now as Two Toes lay in the brightening dawn under the big boulder high up in the Twist Hills. His foot wound had long since scarred over. He had mated for the third time. His bitch's den was at the head of the draw that ran to Green River below.

His yellow eyes with their slit pupils never stopped moving, surveying the benches as they dropped down hundreds of feet to the river. His cocked ears alternating forward and back now locked in the front position as distant chatter of magpies suddenly grew extreme. The coyote's head rose from his forepaws.

As the birds' raucous calls and responses increased in intensity, Two Toes sat up quickly. His eyes and ears pointed at the river, his nose sniffing the breeze for any strange scent. Then his head thrust forward and froze. Down where the wash met the river bed there was motion in the heavy brush. A horse and rider moved out of the brush and came slowly up the sandy bottom of the wash. The rider was leaning forward, head down, looking for sign in the sand. Two Toes, motionless, watched closely from a half-mile above.

The man reined up his horse, removed his dusty, sweat-stained hat and wiped his forehead with his sleeve. The March sun was already warm. The man sat still in his saddle, raised his head and looked up towards the buttes at the head of the canyon, in Two Toes' direction. He touched the horse's flank and continued up the wash.

After a ways, the rider stopped again. He stepped down from the saddle, ground-hitched the reins and walked over to a large greasewood bush, checking for signs around the bush and for several yards along a cut bank. Then he remounted and slowly, eyes fixed on the ground, rode out the mouth of the wash, around the cut bank out of sight.

A low growl rumbled in Two Toes' throat. He recognized the sorrel horse with the blaze face and three stocking feet. He recognized the tall, stoop-shouldered rider. It was the same man who had ridden out of the draw when Two Toes was a pup, pulled his gun from the scabbard and shot Two Toes' brother. It was the man who had rounded the boulder the day Two Toes had been caught in the trap. Last spring, the same man had found Two Toes' den, killed his mate and pups.

The coyote couldn't have known this, but the man was the trapper who had given Two Toes the name that was to start a legend in the Green River country of eastern Utah. What Two Toes did know was that this man was the enemy. And he was dangerous.

The man's trap sets and baits were all over the range. Two Toes had visited many of the traps with the man's scent mixed in with the smell of coyotes that had been killed then thrown in the brush.

With animal cunning, Two Toes had avoided every one of the traps. Now, he slipped away to hunt. He headed in the opposite direction from where the man had disappeared in the draw below.

THREE

▲ ▲ ▲

Trapper Jack

HIS FRIENDS always said Jack Willig was half-coyote. But it was the human side of him that rankled this morning. The run-in with rancher Ty Bingham had set the government trapper to brooding, a mood he wasn't used to.

Willig had faced frustration before, trying like hell to trap or den troublesome coyotes with the angry sheepmen badgering him week after week; but these problems usually resolved themselves with the result of his trapping skill that had taken years to master.

Willig was a damn good trapper and he knew it. He was jealous of his reputation. He was a man of action. He was proud.

He'd had all winter to bury his trouble with Two Toes. But now, thanks to Bingham, the aggravation had kindled again.

It had been at Ashton's Mercantile Store in Vernal, where Willig had bought a new fry pan along with his weekly supplies. Nearly every weekend he returned the 30 miles or so to the ranching and farming town, the Uintah County seat, where he lived.

He was loading his pickup when the sheepman appeared and beelined for him.

"What the hell're you doin' in town?!" Bingham had growled. "I thought you'd be out trapping for that sonofabitch coyote that's cost me the last two lambing seasons. Have you caught that damned Two Toes yet?"

There is nothing subtle nor civil about a sheepman in spring. Willig knew that. The only things on a sheepman's mind in spring are getting his sheep to the ranch, getting them sheared and getting the biggest lamb crop he could. Everything else, including God and family, are secondary. So it was with Ty Bingham.

Bingham was a man who would be polite and generous any other time when his very livelihood wasn't hinging on making an extra 10 to 15 percent profit on his lamb crop after two lean years. He'd grown red-faced the moment he'd seen the government trapper in town.

Standing nose-to-nose with Willig, he hadn't backed off, and the trapper had done nothing further to rile him.

"I'm camped now in Squaw Wash at Badger Spring," Willig had responded slowly, as men who spend most of the year away from civilization are prone to speak. "I'm putting out more traps. I'm just starting to look the country over. No sign of him yet."

"How come after two years you haven't got that coyote?" Bingham had retorted sternly, still in the trapper's face. "By God, if he shows up again, you'd better get 'im. You better kill that sonofabitch before my lambing herd gets there."

Then his tone had grown even colder. Looking the trapper square in the eyes, the rancher had added: "You'd better get 'im this time."

Before Willig could reply, Bingham, having said what he'd said, had turned on his heels and stalked off. All Willig could do was slam the pickup door, start the engine and shift into gear.

Now, standing in his sheep wagon the morning after, he still bristled, remembering the exchange. *"How come after two years you haven't got that coyote?"* He poked a lighted wood match through the hole of his Coleman lantern. When the mantle popped and lit, he pumped it some more for the white gas to sustain the blue flames, and hung the lantern back in the screw hook in the wooden bow of his sheep wagon. Soon the coffee boiled and he set it on the back of the stove. He poured in a cup of cold water to settle the grounds. He wished his temper were so easily relieved.

Willig cracked four eggs and laid four strips of bacon in his new black iron pan freshly broken in by hot oil and salt. He already knew the score with Bingham. He'd heard the same refrain

10 times the year before. He knew how sore and worried the sheepman was, even though Bingham's herd had just started up the stock driveway from the winter range. He guessed that Bingham blamed him for his desperate financial straits. Willig sensed that the sheepman believed that damned Two Toes was the reason for every sheep lost on the trail.

The first year, the trapper had been jawed at more in a teasing manner by the sheepmen, each of whom had had to endure two weeks of Two Toes' slaughter as his herd moved through the coyote's territory on the west side of the Green River. What the hell—Willig had a coyote he couldn't catch? Imagine that, they'd said.

The second year their comments grew nasty: Why they hell can't you get him? they'd said. They were all losing too many ewes and lambs and they didn't care if he had to stay out there a month, they wanted that coyote nailed. Too often, the trapper had caught a dirty remark or been the butt of some wisecrack.

And then the stories had spread. Word got round that every outfit was getting hit by this stealthy killer and no one could do a thing about it. Fears fueled the rumors, which spread like wildfire. The coyote leaving the two-toed mark hadn't killed 10 sheep, but 100.

Tall tales, Willig knew. But there had been no relief. Two Toes didn't go away. Always it was his telltale paw print leading away from the traps Willig found dug up and sprung. More than once he'd come upon a trap set up with a dead rabbit, only to find Two Toes had pissed on it as his calling card. Always it was he—Two Toes—who seemed to howl at night on the west side of the Green River in the Twist Hills area, letting Willig know he was still there.

Like all trappers in the West, Willig hated coyotes, but it was a love-hate relationship. He respected them as the most difficult animal to catch. Yet he knew they were vulnerable. They were creatures of habit. And with Two Toes, that would be the key.

Using all his tracking skill, Willig traced one of Two Toes' routes. He found where the coyote frequently hunted in a flat of sagebrush and rabbit brush that served as winter cover for a bunch of jackrabbits. The trapper saw that when Two Toes caught a rabbit near the river, he'd head for a rocky point where there was an old greasewood bush and deteriorated calf bones that served as a pissing post. And every time Two Toes came to this post, he'd piss and scratch, leaving fresh marks.

So Willig set a trap with fish scent along this route. But when he checked it again, it was sprung. No coyote. He set a trap with a sex scent. It, too, was sprung. No coyote. So he set a trap with rotted deer meat scent. Again, the coyote had somehow known it was there.

Then Willig reached deep into his sack of tricks and tried a blind set right at the pissing post. He dug down a few inches and set the jaws of the trap, covering the pan so no new dirt got underneath. He carefully camouflaged the scent-free trap with dirt and brushed the area clean of any trace. Then he set a branch behind the trap, and a stone in front, so that a coyote trotting down the trail would step over the stone in the space between it and the branch—into the trap.

But when Willig checked the set again, it was undisturbed. Two Toes hadn't fallen for this trick, either.

It had made Willig even madder.

Now a third spring was almost here. Willig could feel a knot beginning to form in his stomach. He'd never faced a coyote he couldn't catch eventually; but he'd never faced this kind of coyote before, either. He had to catch Two Toes this year. He had to catch Two Toes or the sheepmen of this region would make his life miserable.

Trappers with the U.S. Biological Survey's Control Division were paid to work year-round. Over the winter, Willig had put 25 poison stations of strychnine-laced sheep and horse meat throughout the Twist Hills and the Green River breaks. He'd picked up the stations last month. Many had been well-eaten. Willig had spent more time than he should have, looking for dead coyotes and hoping to find among them the one with the right-front paw minus two toes. He had found quite a few dead coyotes, but his hope to find that certain one proved in vain.

Now, a week before spring, Willig was working the territory ahead of the sheep coming up the trail off the winter range. He still had 15 or 20 good days before the first herd arrived. His wagon parked in Squaw Wash was near the first sheep camp north of the swinging bridge above Ouray. It was the first camp the herders would hit after they crossed the Green River on their way to the home ranches.

The herders all knew if anyone could catch Two Toes, it was Jack Willig. It was said by those who knew him that he knew what a coyote would do next just by reading its tracks. He could tell where it was headed, where it came from. He could tell a dog coyote track from a bitch track. He could recognize a coyote track as the same one he had seen months before, miles away. He read sign like the alphabet.

Willig, checking the ground from his saddle, always paid attention to how the coyotes were moving, whether they were hunting or had just made a kill. He took stock of how big they were and how old they were. From such astute observation, he could tell if they were hunting food, heading for water or looking for other coyotes.

If there was fresh snow, Willig would pick up a fresh coyote track and follow it all day just to learn its habits. He might follow a crazy trail as the coyote checked a sand hill for kangaroo rats, trotted over to a large bush checking for rabbits, went a mile away to hunt a prairie dog town. Sometimes a coyote covered many miles before making his kill and satisfying his hunger.

Willig absorbed it all. Most who knew him agreed he was "coyote smart." He knew all the tricks of the trapping trade. He had started young.

When Willig was a boy growing up on his father's ranch in central Utah, a grizzled old wolfer was working the Fish Lake Mountains and out on the San Rafael Desert. The old trapper had taught young Jack how to gather the new sagebrush branches covered with leaves and buds, fill a wash tub with the sage, cover it with water and boil it for two days, then immerse the traps in the purple sage water for two or three days more. The traps were then hung up to dry, a purple sheen to the metal and all smell of metal and man wiped out for a good year.

The old trapper had instructed how to bury the used canvas—for trap pan covers, gloves and ground cloth—in a pile of cow and horse manure for a week to kill all man smell. He'd explained that range cattle and mustangs covered the Utah deserts and their scent wouldn't spook a coyote in the least. He'd demonstrated how to make a fish scent by putting fish, usually carp, in a five-gallon tin and letting it rot down set in the sun, then, when it was thoroughly putrid, adding enough mineral oil to fill the tin and stirring it well every few days so in a week he had a bottle full of the scent oil for his trap lines. And the wolfer had taught how to make what he called "passion scent" by removing the sex organs and glands, bladder and urine from the animals he skinned for furs in the fall, putting the parts and the urine in a can and making it up the same way as the fish scent.

He'd shown Jack the rudiments of trapping, and Willig carried on to learn more on his own. At 40, he was one of the best coyote trappers in Utah, if not the West. He had worked for the government for several years and every year he was at or near the top in the count of predators taken. In Utah in 1941, between the government trappers and the bounty trappers and the farm and ranch kids, there were probably 3,000 Utahns going after coyotes and muskrats. In the top echelon was Willig, a master trapper. A century before he'd have been a mountain man.

Willig was glad he'd made a career out of trapping. He much preferred it to cowboying, which could have become his livelihood had trapping not gotten in his blood.

Willig had been born on his father's small ranch in 1901, and after he'd gotten out of high school cowboyed for several ranchers in the area. But his love of the wilds and solitude was too firmly ingrained to keep him hitched solely to buckarooing; he'd trapped coyotes and bobcats, muskrats and mink for fur money on the side.

Finally he'd quit his job and trapped full-time. From 1919 to 1929, Willig made good money. His furs always topped the market. During the 1920s, long-haired fur was the style. Willig's prime pelts would fetch up to $25 apiece.

The Depression ruined the fur market. What's more, the livestock men, belts tightened to weather the hard times, stopped paying bounties on coyotes or bobcats. Willig might have gone back to cowboying except that the U.S. Biological Survey was employing full-time trappers. Willig got himself hired and was assigned to trap for the many sheepmen who ran their herds in the Uintah Basin in northeastern Utah.

Willig's lanky six-foot frame was stoop-shouldered from all his years spent hunched over in the saddle, searching for tracks and sign on the ground. Crows-feet lined his deeply tanned face, and his pale blue eyes squinted from sun and glare from the winter snow. He was lean as a whip and used to long hours and hard work.

Willig loved being his own man. He loved being out where no one was looking over his shoulder, telling him what to do. He loved that his work bore direct results that told him whether he was successful or not. He either caught coyotes, or he didn't. He loved the daily challenge.

Every day, Willig rode his trap line for miles, usually from daylight to dark, checking the traps he'd set and knowing the location of each as well as a man knows his front porch. Each time he approached a trap, there'd be anticipation. Willig loved the thrill of the hunt. He would stay in this line of work the rest of his life. It was all he knew how to do. It was the only thing an independent and competitive man like him wanted to do.

He was still mulling over the encounter with Bingham as he watched the bacon and eggs sizzle and pop in the frying pan. When they were ready, he slid two eggs and two bacon strips onto his plate and put the rest on a slice of bread to wrap in wax paper and put in his saddle bag for lunch.

It was now final in Willig's mind. He wanted Bingham off his ass. He wanted all the sheepmen off his ass. There he was, out working twice as hard as them and their herders, put together.

He wanted it done with. And he knew the only way to get it done with was to get that Two Toes.

Willig would catch the coyote. He was certain of that. He would scalp him and take the two ears held together with a piece of hide and add it to his other scalps to present to the Control Division supervisor when he came that month.

And there was something else Willig would do.

He would cut off the coyote's right-front paw. He would wave it in Ty Bingham's face.

▲ ▲ ▲

It was just breaking daylight as Willig saddled Sontag. They were old partners. Willig had ridden the sorrel horse for seven years. Sontag was a well-trained trapper's horse. He stood 11 hands high and weighed more than 1,100 pounds. And, like Willig's gear, the horse with the blaze face and three white stocking feet was rugged and tough. Sontag carried the steel traps, scent bag, rifle, trapper's pick, saddle bags and slicker easily throughout the long day, and never raised a fuss. He didn't spook when the steel traps rattled or when Willig jumped off, pulled his rifle and shot at a coyote or bobcat. The horse was now 10 years old. Willig knew he could never replace him.

He patted Sontag's rump. With methodical motions, the trapper loaded up the tools of his trade. The traps and his gloves were already rolled up in a piece of canvas tied behind his saddle. He looped his canvas scent bag over the saddle horn and let it hang down the right side; the bag held his bottle of scent, the torn canvas squares to cover the pans of his traps, a pair of pliers, a small roll of wire and pieces of wool. Then Willig slung his trapper's four-pound hammer with the curved, sharpened pick on the other end over the horn to hang down on the left side. He used the hammer-pick to drive his trap stakes into the ground and to dig dirt loose for the trap set and chain.

Willig looked forward to checking the traps this day. He'd used a new scent this past winter and he was sure it would lure Two

Toes. Willig's two regular scents—the fish scent and the passion scent—hadn't caught the coyote. Neither had the blind set. But last fall, he had gathered up some deer and antelope hides along with the musk glands cut from inside their hind legs. He'd cut the hide with the fat on it into strips two feet long and put them in a five-gallon tin, adding deer brains, kidneys and bladders. When it was all thoroughly rotted down, he'd added enough mineral oil to make paste.

Willig had left nothing to chance. He'd tried the scent out on dogs in town. He'd put a dab of paste on a stick and toss it in the road when a dog headed his way. Each time, the dog would stop, nose up, locate the smell and move right to it. The dog would kick and scratch and paw at the stick, sometimes rolling on its back over it. Sometimes it would even pick the stick up in its mouth.

Willig had marveled at this. He'd never seen anything like it. It gave him faith in the scent. He knew it would get Two Toes. It had to get him this time. Of course, maybe he wouldn't even need it. Maybe he'd find the bastard's poisoned carcass while riding his trap line today.

Willig finished tying up his gear and swallowed a last cup of coffee. Then he closed the doors of his sheep wagon, dropped the bacon-and-egg sandwich in his saddle bag and mounted up.

Willig rode north, up the west bank of the Green. He moved back and forth, cutting to the water to check the sandbars where tracks were easily made and seen, then up a wash for a ways. He rounded a bend, sending a flock of magpies breaking from the river and screeching into flight. He cut over along the breaks where the hills dropped abruptly to the water and rode up the bottom of the washes to check sandy soil there.

Ahead of him now at the mouth of a wash stood a greasewood bush 10 feet high. Between the bush and the high dirt bank behind lay a deer carcass. Even from a distance, Willig could see it was a coyote kill. It was easy to read what had happened. The doe had been caught in deep winter snow. Escape impossible, she had backed up to the dirt bank to fight off advancing coyotes.

All that was left now was her skull, rib cage and leg bones, along with scraps of hide and some hair.

Willig tied Sontag to a small sagebrush and stepped carefully onto the hard pan and rocks. Approaching the carcass, he stopped suddenly and half-jerked back as if hit, sucking in his breath.

There, plain and clear in the dried mud, were perfect tracks of a coyote. The right-front foot was short two toes.

Willig cussed under his breath. He cussed again out loud. Kneeling, he slowly traced the edge of the track with his thumb. It had been made about six days ago. There had been a late snowfall of a couple inches and the melting snow soaked into the top two inches of soil. This meant that Two Toes had survived the winter and the traps and poison baits Willig had set out. It meant that Two Toes had mated, and now would soon have pups to feed. It meant that he would be hunting for eight or nine mouths, including the bitch's. And he would be hunting for sheep.

The trapper swore long and bitterly.

He stood and peered up toward the Twist Hills, up the draws and gullies where bitch coyotes could soon be denning and raising pups. Squinting, he scanned the endless series of ledges. They seemed to mock him.

For all Willig knew, Two Toes was watching him this very moment, invisible in the terrain even though the trapper, like all outdoorsmen, could spot an unnatural break in the scene a quarter-mile away. Willig knew that Two Toes knew him. It was a half-mile from this point that Willig had found Two Toes' bitch's den the year before. The bastard coyote was somewhere out there now, Willig felt sure.

The trapper walked back to Sontag. He removed a trap and stake, his hammer pick, scent bag and ground cloth and slowly stepped back to the carcass. There, he noted several fresher tracks and scratches in the hard pan close to the rib bones. That was the right spot for the trap.

Willig took his time. He pulled on his gloves, then carefully spread his canvas ground cloth two feet from the rib cage. Where the coyote scratches disturbed the silt soil, he dug a V-shaped hole four inches deep to hold his trap. He set the dirt removed from the hole on the canvas cloth in front of him. When the trap sat solidly in the hole without tilting or wiggling, he drove the steel stake into the ground just off the end of the trap springs. Then he coiled the eight-foot chain and set it level with the springs so it wouldn't stick out.

Willig put the trap across his knees and closed the springs so the jaws fell open. Gingerly, he flipped the trigger over the inside jaw with his left thumb while raising the trap pan with his right index finger. Holding the pan tight, he slipped the trigger into the groove on the pan, then slowly released his grip on the springs.

The trap was set. The trigger held the inside jaw tight; the pan slot held the trigger firm. The inside jaw held down the springs and the outside jaw lay back free. It was ready to go on the ground.

Cautiously, Willig set the outside jaw up in the air so he could cover the pan with a four-inch square of canvas. Set down, the pan was two inches off the ground. No dirt would get under it because of the canvas cover; that meant the slightest pressure on the pan would push it down, releasing the trigger from the slot. The springs would instantly slam the jaws shut on whatever stepped on the trap. And the unfortunate prey would be held tight. The jaws, offset and toothless so as not to tear up the foot locked in it, would hold it firm so that the animal could not chew free.

Willig tucked the cover under the pan then slowly laid the outside jaw down so it was flush with the inside jaw and the trap was open. Now he set to camouflaging the trap. He scattered dirt over it until it was completely covered. With a sage branch, he brushed the ground until there was no trace left of his work. Then he reached into his bag for the jar of his new scent—the special one made from deer and antelope hides and glands.

Willig held the jar away from his face, wrinkling his nose at the putrid rotten smell. He picked up a small piece of rib bone from the carcass. Wadding a blob of wool on the end of the bone, he daubed the wool into the scent jar and inserted the scented

rib back under the rib cage of the carcass, right behind the trap set.

Willig managed a smile. Any coyote lured by the scent and sniffing around the rib cage would spring the trap not knowing it was there.

Now the trapper carefully picked up the four corners of his ground cloth. He carried it down to the river and threw the surplus soil from digging the trap into the water. He gathered the remainder of his tools at the trap set and slowly backed away, brushing out his footprints with the sage branch until he'd reached Sontag.

Back in the saddle, Willig surveyed his work. It was perfect. No sign or smell left, and a new scent that would be irresistible to coyotes. Already, in his mind's eye, he could see Two Toes—a coyote with a fierce will to live—spinning in the trap, snarling and thrashing as Willig rode up to it the next time. He couldn't wait. He would wave his left hand out of reach of the snapping jaws to divert Two Toes' attention, and with his other hand bring down the hammer onto the base of the skull, instantly killing him.

Then he would cut off the famous front foot.

FOUR

▲ ▲ ▲

The Sheepman

TY BINGHAM drove his pickup truck southeast on the rough and dusty road of the Leota Bottoms, rumbling through drought-stricken country that seemed more desolate and disturbing every time he passed through.

The rancher had left Vernal just before daybreak, headed for his sheep camp now set up at Willow Creek. Looking over the abandoned Bottoms, he found it hard to realize there were now no cattle, sheep or horses as far as he could see. Just a few years before, this valley had been dotted with farms: a busy, thriving community. As a white-tailed jackrabbit darted across the dirt road yards in front of his pickup, as if fleeing the devastation, he thought: How true the old saying, "Not enough graze for a jackrabbit."

Here and there in fields sat a rusted threshing machine, a hay baler, an old truck, its hood up and tires flat—as if someone had been working on it then just walked off one night and left. Bingham could never stomach how pathetic it was to see all that equipment gone to waste.

On either side of the road here, fences built to keep out rabbits and rodents still surrounded barnyards; but instead of chickens or pigs in them, the yards were now strewn with dead branches, boxes, bottles and cans—the litter of abandoned homesteads. In one front yard sat a washing machine and stove, probably hauled from the empty house by scavengers who'd then decided on better pickings. In a field beyond, a solitary tractor stood like a mute sentinel protecting a vanishing trace of civilization.

Caked with dust and piled underneath with tumbleweeds, the tractor would be undriveable, Bingham knew, even if its owner had somehow returned to reclaim it, for its parts had been cannibalized by farmers or ranchers who'd stayed on longer to fight the futile battle with the unending drought.

No one had foreseen this state. The Bottoms had been rich soil left from a prehistoric lake bed that caught rain and snow runoff. In the early 1900s, the government blocked off the range land into 160-acre plots and made them available to veterans of the Great War. Many had started farming there with high hopes. Drilling found water 100 to 200 feet below the surface; farmers had built small reservoirs and filled them with enough water to irrigate small grain and alfalfa fields. Late spring storms even yielded a crop of grain and corn for the few who dry farmed.

The average farmer got by fine raising grain, corn and alfalfa, plus running a small band of sheep and a few cattle. Every family had milk cows, chickens, pigs and turkeys and a vegetable garden. Every farmhouse had a root cellar filled each fall with canned vegetables and fruits, onions and potatoes. The families were self-sufficient. They could survive even if they only earned $100 cash a month.

Fifteen years later, drought had reduced the fertile Bottoms to a dust bowl. No one had ever seen anything like it. The dry stretch of weather that began in the region in 1931 was unheard of, a first for white men in the West. Every year the farmers thought it would end, that a good year would yield the fruits of their patience and prayers. But a good year never came. There was just more scant rainfall and scarce winter snow; more parched soil, more bitterness, more growing despair.

At first, the farmers tightened their belts. They allayed concern with the knowledge they could raise what they needed to feed themselves. But then their reservoirs and wells dried up, their crops burned, their fields were overrun with weeds. By 1934, many of the farms had dried up. Suddenly, the families of the Bottoms were choked out of existence.

One by one at first, and then in bunches, they were forced to move away. They packed what they could onto trucks or pickups and pulled up stake for Salt Lake City or Ogden or Grand Junction—or that great star, California. Their farms and ranches lay fallow. The banks did not want them; they were worthless, couldn't be sold. By 1935, most of the farms were vacated. Finally, even the most stubborn clingers-on up and left.

Bingham shook his head, imagining the agony and misery of the farmers as they drove away from their hopes and dreams of a bright future. He passed the farm that had been owned by Pete Johansen and his family. He remembered how they were hard-working and thrifty, raising two girls and two boys. Bingham recalled how the boys would ride their ponies clear down to Bow Knot Bend when his lambing herd was camped there to ask Billy Butts if he had any bum lambs they could have. The sheepherder always tried to hold a bummer or two for them, and in 1933 one of the lambs he gave to them won a blue ribbon in the 4H Livestock Show in Vernal. But that was eight years ago.

Now the front door of the Johansen house jagged crookedly ajar from a busted hinge. The front windows yawned with teeth of broken glass spikes, and the curtains hung forlornly, darkened with dirt. The red fence around the little front yard was almost covered by vegetation—tumbleweeds and Russian thistle, branches and leaves from the dead and dying trees. Nature, encroaching at its slow but tireless pace, was reclaiming the land.

Bingham was glad when the road left the Leota Bottoms and headed down a ridge toward Ouray Trading Post. It was hot and stuffy in the cab with the windows rolled up against the dust. He would buy a bottle of root beer at the post and take a breather. The neglected farms in the withered terrain had also filled him with foreboding. Bingham knew that he was blessed that the winter and summer ranges still had sufficient graze and browse, that Ashley Valley where his ranch was had water from running streams. Still, he'd had to borrow $5,000 from the bank. The drought threatened him, too.

The brush along the Duchesne River a few miles to the south came into view, and off to the east Bingham made out the tops of the cottonwoods along the banks of the Green. He had driven this route 500 times, easy; but it still was with a sense of appreciation that the sheepman peered out across the Green River as he drove, to where the red and yellow hills formed an escarpment that rose up from the desert that ran from White River on the north to the Book Cliff Mountains on the south. There, at an elevation of 5,000 to 6,000 feet, stretched thousands of acres of native grasses and brush, growing hardy and high in protein for the cattle, sheep, horses, deer and antelope that made it their winter feed. The desert had been livestock range for more than 50 years. Bingham sheep had wintered there most of them. It was home. In his heart of hearts, Bingham knew he'd never leave.

Ty Bingham was all sheepman. His father had been a sheepman before him and as Ty grew up, he'd spent all his spare time working beside his pa. Like all children of ranchers, Ty had practically been born on a horse. He'd also learned early on to drive the pickup, run the wagon team and tend camp. Working all summer on the ranch as a boy, he'd learned to shear, brand and earmark. He'd learned to "mouth" sheep, telling their age by checking their teeth; but he could usually pick out an old ewe or ram just by looking at it. Yes, he'd learned everything there was to know about sheep: forming up herds; putting them on the winter range in the desert; bringing them in for lambing and shearing; contracting and organizing the shearing crews that came through on their circuit from Texas or New Mexico or Arizona, up through Idaho and Montana; forming up herds again for the summer range on the forest.

By the time the elder Bingham died, Ty was running the entire outfit and doing an excellent job of it. He was 37 when he stepped into his father's shoes in 1923; by 1935, he was recognized as one of Utah's outstanding sheepmen. Ty was intelligent and well-educated—he'd earned an agriculture degree from Utah State College—and he was calm and collected, kind and even-tempered . . . except, of course, in spring, when all sheepmen grew testy. The tougher things got, the antsier they'd get; Ty Bingham was no exception. But like all sheepmen, he was wedded to his work. And his reputation was that he handled men well and he was fair.

Bingham wasn't large in stature—a shade under six feet—and his voice was soft; but his entire bearing was that of a man who knew what he was doing. His was a well-known and respected family, had been for 70 years in the valley around Vernal, and Bingham was regarded as a leader. He had been elected president of the Utah Wool Growers Association for two terms. Now 45, he was serving on the advisory board of the newly formed federal Division of Grazing. The sheepmen were happy to have him for a spokesman.

Bingham wouldn't admit it or side in with the feds, but he saw the need to change with the times. Before and just after the turn of the century, all sheep and cattle men had roamed the federal ranges uncontrolled, their own bosses. In critical years when resources grew scarce in Montana and Wyoming, Utah and Colorado, sheep and cattle outfits going for the same grazing grounds collided in conflict that spilled over into bloodshed in range wars that became famous. In spite of such consequences, the average livestock man believed that the range was his to use and no federal official had better stick his nose in and tell him where and when and how he could graze it.

Bingham was one of the few who didn't bellyache or buck when the federal government began asserting management of the range in 1935 to prevent overgrazing and soil erosion and to allocate resources among all outfits. He saw the wisdom of paying the Division of Grazing a cent-and-a-half per sheep for each month his herds were on the range. He knew the money needed to be spent on range improvement, putting in corrals and roads, developing springs and water troughs and reseeding grazing ground. He knew the range had to be managed to be preserved. He didn't need to think about disasters like the Leota Bottoms to grasp the importance of planning ahead.

It was almost 8 a.m. as he pulled up to the front of the trading post and killed the pickup's engine. He sat for a minute, watching a slight westerly breeze pour dust over the truck. Then he stepped out. A grimy brown cloud of dust stirred up by the pickup hung over the road as far back as he could see.

Bingham clambered up onto the wood plank porch. Well, one thing that likely wouldn't change as long as he lived was this flat-roofed trading post of cottonwood logs chinked with red clay from the Duchesne River bottom. There was a solid permanence to it. The post on the Fort Duchesne Reservation had been built in the 1880s for the Ute and Uncompahgre Indians. But as far back as Bingham could remember it had been a general store serving not only the Indians but ranchers, sheep and cattle men and the occasional hunters, trappers and prospectors who happened through. Under the familiar black letters on the front that read "OURAY TRADING POST" was a smaller sign noting it was a post office, too. The gas pump out front was the only one within 20 miles. The post was a fixture. Osiah Portle had been running it more than 30 years.

Bingham brushed his sleeves and pant legs with quick swats. He pushed open the heavy frame door and stepped into the big store room. Portle, in his flannel shirt and black suspenders, immediately appeared in the doorway that led from the back.

"Hello, Ty, how are things?" the poker-faced storekeep said, the tips of his gray mustache drooping as always.

"Too damn dry and hot for March, Osh," Bingham replied. "Coming across the Bottoms the dust just about choked me."

"How about a cold root beer?"

"Sounds good." Bingham moved toward the counter.

He tipped the cold bottle of Hires up and the sweet brown liquid fizzed on his tongue and worked down his throat, leaving a musky aftertaste. It was an old sensation, anchored in memories and times dating back to his first trip with his father out to the Green River country. The taste all fit in with the mingling aromas of coffee and spices and leather and wool blankets in the trading post, which was an endless bazaar of barrels, bins and shelves loaded with a little bit of everything: coal oil lamps, turpentine, Levi's, jackets, shirts, gum boots, guns, ammo—whatever one needed in these parts. And whatever the store didn't have, the storekeep could order. The Ouray Trading Post was where Bingham, riding in his father's buckboard, had visited and savored his first stick of licorice.

"When do your sheep cross the river?"

Portle's question broke Bingham's dreaming.

"Should be by the end of the week," the sheepman replied. "Billy Butts should be breaking camp at the mouth of Willow Creek today. I'm headed out there now with supplies."

He took another slow swig of the root beer. "Many of the herds showing up?"

"Hasletts are over at Lizard Springs and I guess most of them are on the move," said the storekeep, the fount of information in these parts. "Buckwalter, Thompson, Sundstrom, Miller and Chance are all on their way north."

Bingham nodded. "How are the coyotes this spring, Osh? Thick as ever?"

"Haven't heard recently," the storekeep replied in a monotone. "But there was some trouble with coyotes this winter out at Bonanza and on Mustang. Buckwalter lost quite a few sheep in December and January."

Then, remembering the $25 bounty Bingham had offered the year before, he added, "Anybody get that Two Toes yet?"

Bingham gulped involuntarily. The carbonated drink gurgled up harshly in his throat, making him cough.

"That damn coyote has cost me a lot of money the last three years," he said, regaining his voice.

Bingham cleared his throat. "I saw Willig the other day. He's working the stock trail from here to Vernal right now. Looks like my sheep are going to be the first ones up the river. By damn, he better get that coyote before I get there. Last spring, the bastard killed one or two ewes and lambs every night. Followed my herd clear to Brush Creek."

Portle raised his eyebrows.

"The Indians are complaining about the coyotes killed by poison," he said. "Maybe Two Toes took one of the baits —"

Bingham cut him off. "No one has brought him in yet," he said. "If he hasn't taken a poison bait by now I doubt he ever will. That sonofabitch only eats his own fresh kill."

His face hardened. "By damn, it better not happen again this spring."

Bingham sat silently for a time. Then he finished his bottle and slapped a nickel on the counter.

"See you tomorrow on my way back to Vernal, Osh."

Outside, he started his truck, put it in gear and pulled out. He wound his way across the flats and the Green River bottoms that flooded in high water but now were cracked and dry and covered with sun-browned cockleburs. He made a mental note to keep his herd away from the flats. A sheep fleece full of the spiny, thumbnail-sized 'burs lowered the price of the wool.

As he approached the Ouray bridge across Green River, Bingham put the truck in low gear and slowly crawled up the dirt ramp. The 150-foot span was a swinging bridge 12 feet above the river. It never failed to fill a traveler with butterflies no matter how many times he crossed, and that included Bingham. The bridge was held up by four-inch steel wire cables strung from six-inch steel posts anchored in concrete blocks at either end. From these cables dropped the ties that held more cables, supporting the cross planks that were the road bed for the bridge. The planks were four inches thick and 16 inches wide. They'd been left loose to grind against each other beneath a vehicle's wheels. There was just enough width on the bridge for a small truck.

The bridge began to sway the moment Bingham inched his truck onto it. The pickup's weight depressed the planks like piano keys and those in front rose halfway up the radiator as the truck crept forward. The planks creaked and groaned beneath the wheels like lost souls. The timber rattled and crackled and the cables screamed in an eerie chorus that Bingham never got used to. It was a real experience each time crossing the bridge.

When he was finally safe on the east side of the river, Bingham parked and walked back to kick a few loosened planks into place. Then he got in his truck. He took the south fork in the dirt road and headed down across White River to the mouth of Willow Creek, where Billy Butts was camped.

FIVE

▲ ▲ ▲

Keep Your Rifle Handy

BILLY BUTTS watched the wave of dust rolling up the truck trail that led from Ouray and squinted until he saw Ty Bingham's blue Chevy pickup emerge. He was tying his horse to a rear wheel of the sheep wagon when his boss pulled up.

"Thought you'd show up this morning," Butts said, stepping to the front of the wagon as Bingham climbed out of the truck. "Hot coffee's on the stove."

"Good, I'll take it," Bingham said.

As he poured a steaming tin cupful, Bingham smiled to himself. Butts had made an extra-large pot. There was never any surprising this herder, no getting an edge on him.

Butts was camped near the mouth of Willow Creek where it flowed into Green River five miles below the Ouray bridge. The camp was close enough that Bingham could reach it after a couple hours drive. It was now about half-past 8. But even when Bingham hit Butt's camp at daylight, he never caught the herder in bed. Usually, the sheep were already off the bed ground and being moved out on the range to graze. Butts was all sheepherder. There were none better.

If the grazing ground was close to camp, Butts would leave one of the dogs to watch over the sheep at noon and return to the wagon for lunch. If it was some distance, he would pack his lunch in his saddle bag. He would always have his herd back on the bed ground an hour before sunset. That gave him enough time to cut wood for the stove, fetch fresh water, grain his horse and take care of whatever else needed doing before it got too dark to see. Then he'd light the Coleman lantern. As it hissed and popped in the wagon he'd start his supper.

If anyone happened to be traveling close to Butts' camp around nightfall they'd go out of the way to stop at his wagon, hoping to catch the herder at meal time. Butts' sourdough biscuits and hot cakes, baked lamb shanks and ribs and berry cobblers were famous far and wide.

Bingham reflected that William Butterman had lived up to his expectations, and then some. He was the best herder he had ever known. Billy Butts knew sheep, both on the range and at the ranch. On the ranch, when it was breeding time, Butts would put the rams in the herds at the right time and immediately get rid of bucks that didn't measure up. He'd keep a careful eye on his young ewes to make sure they got bred their first time, and if any refused a ram, Butts would cut her out and tie her up so she could be easily mounted.

He had also persuaded Bingham to try the breeding markers on his bucks. It was an innovation Butts had evidently learned in Texas, and it yielded impressive results. It was so simple. A harness would be placed around a buck's chest. In the harness was a large sponge bag filled with a perforated container of paint. When a ram topped a ewe, a dab of paint would mark her back. The breeding markers made it easy to keep track of which ewes had been bred and which ones were missed. Bingham's lamb crop percentage had gone up the very first year.

When shearing and docking time drew near, Butts would organize for the hectic days ahead. He'd make sure the shearing pens, gates and alleys were in working order, and that the scaffold that held the wool sacks while they were being filled and stamped was repaired. Then everything, hopefully, would go like clockwork. The sheep would be corralled at daylight. Then the lambs would be separated from the ewes into a different corral, leaving one full of ewes ready for shearing, right next to the shearing stalls. In the corral full of lambs, the bucks would be castrated and their tails docked. Here the accurate count of buck

and ewe lambs would be taken to establish the ratio of the lamb crop to bred ewes for that year. At the end of each day, the lambs would be turned into the corral of sheared ewes to once again be mothered up. When shearing and docking were over, the summer bands would be put together, ready to head for the mountains and the summer range.

Yes, matters were in good hands with Billy Butts around, Bingham thought. He never had to give the herder many orders. He hoped to keep Butts around as long as he could.

When Billy Butts had asked Bingham to get him two collie pups that were advertised in the Vernal newspaper, the two had gone out to take a look together. The Scotch shelties had good breeding, and Bingham hadn't hesitated buying them. Before the summer was over, the quick, alert, black-and-white pups were fast becoming good sheep dogs under their master's guidance. Before they were a year old, they only needed a soft word of command and to be pointed in the right direction with a wave of his hand.

Now the shelties were three years old. Butts only sent them out when sheep were splitting off from the herd or had fallen too far behind. The dogs would quietly go about their work, with the same sort of efficiency as their master, barking and nipping heels only when called for.

Butts soon became known for his well-trained sheep dogs, thanks to a trick he liked to do when he went into town. Before going into a store or cafe, he'd set his Stetson on the sidewalk and place his leather gloves on top. "Guard," he'd say. At the command, the dog would stretch out beside them on the sidewalk, nose on front paws. The hat and gloves would be safe until Butts returned. No one would touch them. Once, he even stuck a $10 bill in the hat band.

Having Billy Butts working for him was like having an ace in the hole, Bingham reflected, sipping hot coffee and watching the band of fat, woolly ewes moving slowly way off in the distance, grazing at their own pace. His herder was an extra bit of advantage in the current circumstances. Who knew, maybe having Butts would be enough to swing things in his favor this year. If they could only get the herd back to the ranch with little loss of ewes and lambs.

"Are you ready to head for the river?" Bingham asked.

"Planned on starting tomorrow," his herder said. "If you'll move the wagon to the campsite in the cottonwoods this side of the bridge, I'll have enough graze for the sheep till next week."

Butts thought for a moment, then added, "I rode over there yesterday and that bench land up east of the river has real good feed on it this spring. The sheep will do fine there till next week."

Bingham sipped his coffee. "All right," he said. "If I pull your wagon there on my way back, can you reach it with the sheep by night?"

Butts shook his head.

"No, but I can bed the sheep about four miles this side of there tonight and move them on in tomorrow."

Bingham's hand holding the coffee cup stopped halfway to his mouth. Coffee splashed over the sides, burning his fingers.

"What about coyotes?" he asked, flicking his fingers and looking straight at Butts. "Not a very good idea to leave the sheep alone for a night. The last thing we need now is to lose some lamby ewes to coyotes."

Butts winced slightly. He remarked to himself that his boss' edginess had bloomed sooner than normal.

"I haven't seen any coyotes for several days," he replied. "I cut the draws and sandy spots yesterday and didn't see a single coyote track. The only coyotes howling have been across the river and up north."

He could see his boss was not convinced.

"Besides, I'll bed the herd down and stay there till midnight before I go to the wagon and I'll be out there again in the morning about 4:30," Butts said.

That would be an hour before daylight. The herder knew no coyotes would bother the sheep between midnight and 4:30.

Bingham stood silent a minute, staring at his boots. Then he tossed the remaining coffee on the ground.

"By damn, it's a good thing that cussed Two Toes is on the other side of the river," he muttered. He turned to his herder with a hard look.

"I saw that trapper, Willig, the other day. He hasn't caught 'im yet. If that coyote hits us again this year, I'm gonna blister someone's hide."

Butts nodded.

The day before, Joe Gander had stopped by on his way up Willow Creek and told Butts about seeing Willig riding a trap line north of the trading post. Willig hadn't even stopped to talk; he'd just ridden by with a wave of his hand. It was obvious that Willig hadn't caught Two Toes yet. If he had, he would've stopped to talk about it.

"I think Willig's trapping the stock driveway on the west side of the river," Butts said. "That's where the coyote must have his den."

"You keep your rifle with you all the time from now on," Bingham said, as if not listening. "Can't miss a shot at that coyote 'cause you're not carrying your rifle."

Butts merely nodded again.

Bingham helped the herder pack the sheep wagon for the move. Then the sheepman backed his pickup to the wagon tongue and hooked it to the trailer hitch.

He turned to Butts one more time.

"I'll park the wagon at the cottonwoods. See you Wednesday."

He started the pickup, put it in low gear. And, wagon in tow, he slowly pulled onto the dirt road, and headed toward the swinging bridge.

▲ ▲ ▲

SIX

Pups to Feed

THE HOLE was freshly dug in the high bank in a dry wash that ran below a red rock ledge that curved out to a pla teau. Two Toes, come into the draw, lowered his head into the hole and crawled inside a short ways.

He whined into the cramped darkness. His bitch answered him in kind.

The dog coyote could hear mewls of the new-born pups, and the sound of the bitch licking the last to emerge from her belly. An instinct, ancient and absolute, informed him that long days lay ahead. His mate would now devour everything he brought. She was nursing seven pups.

The sun was setting behind the high rocky crest of the Twist Hills now, sending shadows running down the plateau toward the east. Two Toes, returned to his lookout under the red sandstone ledge, cocked his ears toward the river below. Magpies were scolding each other madly, darting among the cottonwood branches.

The coyote trotted along the south rim of the plateau, into the setting sun. He dropped into a draw and minutes later was hurrying through the wash bottom leading to the river. When he emerged at the riverbank, his nose lowered to the ground. He was cutting sign across the river bottom this way when he suddenly stopped.

It was a horse track he'd sniffed, and it was fresh. Two Toes back-tracked the trail at a trot, following the hoofprints. He found they had come from around a large patch of willows. He followed the horse tracks across a sandbar along the main riverbank, and then into the mouth of a large wash that emptied into the river. It was in the middle of the wash when the coyote stopped again and lifted his nose. A slight breeze was coming down the draw. He moved his head to catch it. The breeze carried on it the faint smell of man and horse, but there was also another smell, unfamiliar, mingled in. Then the coyote's ears cocked. From somewhere nearby there came the muffled sound of scratching.

A hundred yards ahead, a large greasewood bush backed up against a high cut bank. The raspy scratching was coming from there. The coyote moved forward, cautiously. At 50 yards, he circled to the right, getting downwind from whatever it was that was giving off the strange smell. The scratching grew louder. And then Two Toes was close enough and at an angle to see behind the greasewood bush to the noise's source.

A large, furry porcupine was pawing at the hard pan. Two Toes slowly circled closer. He saw the trap clamped onto the porcupine's hind foot. The waddling critter had been feeding on green clover along the riverbank when it had accidentally stepped into the trap.

Scratching with futility at the ground, it dragged the trap to the end of its chain as it climbed up the greasewood. But escape was hopeless. The trap caught up between two large branches that formed a fork on the bush and the porcupine, struggling with the heavy trap, keeled over backward and hung, dangling, unable to move.

Two Toes came around the other side of the bush. The strange smell was overpowering now. There, ahead, lay a rib cage of a deer. The strange musky smell was coming from its bones. Two Toes sniffed again. He felt a strong urge to lie down and roll on his back near the bones—but fear stopped him. A fear born from experience. The smell of horse and man still lingered faintly, and the coyote remembered from the past about coyotes and rabbits, badgers and skunks, caught in traps and dead, some rotting away.

Two Toes walked back to the bush. The upside-down porcupine hung, its head inches from the ground, its big hairless belly a wide-open target. Two Toes hesitated. Another memory, a very early one, played in his mind. When his bitch mother was training the pups, she'd whipped him off of a porky's scent; but being the ornery little cuss he was, he'd rushed ahead anyway and took a grab at the larger animal. His reward as he touched the hair were two quills hidden beneath that stuck into his upper lip. The shock of the barbs and their extreme pain for two days proved an unforgettable lesson.

The smell of the porky spelled danger to Two Toes; but its helpless predicament was too inviting. It proved to be no trick at all for him to rip open the quill-less throat and belly. After he'd eaten his fill for himself and his mate, Two Toes turned sideways and lifted a leg. A stream of urine sprayed the porky's carcass, and then the big coyote moved over to the trap and repeated the performance, followed by backing up kicking and scratching the dirt.

He turned and scrambled out of the draw and headed up the plateau. His route took him almost to the plateau's head, where he crossed to the north side and jumped up onto a sandstone ledge that curved to the dry wash where the dug-up dirt at the foot of a bank showed him the den was.

The bitch came to the den's mouth in response to her mate's whine. She found the vomited-up porcupine meat in a pile and gobbled up the red chunks. Two Toes sat and watched. It was almost night. When she disappeared back into the den he scrambled up the bank and stood on the edge of the draw, his body a dim silhouette in the blue light of the dying dusk.

The night breeze brought no warning smells, but Two Toes' ears lifted at the hoot of a distant owl perched in a riverbank cottonwood. Far to the south, a hunting coyote barked, a harsh staccato briefly answered in turn by three others. Exclamations of territory.

No dangers loomed in the night's offing. Two Toes returned to his lookout bed under the rimrocks. He curled up and went to sleep.

▲ ▲ ▲

Dawn had yet to break when Two Toes stretched long and hard with a big yawn and sat up, perfectly still, ears cocked and alert. No sounds came. Soon he was trotting southwest along a table-top plateau that led to the Indian farms scattered along the east side of the Duchesne River.

Mice and ground squirrels would not suffice now that the pups had been born. Two Toes was after bigger game. He covered the three miles to the outlying farms as the sky was paling to light.

Every winter, especially in deep snow, Two Toes hunted this settlement. Most of the Indian farms were poorly maintained, the legacy of a people severed from its past and pushed to its knees, its spirit badly crushed. Some will or initiative went want-ing for many; their farms' pens, pastures and corrals were usu-ally in such poor repair that if the chickens, geese and livestock weren't outside the fences, it was easy for a coyote to get in.

Two Toes stopped behind a large rabbit brush and checked for scents coming from the farm buildings. A myriad of smells spewed forth: horse and cattle, pigs and sheep, and also the Indians' mongrel dog, the big coward. The coyote watched and waited, still as the terrain. He waited for an opportunity.

Presently, a rooster crowed his morning's greeting, and hens started from the chicken coop. They moved jerkily toward the corral fence facing the invisible coyote, scratching for seeds and grain in bare spots on the cold ground. In the corral, a horse nickered. The sound of the large beast rubbing its neck against a post vibrated softly across the open ground. But there was no sign yet of the mongrel dog, the black-and-tan menace that could sound the alarm in an instant. He was still asleep. Two Toes stared at the house. No sign of movement there, either. No lights. No smoke from the chimney. No people sounds, at all.

The chickens were poking in earnest now at the ground. They were joined by the big red rooster emerging from the coop. The chickens scratched and picked at the earth and moved through the fence into the pasture. The rooster, taking charge of his harem, ran at the leading hens, clucking loudly, and took over the scratching position of the first. The hens moved off in separate directions, pecking up the seeds of grain. One uncovered a trail of spilled wheat and clucked noisily, eating up the kernels as fast as she could. The greedy rooster rushed to get ahead of her.

Two Toes, flattened perfectly motionless in the pasture grass, lying unseen, watched the chickens feed toward him. His eyes were trained on the hen not 20 yards from his nose when the red rooster suddenly ran between the hen and the rabbit brush. In two leaps, the coyote had the cock by the head in his mouth. As the bird let out a frantic squawk the other chickens ran cackling back through the corral fence.

The rooster had no chance. His wings flailed uselessly as the coyote, half-carrying and half-dragging the flopping fowl, ran for a heavy stand of rabbit brush and greasewood that marked the mouth of a draw coming out of the small hill just north of the farm.

The Indians' dog, a mean-looking cross between a shepherd and a hound, was awakened by the cackling commotion. He ran out from under the back porch of the frame house, barking and growling. The mutt crawled between the bars of the corral and began to race across the grass pasture; but when he caught the smell of coyote, he stopped immediately, hackles raised on his back, and barked at the top of his voice.

A door opened at the back of the house. An Indian clad in long underwear yelled at the dog, then went back inside, slamming the door. The dog, abandoned to his own bravery, growled and walked stiff-legged to the rabbit brush where the coyote had lain. Cautiously, he sniffed until he was sure the invader was gone. When he felt entirely confident no coyote lurked in the nearby brush, to suddenly appear with fierce snarls and run him back, he lifted his hind leg, made his mark, scratched up the ground and trotted back to the house, growling all the way.

High on a ledge some distance away, Two Toes dropped the limp rooster and surveyed the farm below. He was free of pursuit. He ate the bird, bones, feathers and all, and with a last look down the draw to the farm, climbed up on the flat table and trotted east and north, toward his mate's den.

SEVEN

▲ ▲ ▲

A Sprung Trap

J ACK WILLIG was in the saddle before dawn, eager for the day ahead and spurred on by a tickle in his gut.

He had a lot of miles to cover. First priority was checking the hills west of the Leota Bottoms next to the abandoned farms. A year before, he'd taken two dens full of pups there. Coyotes could be denning there again this spring. He would spend hours checking the washes and gullies for tracks and lay more trap sets with his new scent.

Then there would be something else Willig would do. He would check the trap set with the new scent he'd made at the bones from the deer kill. That was what filled him with excitement.

There is a feeling a trapper gets after he finds fresh tracks in an area well-traveled by animals, and he's laid down a good set leaving no traces and everything's just right. It's a certainty; a sense of anticipation of success. It makes him feel whole. And it makes the long hours in the saddle melt by.

Everything felt just right now for Trapper Jack. First, he knew Two Toes would go out of his way to check a popular pissing post like the deer bones near the big greasewood bush on the river. Many coyotes had visited there; Two Toes would, too. Second, the missing piece of the puzzle had been found. Up to now, Two Toes had flushed out every one of Willig's traps; he'd out-foxed him every time. But Willig would get the coyote with his new scent. He'd end this game. He'd win it this time. He felt sure.

Willig rode north as far as Wonsits Valley, to the old Indian campsite on Green River, then swung west toward the Leota Bottoms, checking all the time for signs of denning coyotes. There were scant tracks and no den sign clear to the abandoned dry farms, though there was plenty of game. As he passed a fence corner piled up with tumbleweeds, a big white-tailed jackrabbit that had crouched in the cover sensed it had been spotted. With big long jumps, it burst out of the brush and loped across the front yard, its ungainly ears like long socks pulled back in the wind.

Prairie dogs, kangaroo rats and jackrabbits had overrun these empty, unplowed fields, which now were happy hunting grounds for hawks, owls and coyotes. Willig moved his horse through the dry, dusty soil. There were a few fresh coyote tracks, but none were those of the animal he was looking for. At the heads of two washes where irrigation water from Pelican Lake had once flowed down to the farms, he set two more traps.

Willig worked his way along the south edge of the bench land, and spotted a filmy curtain of dust that had been kicked up a half-hour before on the truck trail ahead. The way it hung in the quiet lonesome of the range, sunshine filtering through, would have filled a city person with melancholia. But not Trapper Jack. He was at home on the range. He took stock of everything from his nose to the horizon, and the dust cloud was just one more sign for him to digest. He gathered it had been left by a pickup going from the trading post toward Halfway Hollow and the highway. It was some sheepman going to town, probably. Maybe it was Bingham.

That thought made Willig press on with more determination. He wanted to get his tracking out of the way.

The trapper checked the gullies where he'd dug out dens in years past; but none of the holes had been freshly cleaned out. So far, the sandy bottoms of the washes showed little coyote sign, and there were no tracks that increased in number to indicate a live den. A skilled trapper will follow such tracks knowing that as he gets within a half- to a quarter-mile of a den, they would begin to crisscross, old and new, going in every direction—almost always left by coyote parents heading for hunts. He would have to sort out which ones led to the den and which away from it. Which were those of the dog and bitch and which tracks of other coyotes? And was there really a den, or was there a dead cow or sheep or horse close by that all the coyotes were feeding on?

An old hand like Willig could often get it sorted out in a few hours, though sometimes it took a day. To him, a den was like the hub of a wheel, and the tracks were like spokes fanning out in a large circle, all leading back to the same center. If he was certain of a den, he would search out a good fresh track to follow. If the track wandered, say, from a rock ledge up to a sand hill and over to a clump of rabbit brush, Willig knew the coyote was hunting, and hence going away from the den. But if the track led steadily in the same direction with no hunting moves, he could be sure the coyote was heading back to the den with food for the pups.

But there were no telltale tracks this day. It was evening now. Willig and Sontag had covered a good 20 miles of rough travel and were still a couple hours from camp. Another day, Willig would have headed immediately back to Squaw Wash. He was tired and thirsty, and so was his horse. That normally ended his day's work. But not today. This was the hour he'd been waiting for.

He turned north, toward the big horseshoe-shaped bend on the river that lay east of the Twist Hills. As Sontag dropped down off the last bench to the river bottom, Willig could hardly keep from spurring him into a trot. Shadows had fallen across Green River by the time they finally rode around the high riverbank to the trap set at the bones and rib cage of the dead doe.

Willig rode up to the big greasewood and reined up his horse. He sat motionless in the saddle, his glazed eyes staring ahead. His shoulders sagged as the breath exhaled his lungs. The scene unfolded in a second: the porcupine carcass hanging absurdly upside-down from the greasewood; the trap clamped on its left hind foot; the meat ripped from its bones, but with the hide and quills, head and clawed feet intact.

Willig slowly looked down to the fresh turd and urine spots on the ground in front of the porcupine and—the final blow—the fresh coyote track. The two middle toes were missing. Willig sat numb in the saddle for several minutes.

"You rotten sonofabitchin' four-legged bastard," he finally muttered, with icy calm.

It was dark when he arrived at camp. He reined Sontag up at the rear of the wagon and swung down. Slowly, he took his rifle out of its scabbard and leaned it against the sheep wagon. He hung his trap bag, scent bag and hammer on a hook on the side of the wagon. He loosened the cinch on the saddle and threw it over one of the rubber-tired wheels, then put the blanket and bridle on top of that. He grabbed up the grain bucket from under the wagon, filled it from the oat barrel and set it down for Sontag. He felt he was in a daze, but wasn't sure why.

Willig climbed into the dark wagon, groped around for the lantern and set it on the table. He primed it with quick, strong pumps. He thumbed a match, twisted the valve a half-turn, and when the mantles popped into light, opened the valve wide and hung the lantern from the hook in the ceiling bow.

It was when he started to sit that his temper blew.

"You r-r-rotten s-s-s-onofab-b-bitchin' f-four-legged bastard!" he shouted, at the top of his lungs, smashing the table with his fist.

"You r-rotten s-s-sonofabitchin' b-bastard, I sh-should've had you!!"

Willig banged the table and cursed Two Toes. He hammered it some more and cursed all coyotes. Then he cursed Ty Bingham, sheepmen in general, and, lastly, his own stupid luck. The lantern above swayed gently, sending an orb of light back and forth in the cramped quarters, hissing softly.

It was several minutes before he suddenly became aware of a voice. It sounded like another person shouting in the wagon. But it was his voice, in a stuttering rage, and it recalled for him a maniac drunk he'd seen once in a back street in Ogden, frothing and flailing at some invisible demon while onlookers guffawed at the gutter rat who'd got hold of a bottle of bad Prohibition moonshine.

As if awakening from a far-off place, Willig looked up strangely at his clenched hand suspended above the table in the yellow lantern glow. He found he was breathing hard, and when he brought his fist down again he felt the impact and the vibrations and let it stay there, the fingers slowly uncurling until they pressed flat against the wood, solid and real.

Willig fell silent, face red, veins standing out on his neck. The rage ebbed away, releasing a slow chuckle that grew into a laugh. He rubbed his sore hand and swore again, quietly. He stood and stared into the square of glass he used as a mirror. The face that looked back in the dim light wore a wry grin.

"Man, you sure let go of that one," he said.

Willig shook his head slowly to clear his brain, and felt the ache in his neck muscles. He poured himself a cup of cold morning coffee from the pot on the stove. He swished the sourness around his mouth, then took the lid off the frying pan and wiped up the cold bacon grease with a slice of bread. He chewed it slowly and washed it down with the bitter coffee.

He was back in the real world now. Already, his mind was spinning new plans. It would continue to do so as he slept. He turned down his quilts and heavily pulled off his boots and socks, Levi's and shirt.

Crawling into bed in his longjohns, he reached up and turned off the lantern. He was almost asleep before it quit sputtering.

EIGHT

▲ ▲ ▲

To the Swinging Bridge

THAT MORNING, Billy Butts had sat in his saddle and gazed north at the hovering dust kicked up from Ty Bingham's truck as it had disappeared over the distant ridge that morning. It was evening now, and Butts, riding steadily north, had settled into a reflective mood.

William Butterman had done enough living to know that hard work alone did not lead to success in the sheep business, or any livestock business, for that matter. He knew that mysterious force called luck, for lack of a better name, somehow always found a way to intrude into the mix. It was what put the fickle in fate. It was what set an innocent man in the right place at the right time, or the wrong place at the wrong time. It was what had landed himself, after a long and twisted chain of events, out West.

As Butts cut north to round up his herd, crossing a draw and climbing up onto a flat, he considered he was trusting his luck right now. His plan was to sleep in the sheep wagon, after gathering and bedding down the sheep. Then tomorrow he would move the herd to Green River, not far from the crossing point at the swinging bridge. While this plan meant leaving the sheep alone during the deep hours of the night, far from the wagon where he'd sleep, Butts believed it'd be OK. He felt lucky. He rode steadily north for two miles, his two dogs trotting behind.

The horse picked up the sheep bells first. It flicked its ears straight ahead. Butts rode up on the mesa toward the tinkling bells and stopped at its edge. Looking down into the shallow valley that stretched a half-mile to the next hill, he saw the herd was split. Some were feeding down the valley heading north, the others up it going south. A half-mile separated the band.

Butts called his dogs with a sharp whistle. With his index finger, he pointed one to the left and the other to the right. They responded on cue, darting forward in different directions with uncanny speed toward the south-moving sheep. Born with the pack-hunting instincts to nip at the heels of animals much larger and move them around, they'd long since been trained to obey hand signals, after mastering the verbal commands to "heel!" or "fetch!"

Butts loped up the valley, sweeping wide until he was 200 yards ahead of the wayward band. He swung his horse around and started moving across in front of the black bellwethers, the castrated buck sheep. The wethers were larger and more aggressive than the ewes, and so the band followed them as leaders, but also because they responded to the bells hung around the wethers' necks.

The Scotch shelties were now on either side of the south-facing band. With Butts yelling and waving his Stetson and the dogs barking and nipping at the wethers' hind legs, the separated half of the herd turned and headed north toward the rest of the band. Butts moved the sheep steadily, giving them little time to graze. Before long, the herd was bunched. He called the dogs back and let the herd graze at its own pace, moving slowly north.

At sundown, the herder headed the sheep for a low, round hill. As the dusk thickened they bedded on the knoll, tired from the long drive. They were nice and quiet on the bed ground and even the bells on the black wethers ceased to clang. From his spot on top of the knoll, Butts surveyed the herd. He quickly counted the black bellwethers that stood out in the sea of white. There was one black for every 100 sheep; Butts spotted seven and thought he saw the eighth, though now it was too dark to be sure. He didn't worry, though, feeling lucky as he did. He counted the blacks every night at dusk and repeated the process every dawn as he moved the sheep off the bed ground. He knew tomorrow morning he'd be adding up eight blacks.

Butts pulled the saddle and blanket off his horse and with the upper side of the blanket rubbed down the sorrel's back where it was hot and sweaty. The horse was glad to have the weight off. Butts slipped the bit out of his mouth and tied the reins around the saddle horn. The sorrel moved off to graze.

The herder stretched out tired and lazy against a rock. It was a clear night. The moon would be coming up shortly, and lots of stars. In a few minutes, he was lying on his saddle blanket below the rock, his head on the seat of the saddle. He could just make out his horse grazing, head down, 200 yards away.

The canopy of space enclosed the night. Butts picked out the Big Dipper like an old friend in the crowd of white glitter, traced down its bent griddle-like handle and out to the North Star. It was a beacon pointing the direction the herd was heading. Then he moved up and back the other way along the line that formed the handle to the box-like Little Dipper.

The endless constellations blinked out their eternal dance as Butts allowed himself to nod off. When the diamonds that filled the heavens suddenly melted into snowflakes falling, the herder's eyelids shut fast.

▲　▲　▲

Billy Butts woke with a start. He was cold and stiff. The moon had come up, a scythe-like crescent. He pulled his Ingersoll out of his shirt pocket, thumbed a match and saw it was 10:30.

The sheep were quiet and his horse was out of sight. Butts untied his Levi's jacket from behind the saddle and slipped it on. He started walking in the direction his horse had been grazing before he'd dozed off. He caught up with him on the other side of the shallow valley, untied the reins and led him back, stopping several times on the way to pick up pieces of dry sage and slip them under an arm.

At the rock, he dropped the reins. He piled up the sage branches in a little hollow spot and began stripping the shaggy bark off a limb to make tinder. It lit easily from a match. Soon the herder had an Indian fire going, small enough to serve his needs and yet not throwing much light.

He settled down next to the flames, taking in the heat radiating from his side and also reflecting off the rock on the other. His hands and legs were quickly warmed by the glowing coals. The dogs hunched and lay behind, heads on paws crossed under chins.

The moon hung high now, and bright. A dead still had descended. From far down toward the river, a hunting owl hooted and was answered by its mate. But the only noise from the herd was an occasional cough from dry grass seeds stuck in a throat. When the orange coals began to fade and die out, Butts rose. His dogs would stay behind.

The herder saddled his horse, put the bit in the horse's mouth and buckled the headstall. He was about to step into the saddle when a coyote barked, quite a ways off to the northeast. He immediately stood still, waiting to hear if other coyotes howled or barked in response. He waited an entire minute. None did.

Butts drew a sigh of relief. At least it wasn't a pair or a pack of yearlings out hunting. But the coyote's bark had been like a distant bugle call, instantly filling him with a dread and loathing that lingered, giving a little edge to his nerves that made him feel maybe he wasn't so lucky, after all. The bark had roused in him fear and the resolve to shoot any of the bloody bastards that showed itself in the days ahead.

Butts tarried 15 minutes more at the rock. It stayed quiet, so he mounted up and headed for the cottonwood grove and the spring where his boss had left the sheep wagon. Around midnight, he saw the white cover of the wagon ahead. He quickly removed the saddle, gun, bridle and blanket from the horse. The hobbles were on a hook on the side of the wagon. He fastened the heavy buckles, strapped with a stout piece of latigo on a D-ring, around each of the horse's front legs. Hobbled by the buckles and chain, it could only walk or hop along slowly now. Butts found the small bucket by the sheep wagon, filled it with oats, and set it down for the nickering horse.

Butts was hungry, too. Inside the sheep wagon, he lit the Coleman lantern and made a fire in the stove. He reached under his bedroll, pulled out a white flour sack and took out the hind-quarter of a fat wether he had butchered over a week ago. The cheapest meat a sheepman can give his camp tender is from his own herd, and a wether has the most meat.

Butts was like a short-order cook with the mutton. He cut four slices of round steak out of the leg, floured and salted the steaks and set them aside on a plate. He wiped the bottom of the frying pan in bacon grease and set the pan on the fire on the back of the stove. He took a kettle from the storage space under the bench seat and fished two cold boiled potatoes from it. He sliced the potatoes into the hot frying pan and added more slices from a white onion. He put a lid on the pan and let it all simmer while he set a fresh pot of coffee on the stove.

Butts stirred the potatoes and onions until they were nicely browned and spooned them on a plate which he set on the back of the stove to keep warm. The sheep wagon filled with savory smells. The herder's mouth watered. He got the pan hot again, coated it with more bacon grease and plopped in the steaks to fry. The coffee boiled and he put a cup of cold water in to settle the grounds. Then he removed two cold baking-soda biscuits from a second flour sack. Soon he was putting lamb steak, pota-toes and onions on his plate.

Butts ate his dinner with relish, licking his fingers. He washed down with coffee the last of the two steaks he'd devoured, and picked meat from his teeth with a wood sliver. Then he set the coffee pot on the back of the stove for a quick cup in the morn-ing. He wrapped the other two steaks with two slices of sour-dough bread up in a small white salt sack for his lunch the next day. It was long past midnight when he crawled into bed.

Four-thirty came fast. Butts woke by his internal clock. He made a quick fire in the stove and the coffee boiled while he saddled his horse. Two fast cups, and he was headed for the bed ground on the knoll.

It was just getting daylight when he reached the herd. Half the sheep were already up. Butts pointed the direction he wanted them to take and the dogs soon had the entire herd moving out to graze. He rode slowly around the bed ground, counting the blacks, his quick eyes missing nothing. There were no sign of lambs born in the night, or sick sheep. He continued on, making a wide circle around the outside of the bed ground, checking for fresh sheep tracks that would mean strays. He watched closely for any sign of coyote. Seeing none, he again felt lucky. The herd had not been hit during the night—he had guessed right again.

It was late afternoon when he sat in the saddle, finishing his cold lunch. The herd had moved along quite well, and was now only a mile or so from the cottonwood campground. Not long after, a bellwether and others at the lead smelled the water from the Green River. Quickly, with lots of bleating and baa'ing, they headed for the river.

Soon, they were all scattered along the edge, drinking.

NINE

▲ ▲ ▲

Tight Budget, Tight Dollars

O NCE EVERY SPRING, the weight of family history came
bearing down on Ty Bingham. It was usually at a time
like this—sitting in the house his father built, at the old
oak roll top desk in the parlor room that Ty had converted into
an office, working over the cost estimates for the coming year.

His grandfather, Sessions Bingham, had come to Wyoming from
Iowa with a small band of sheep in 1869, and never gone back.
He found himself a nice creek and a good home-ranching site
and built a sturdy log cabin and corrals. The good sheepmen
made it where the careless ones didn't, and Sessions Bingham
had put in the hard work and sweat and gambling and pure cour-
age that it took to succeed. His oldest son, Heber, had carried on
the legacy, through fat times as well as blizzards and storms, dry
spells and the killings of wolves and coyotes and other predators
that constantly threatened ruin. By the time he passed on in 1927,
he'd turned over to his oldest son, Tyrus, a ranch with nearly
1,000 head of sheep and acreage added from three neighboring
operations that had gone broke over the two generations since
Sessions Bingham had disembarked from the Union Pacific cars
at a remote rail head in wild Wyoming.

"You are going to own and run one of the best sheep outfits in
Utah," Heber's father had told his son not long before he died.
"You have worked with me since you were 6 years old. I am
leaving it in your hands. Take care of your mother and be a good
sheepman."

Ty had.

He moved his family into the home place his father had built in 1891, a year after Ty was born, so that his mother would not go through the trauma of being displaced from her home after all those years. Like with so many long-married couples, she followed her husband in death soon after, and Ty buried her in the Maeser Cemetery alongside his father, as they had wished. As the family's new patriarch, he worked unwaveringly to continue the legacy passed onto him.

Over the next 10 years, Bingham steadily built up the herd, increased the range capacity and solidified water and range rights. He was now running nearly 1,500 sheep, counting ewes, lambs, bucks and wethers, plus about 150 carry-over yearling lambs to replace the ewes that were culled out because they were old or crippled. Every spring, any ewe that did not have a lamb was cut from the herd to be sold for wool and meat, and replaced by a holdover yearling that was ready to breed.

Through such painstaking management, Bingham had by 1937 increased the number of lambs docked at shearing time from 70 percent to more than 80 percent of his bred ewes, so that those 1,000 ewes were putting 100 more lambs into the herd than when his father was alive.

Like all sheepmen, Ty Bingham was proud of his work. Ranchers like him furnished the fleece for most of the wool clothing in the nation. It was the stalwart sheepmen who put good lamb in the market. They fulfilled a national need, just like the cattlemen and the corn-growers.

But now it was 1941, and America, and the world, had been mired in a great depression for more than a decade. Wool had sold for as low as 5¢ per pound, and a leg of lamb did not bring much more than the price of hamburger. To top it all off, the drought in the West was ravaging the range. And for the first time in his life, Ty Bingham was worried about bank loans.

In each of the past three years, he'd borrowed money from the Bank of Vernal. Betting against his yearly profits, he'd built new lambing sheds, drilled another well on the home ranch and bought a new mower and baler to put up the much-needed hay for feed during the winter. His only hope to ride out the drought was to turn a profit and not go under, as so many others had. But the amount of profit he needed to turn to stay afloat grew greater each year.

As Bingham worked over his numbers now, running through them again and again, he understood with no shadow of a doubt that his income estimates depended entirely upon the lamb crop he could take to market in the fall. This year, the difference between 80 percent and 90 percent meant the difference between survival and failure. Devastating failure, in fact. He needed those extra 100 lambs. He needed the extra money, or he'd be done.

Bingham knew he was taking every possible step to ensure a high percentage lamb crop. Each year now, every one of his bucks wore the marking collar so that no unbred ewe could go unnoticed. If a ewe did not show the daub of red paint on her back from being topped by a ram, she was put in a small pen where the ram was sure to breed her. If a ewe was old or sick and had not lambed the previous year, she was gone that spring, cut out of the herd and sold. If a ewe had a lamb but rejected it, she was tied to a sagebrush so that the lamb could suck. And as soon as it had nursed a time or two, the ewe claimed it and the pair was turned loose into the herd.

If a ewe dropped twin lambs and did not nurse both, rejecting one, the ewe would be tied to a bush or stake until it let both lambs suck. If a ewe lost a lamb, it was skinned and its hide tied onto a "bummer" lamb that had lost its mother. Then it was given to suckle to the ewe that had lost its lamb, for she would now identify the smell of the bummer as that of her own.

Bingham knew that with good herders taking good care of the lambing herd, a 90 percent lamb crop was possible. And he knew that coming out with 90 lambs for every 100 bred ewes would cover the expenses of operation and the bank payment. The Bingham legacy would be preserved.

The sheepman, sitting in his chair in the converted parlor of the main house where his parents had once entertained a Mormon apostle, was resigned to the fact he had to make it this year. Should he come up short—seven decades of Bingham blood, toil and tears would be for naught. Last year he had not turned the corner. Bingham had had to roll his bank debt over for one year more. Each year for three years now, he had borrowed $10,000 to carry his annual budget. The first two years, he had paid off only $6,000 each time, forcing him to renew the loan plus ask for $4,000 more. Each time, that had dug the hole a little deeper.

This last time, he could see the concern in the bank president's face. Adair Johnson, 6-foot-5 and ramrod-straight, with a full head of iron-gray hair and a dignified manner as if he belonged in the British Parliament, had looked at Bingham solemnly and said, "Ty, I will carry you one more year, but we are short of cash and long on loan collateral. We have sheepmen, cattlemen, farmers, timber men, oil men and town businessmen, all trying to hang on, and we cannot go any further with you. So the shipping of lambs in October is pay-up day."

Bingham knew by Johnson's tone that the banker had made this speech 20 or 30 times before. He knew the Bank of Vernal had had to close on the mortgages of homes and also on chattel mortgages on trucks, balers and other equipment, horses, cows and sheep. It couldn't divest of what it already had. It, too, was in a bind.

Ty Bingham's pastures and hay land were mortgaged and there was a chattel on his sheep. He was facing disaster, just like the erstwhile neighbors whose ranches his grandfather and father had bought up. It was as simple as that. And there was nothing to do about it, but bite his lip and work even harder. Defaulting on the loan would mean he'd lose his collateral, And the minute that happened, he was through.

Bingham went over his numbers one final time. By his exhaustive calculations—after all his planning, saving and figuring—the only place he could see some daylight was in reducing the coyote losses to his herd.

Some of his sheepmen friends said that coyotes cost them at least 20 percent of their lamb crops. Two or three even claimed a

40 percent loss, though Bingham didn't believe them. He knew that some sheepmen were nothing but lazy, or loved to drink and play cards in town instead of checking up on their herders. Some had even hired herders for half the going wage and gotten what they deserved—next to no care of their sheep. Bingham even knew of one shiftless, no-good herder working for his neighbor, John Schackling, who blamed all the sheep losses on coyotes. This very same man never got out of bed before 9 a.m., rode around the herd until late afternoon and then headed for the sheep wagon, letting the herd bed down for itself until he rose at 9 the next morning.

But Bingham had Billy Butts. And the numbers he'd worked up said he had a chance. This year, he'd have everyone working to save every lamb possible. Billy Butts would skin the dead lambs and find the bummer lambs that had lost their mothers, identifying them by their constant baa'ing and looking for a bag full of warm milk. He'd tie up the bummers with the dead lambs' hides and pair them up properly with the lambless ewes, whom he'd spot by their big bags. Bums could get weak and skinny within a few days, and if there were too many in the herd, Butts and Bingham would load them into the pickup so they could be taken back to the home ranch to be bottle-fed.

Bingham's grandpa and his pa had made it through thick and thin, and by God, he would, too. But it would not be easy and he would need some luck. Luck that there wouldn't be a sudden freezing snow. Or an outbreak of scabies. Or too many strays drowning in the river. Or coyotes hitting him too hard, like the past two years.

And that's what it finally came down to, Bingham decided, sitting in his parlor.

Good sheep herding could handle the weather and the disease and keep the sheep moving along the river to the home ranch. It could manage the operation damn well—because Bingham knew exactly how much it cost to bale a ton of hay; how much he had to pay for gas, oil, vaccine, herder's wages, hay hands; exactly what he needed to do to break even.

But there was the wild card, the uncontrollable variable. Coyotes ate into his margin. What could he do about it?

Jack Willig. That's what.

Bingham would have to make damn sure that the government trapper had all the help he could get.

Willig could do only one thing to help, and that was kill coyotes. And by God, he'd have to do it this year. He'd have to keep the coyotes away from his sheep. And he'd especially have to kill that goddamned Two Toes.

Bingham was through scribbling out the numbers. He knew it came down to this: His family's welfare—the whole operation— were at stake now. And where delicate calculations were concerned, the kills by one smart coyote could topple the entire house of cards.

Bingham knew that Willig was riding from daylight to dark, trying to catch Two Toes. But he did not give a damn. If effort was all that mattered, then he wouldn't be in this desperate corner, and neither would the other good sheepmen of Utah. Results were what mattered. What could he do to better guarantee them?

Bingham set down his pencil and closed his books. He was decided on what he must do.

He must get in touch with Willig's boss.

Longer hours, harder work, another trapper—something, anything—just get that Two Toes. Get him off his back forever.

Bingham would get in touch with Willig's boss. He would demand results.

TEN

▲ ▲ ▲

A Herd to Feed On

IT WAS STILL DARK, but the eastern sky bore a dull streak of gray. Two Toes lay curled up in his bed under the rock ledge. He was motionless but for his ears, always straining for the slightest sound.

The wind whistled, so soft and light, as a hunting owl sailed over the top of the sandstone knobs in the pre-dawn sky, gliding silently, looking for pack rats on the ground. The "hoo-hoo-hoo" of a long-eared owl came from the cottonwoods along the river; and, softer, the "hoo-hoo-hoo" from its mate, answering from down the bank.

Two Toes rose. He stretched his front legs out as far as they would go, and craned his head forward the length of his neck. He yawned, his long red tongue curling above his nose, then stood erect, turning his head up the draw toward the den. He listened for any sound from his bitch, who was nursing her hungry pups. But all was still.

The coyote turned again, jumped up onto the rocks above, then again onto the smooth sandstone ledge that ran south. He moved quickly, trotting through the dying night, heading again for the Indian farms along the north side of the Duchesne River. Several miles away, on the bench above the ranch where he had killed the rooster, he proceeded slowly. White curls of smoke were rising from the chimneys. Activity was afoot.

Approaching the head of the bushy draw that ran down to the ranch buildings, the coyote stopped. Noises of horses and the bawling of a calf were coming from under the rim where he was standing. He flattened himself against the dry grass of the bench land. In a few moments, two Indians on horseback came into view. They were pushing three cows and two new calves in front of them. The cows had calved in the last couple days along the river bottom; now, the Indian cowboys were moving them into the corral at the jumble of farm buildings. Two Toes lay motionless until the men on horses and the cattle disappeared around the point. Then he jumped up and loped quickly away.

He hurried in the opposite direction, away from the horses and men. He ran down the bench land, toward the river until the benches ended in a series of ledges, each one falling toward the water like gigantic, crooked stairs. Two Toes dropped down the last ledge to the river bottom and rested, finally, among greasewood brush at the edge of a dry flat.

Again, the bright morning seemed to quicken with activity. The big coyote's ears cocked forward. From very far off, there came the sound of an ax chopping. Two Toes knew it was coming from the trading post, where there were always men. But no scent or smell carried forward the signal of danger. And so he started across the flat toward the river.

He circled around the large patches of cockleburs, for their brown, spiny burrs could catch between his toes, drawing blood and causing pain when he pulled them out with his teeth. At the north end of the flat was a small prairie dog town. Two Toes stood and surveyed it from a little distance. But it was too late. He had been spotted by the alert sentinels, upright on top of the mounds near their holes. They sounded their alarm in high staccato barks, and the few that were feeding on the sparse grass instantly scurried for their holes.

Two Toes trotted on, paying no attention as a dog ran down its hole, its little white-tipped tail waving up and down before disappearing. One of his first hunting lessons as a pup was that if he didn't catch a dog outside its hole, there was no use trying to dig it out. Only a badger, with its triangle-shaped head and big claws, could dig a prairie dog from its hole.

The coyote continued his hunting rounds as he had for his three years, moving from one potential source of food to the next. Now he was running along the faint road flattened by the pickups that came and went across the swinging bridge that led to Willow Creek Road. At a little pool on the river's edge not far from the bridge, he lowered his head to drink. No sooner was he lapping up the cool water than he heard a funny but distinct sound. It was silent again, then the sound carried across the water once more.

It was the baa'ing of sheep.

Two Toes forgot about his drink. He raised his nose, sniffing for any scent on the breeze. The wind was blowing upriver and he could detect nothing.

The coyote worked his way up the road. The bridge rose into sight, its outline stretching over the river. At the span's approach, he hesitated. Another bleat broke the air, heavier, closer than before. It was coming from the brush at the edge of a cottonwood grove, across the water. The sound drew Two Toes forward. He stepped gingerly onto the wood planks that felt alive, gently rocking under his feet as he stopped and tried to balance.

Two Toes was afraid. Men and horses and cars used this bridge. He took another unsure step. The boards vibrated and slightly swayed in the wind. Two Toes was barely on the bridge. He could turn around and be off in a second, back in the safety of the brush. Straight ahead, he would be in the wide open, badly exposed to his enemies.

Again, there came the baa'ing of sheep, louder, clear notes in the daylight. Two Toes couldn't resist. He stepped forward. His front legs found solid planks. Then he shot like a blur across the bridge and was into the first cover of rabbit brush.

He crawled carefully through the brush, senses alert to any hint of trouble. Eyes, ears and nose roamed the air as the sheeps' baa'ing directed him to where they fed on the far side of the cottonwood trees. He was slowly coming up to the band now; he could begin to smell the mustiness of their wool. But there was something else in the air: a whiff of wood smoke. It meant fire. It meant man.

Two Toes continued, low to the ground, through the tall sage for 100 yards. As he got close to the cottonwoods, he reached a buffalo berry bush, tall and dotted with the dried orange berries he had eaten occasionally on a meatless morning. Almost immediately, he heard a thumping sound, followed by grunts, on the other side.

The coyote crawled cautiously around the bush. In front stood a ewe, splay-legged, giving birth. With a couple jerks, the new lamb slid out, head first, onto the dry cottonwood leaves. It was a small wet blob, dark from blotches of blood and the bag of water it had left, and still covered in the shiny afterbirth.

Two Toes lunged. Before the ewe could turn to begin licking the lamb's face to free it of the suffocating film, the coyote had lifted the still-blind lamb by its throat and was carrying it off toward the bridge. The ewe bleated loudly at the sight of the dark form, frightened even though it was heading away. She began to waddle off toward the herd, still baa'ing. Two other sheep were grazing nearby. They looked up, baa'ed, and moved meekly away. But with no other sheep around to panic at the coyote's rush, no alarm was raised in the herd.

The lamb quit kicking before Two Toes reached the bridge. With its limp bulk locked in his jaws, he bolted over the boards and into the mouth of a draw that emptied into the river, not stopping until he was behind a clump of greasewood. Panting heavily, he dropped the load and looked back for any sign of pursuit. There was no barking, no crack bursting the air like thunder, no sound or sight of horse, man or dog. Just the faint and occasional baa'ing from the herd of sheep in the cottonwoods across the river, scattered along its bank, grazing eastward, away from the water.

The coyote relaxed. He nosed the kill lying before him. He picked it up by the small of its back and started up the wash. After several hundred yards, he climbed up the south bank and trotted across the bench land that ran north of the Indian farms.

Frequently, he pulled up and dropped the lamb, whose weight, small as its body was, made his jaws ache.

It was warm and sunny. Two Toes put miles between himself and the river. Finally, at an outcropping of rock, he released the lamb and took a long rest, panting heavily. He was hungry. The taste of its wool and blood in his mouth had whetted his appetite. His breathing returned, easy and steady. He moved over to the dead lamb. He bit down at the small of the back. Its bones crunched as he chewed the body in two. Then he tore into the front half, gnawing and chewing until he had eaten all of the meat off the lamb's head, neck, ribs and front legs, picking the half-carcass clean.

His meal done, he picked up the hindquarters and trotted north along the vast bench land, toward the Twist Hills. His kill now weighed about 2 pounds, but every so often the coyote would stop and let it go and rest. Up on the high rock ledges of the Twist Hills, which he had approached from due south, Two Toes swung to the northeast, working his way up on the rock outcropping on the east side of the hills, as if deliberately leaving little sign or tracks.

The sun had sunk low as he rounded his high rock bed ground and dropped down the north side into the wash, directly above his mate's den. At the mouth, he dropped the lamb and gave a sharp bark inside. The bitch came out and promptly sunk her teeth into the fresh kill. Two Toes watched her clean all the meat off the hindquarters. When she'd returned into the den, he worked his way out of the gully and back up to the rock ledge and his bed ground.

The high rocks cast long shadows down the plateaus to the east. Soon, the cottonwoods on the river were in the shadows, which now climbed up the hills on the east side of Green River. As dusk settled a calm over the basin, a coyote howled to the east. He was answered shortly by one to the south. Then a third, on the west side of the river and north of the den, gave a long drawn-out howl, followed by a series of yelps.

Two Toes lay contentedly. He was not interested in the howling. They were expressions of territory. His work for this day was done. But he knew he was not the only coyote hunting for a litter of pups.

ELEVEN

▲ ▲ ▲

A Row Over Denning

A PICKUP TRUCK motored slowly over the high desert, on its way to Cedar Flats in search of a band of sheep heading north for lambing.

Behind the wheel was Joe Haslett Jr., known to everyone as Young Joe, for he was thirty; and next to him was his father, better known as Old Joe, for he was seventy. Old Joe, like Ty Bingham, was a second-generation sheepman. His father had settled in the Uintah Basin in the 1880s. He'd handed the ranch over to his son in 1923. Now Old Joe, slowly, was doing the same with his son.

And so it was the younger Haslett who stared fixedly through the windshield now, while the older sat back, stone-faced, wheels grinding in his mind as they did in every sheepman's head come spring, thoughts fixed on lambing and shearing, plotting two month's ahead. And it was Young Joe who finally broke the silence.

"Dad, there's some dust above that ridge way out there on the right."

Old Joe sat forward, squinted a spell, then said, "That should be Hod and the herd."

Hod Hogan, their herder, was supposed to be on the trail heading toward the river crossing at the swinging bridge. The Hasletts figured he'd be near the old bed ground at Lizard Springs. They'd figured right.

Their pickup crossed a large flat and pulled up on the ridge, following the well-worn ruts of truck tracks that led to the springs.

Topping the ridge, father and son immediately spotted the sheep band moving slowing toward them, about a mile away. Young Joe pulled the pickup up to the springs. The two men climbed out and walked to the water tanks to make sure they were full. The sheep would be dry and thirsty when they arrived.

The fresh spring water was high and cool in the 250-gallon metal tank, which was filled to its seven-foot depth and fifteen-foot diameter. The spigot at one end sent a little sprinkle into the wooden troughs that were full, too, running out twenty feet. At their ends, water splashed out into little rivulets, forming a small stream that followed the low ground, wending away.

Young Joe reached up and dipped his hand into the tank, feeling the water that was being warmed by the late-morning sun. He and his father turned as hoofbeats approached. With a "howdy," Hod Hogan rode past, dismounted, tossed his hat on the ground, then buried his face in the tank's cold water like a dehydrated bear.

The big, heavy-chested man stood back, finally, shaking the water from his hair and wiping his bristly, week-old growth of black beard.

"A warm day and a lot of dust makes that water feel mighty good," he said, as his greeting.

Old Joe grinned. "Where's the sheep wagon?"

"Right where Young Joe left it last, over on Sage Flat," Hod replied.

"Is it all set to hook up to?" Young Joe asked.

Hod nodded.

"Good," said Old Joe, still the one in charge.

He turned to his son. "Why don't you go get the wagon and get camp set up here before dark?"

He turned to the herder. "Hod, you go get the sheep in here and get them watered and bedded down."

That's what I was aiming to do," the herder said, stepping into his saddle. He rode off.

Young Joe hesitated a moment. His father wore a look of concentration. The son could tell he aimed to stay behind. So he got in and drove off without a word.

Old Joe stood for a minute, watching the pickup heading south toward Sage Flat. Then he started walking slowly in a circle around the water tank and troughs. The ground was bare and dusty. No herder had used the water for weeks. The dust would tell much about the coyotes watering at the troughs.

Old Joe made out antelope tracks, old and fresh. He saw tracks from deer, crows and magpies, pack rats and mice. With care, he slowly circled the troughs again. Stooping, and then kneeling, he found another animal's set of tracks fresh-made that morning. There were others, too, weeks-old in mud. It was evident that several coyotes were watering here. It was the only water for several miles.

Absent-mindedly, Old Joe let his fingers dangle in the trough, then lifted the mildly rusty-tasting water to his lips. He stared off toward the ridge for a long time, waiting.

The first band of sheep came over the ridge-top. Smelling water, they started to run. Soon, the ground surged with baa'ing, trampling sheep, stirring up the dust, the leaders' bells tinkling in the early afternoon. The troughs were packed now with sheep, crowding each other, stomping, trying to dip their heads to drink. They butted against the troughs, which were wedged between wooden braces wired to the ground. Dust hung thick and heavy in the air. The water muddied up.

Hod and his two dogs stayed well back from the troughs, next to Old Joe. When the sheep had finally had all the water they wanted, the herder and his dogs, which were a mix of Collies and some short-haired breed, slowly herded the band to the bed ground on a high spot 300 yards away.

"I can hear the truck," Hod said to Old Joe at the bed ground. "Young Joe will be here pretty quick." He led his horse to the spot where they always parked the sheep wagon, in a little clump of aspen.

Young Joe pulled up, got out and dropped the tongue off the trailer hitch. As he unloaded the supplies, Old Joe spoke loudly to Hod, so both he and his son could hear. His eyes were serious.

"There's quite a bit of coyote sign, fresh and old, all around," the old sheepman said. "I don't like it. You'll have to be careful. Check the bed ground if you wake up at night and if the dogs bark or the sheep raise a fuss, get out there quick with your rifle."

Hod nodded. Under the older man's steady gaze, he felt like he had to say something.

"The dogs are good at night for any coyotes nosing around," Hod said, then added, though he didn't have to, since it went without saying, "If they smell coyotes, they raise all kinds of hell."

Young Joe spoke up.

"While I was picking up the wagon, I noticed the feed. It's not too good. I don't think you can stay here a week or 10 days. We'll be back in five. And if the feed is short, be ready to move by noon."

The two men climbed in the pickup and headed for Green River. The elder, again, was lost in thought.

▲ ▲ ▲

Old Joe's face was even more taut a week later, as he and his son pulled up one morning and stopped in front of the Ouray Trading Post.

Ty Bingham looked up as the two Hasletts walked in.

"Are you coming or going?" he asked.

"We're moving from Lizards Springs," Old Joe replied to his family's old friend.

"We'll camp downriver from your camp, Ty."

"I'm moving across the river today, Joe, so you needn't worry about our sheep."

They were standing at the counter, Osiah Portle popping open two more root beers, when Bingham asked, "How are the coyotes? Any problems?"

It was Young Joe who spoke up.

"We've been hit every night," he said. "We've lost two ewes and three lambs. They're hitting us on the bed grounds before

daylight. Hod says they're howling almost every night. He rode around the sheep this morning, about 4:30. Didn't see a thing. 'Course the coyotes didn't hit us neither."

Old Joe's eyes met Bingham's.

"We stopped to talk to Billy Butts," the elder Haslett said. "The coyotes haven't hit him. But he saw Two Toes' tracks a few days back, between the cottonwoods and the river. He had a tight bag ewe but he never could find the dead lamb."

Bingham absorbed the information silently, though his eyes flashed.

"Suppose Two Toes has denned on the east side?" he finally asked. "Maybe that's where your losses are coming from, Joe."

The older man thought it over.

"Could be," he replied. "We've seen fresh tracks around our dead ewes. Haven't spotted Two Toes' tracks, but that ain't saying it's not him nor his bitch."

Bingham's face flushed with dismay. So the furry devil could have crossed the river? No surprise. But now his schedule had become that much tighter, the calculations that much closer.

He banged his bottle on the counter with a gesture of finality.

"We've got to get that damned Two Toes. That's all there is to it," Bingham said. "And that Willig better get his ass out here. And I mean *now*."

Old Joe nodded. It would be a good idea getting the government trapper out to the area while the sheep kills and tracks were fresh. But as he opened his mouth to speak, the sound of an engine roared and died outside. A truck door banged shut. Boots sounded on the wooden porch. The door swung open.

"Speak of the devil," Young Joe said as Jack Willig stepped inside.

The trapper looked at the three sheepmen standing at the counter watching him with full attention. He shot the younger Haslett a funny look.

"What's all this about?" Willig asked, looking from face to face.

The Hasletts, young and old, looked ready to greet him. But Ty Bingham's expression was grim. And it was Bingham who spoke.

Feeling like there was a frog in his throat, the sheepman cleared it. Mindful of the others in the room, as well as his run-in at Vernal, he tried to modulate his tone. But even as the words left his mouth, he could hear how angry his voice sounded. It was higher and louder than he wanted, as if he couldn't control it.

"Hasletts are camped at Lizard Springs and coyotes are hitting them every night," he said. "They lost several head already."

Bingham set his bottle down with a bang, which startled Osiah Portle, forgotten behind the counter.

"They stopped to talk to Billy Butts and he saw Two Toes' tracks a few days back," Bingham said, voice rising. "They were in the cottonwoods near the river. That could mean Two Toes is denned east of the river. I'm on my way over to move camp now."

"Maybe this is a good opportunity to get Two Toes, what with the fresh kills and fresh sign?" Old Joe asked, leaving the trapper plenty of room to reply.

But Willig's voice was flat and blunt: "Two Toes isn't denned on the east side of the river."

This was too much for Ty Bingham.

"How the hell do you know?!" he snapped. "We see his tracks and the killing tells *me* there's coyote dens not far from where both of us are camped!"

Now it was Willig's turn to keep his temper.

"Two Toes has never denned on the east side of the river, and he won't be starting now," the trapper said. "I've taken his den twice the last three years, *west* of the river, and I've seen his tracks on the west side the last few weeks, but I can't get a line on his den."

Osiah Portle's mustache twitched slightly on his poker face.

Old Joe could sense the pressure building to a boil. He spoke up again, in a voice that rang with reason.

"Maybe that's why you can't track his den, because he's on the east side. We are losing sheep. It looks like Two Toes to me."

Before calm could reassert itself, Bingham popped off again.

"You don't know a damn thing about where Two Toes is," he said to Willig. "I'm telling you, you'd better get over to Haslett's camp and find that coyote den. If that damned coyote starts hitting my herd like he's hit Haslett's and you're not over there finding that den, I'm going to call your big boss in Salt Lake and raise hell."

Bingham reached into his pocket and slapped a coin on the counter without looking. "In fact, I think I'll call him anyway. You're not getting anywhere keeping these damn coyotes under control, and their killing is just getting started."

With that, the sheepman stalked past the trapper and stormed out of the store. He jumped into his pickup and pulled out from the porch, headed for the swinging bridge.

Jack Willig's face was red as a beet. He could feel the heat of his blood rush up his neck and cheeks. His breath snorted in his nostrils. He could hardly speak.

Finally, he walked up to the counter and put his fists down, turning the other way from company until he cooled down.

After a minute or two, he turned to Old Joe.

"Tell Hod I'll be over at daylight for two or three days and we'll look around," he said. And without another word, he stomped from the store.

The Hasletts looked at each other without speaking, then walked out a minute later.

When the store was empty, Osiah Portle picked up the nickel Ty Bingham had left on the counter. He spun it around head-to-tail between a thumb and forefinger, flipped it in the air and caught it in the same hand. Then, with the deftness of the merchant, he punched a key on the brass register and dropped the coin into the protruding tray.

His store was well-stocked. It had been open when Indians were still killing white people. It would be open if all the sheep and sheepmen disappeared from the face of the Earth, and Indians were the only customers left.

TWELVE

▲ ▲ ▲

Full Dens

JACK WILLIG was mad clear through. He stood on the trading post porch taking deep breaths, and looking at the dust trail kicked up by Ty Bingham's truck headed for the swinging bridge.

Willig was stirred up himself. It seemed every time he saw Bingham, there was hell to pay, and he was damn tired of getting rawhided. Especially in front of other sheepmen like Old and Young Joe Haslett.

The trapper had no fears over what Bingham would do. He could damn well call his boss. Willig was doing his best. Even if that dad-blasted sheepman somehow managed to get him in hot water over this Two Toes mess, so what? Willig had been looking for a job when he'd gotten this one with the government. He wasn't worried if he had to go out looking again.

But what made him sore was that he hadn't even had a chance to tell Bingham and the Hasletts and the storekeep that he had already taken two dens: seven pups in one and five in the other. What's more, he'd gotten both bitches with their pups, something that happened not more than a few times a season. Not that he'd have volunteered this; he was soft-spoken, not a show-off. But it would have been nice if the conversation had worked around to it.

The first den had come hard. Willig was working southwest of Bow Knot Bend, where an Indian cow had gotten mired in a bog at a dried-up seep. She had died there, the muck up to her belly, unable to move her 1,000 pounds and probably straining and getting more stuck until she'd finally rolled on her left side and died. She hadn't been dead more than a month; the coyotes, crows and magpies had worked her over pretty good. The birds had picked out her eyes and pecked through her back before she was even dead. Now her brown and white hide was beginning to shrivel and curl where the coyotes had torn her open.

Willig had circled carefully around the carcass until he picked up fresh tracks. They were from the same dog coyote he had tracked earlier. Willig was sure the dog was feeding his bitch in her den. Late on the third day of tracking, through washes and along ledges southwest of the cow carcass, he found the telltale sign of fresh paw prints coming and going. He was close. Quietly, he went back to the river and headed for camp. He didn't want to spook the dog or bitch.

Early the next morning, Willig found the den 300 yards up the draw from where he'd turned around the night before. He got the bitch and seven pups and caved in the mouth of the den. The tracks of the dog coyote showed he was an old one, but he sure as hell wasn't Two Toes.

The second den had been almost a total take—pups, bitch and almost the dog coyote. Willig had found it by working up a draw about a mile from the Indian ranches along the Duchesne River and Leota Bottoms. He knew the abandoned farms of the Bottoms were overrun with rabbits and mice, squirrels and birds; that meant they were good hunting grounds for denning coyotes. And it meant there'd be good tracking.

Willig kept to the bottom of the wash, and worked up north of the draw, spotting tracks from coyotes that had dropped down into the draw, and went up out the other side. He located a fresh track coming in from the east side, going up the draw. When he hit another fresh track going down the draw—proof of a coyote going back and forth on hunts from a den—he dismounted, pulled his Winchester from its scabbard and, leading Sontag, worked quietly forward.

He came to a hole that had been cleaned out by a coyote this spring. A little farther up, he ran into more tracks going up and down. He was close to the den. His heartbeat quickened. Willig tied Sontag's reins to a sagebrush, silently pumped a shell into the chamber of his rifle and moved on up. Not 100 yards farther he walked around a bend in the wash and came upon the hole in the west bank about three feet up the side. The mound of dirt was packed with coyote tracks.

Willig's face flushed with anticipation. He cleaned out the entrance with his little metal folding shovel, then removed his Levi's jacket and stuffed it in the hole. If the bitch was inside she would smell the man scent of the coat and not come out. Willig headed back for Sontag. If only all dens were so easy to find.

He was getting a drink of water out of his canteen slung over the saddle horn when, out of habit, he'd carefully looked across the flat to the south. To his surprise, about 400 yards out on the flat plateau a coyote was coming in. It was a dog coyote, and he was coming from upwind so there was no chance he could pick up the scent of man or horse.

Willig knew he had an edge. Sontag was tied up in the shade of the high bank, out of sight. The trapper moved quickly. He capped his canteen, pulled his rifle from the scabbard and carefully peered out over the top of the bank. The coyote was still trotting forward, about 300 yards away now. Noiselessly, the trapper again levered a shell into the Winchester's chamber, took a sight on the coyote, and, not flinching a muscle, waited for his target to come to him.

About 200 yards off, the coyote suddenly stopped and put his nose up, sniffing the air. Willig realized the wind had shifted, now blowing toward the coyote. In a split-second he squeezed the trigger off. As the gun bucked in his hands, he saw the coyote roll over, jump up and disappear at a run into the deep gully. He had missed.

Willig walked to the gully and picked up the dog's tracks. They made him curse. The right-front paw was missing no toes. Two Toes was still on the loose, somewhere in these rocky hills.

Willig walked back to the den, pulled his Levi's jacket out of the hole and put his head in. He could hear the pups whining. He returned to Sontag under the bank, slid the rifle into its scabbard and untied the case that held his denning rod. Back at the den, he opened the case and slipped out his rod sections: six lengths of steel, each two feet long. Special tools of the trade.

Methodically, he assembled the rod, screwing the sections together to their 12-foot length. One end was a wood handle; the other, threaded to screw on any of the three end pieces designed for pulling out coyotes. One end piece was like a sheep hook, for grabbing a leg and dragging out a coyote, especially a bitch digging in sideways, straining against the pull. A second piece was a harpoon head, for probing for a soft spot then jamming it in, the barbs holding fast. It was the third end piece, however, that Willig chose: a frayed burr of steel cable. He screwed it on tight, then shoved the rod into the hole. The bitch coyote would be in front of the pups in a little pocket at cave's back.

About 10 feet in, Willig felt something soft. He whirled the rod quickly around and around. It jerked. He knew the frayed ends of the wires had caught tight in the bitch's fur, making it impossible for her to get loose. The trapper moved backward, planting his feet. His sinewy arms slowly pulled the rod out of the hole. The burr had tightened solid in her chest fur.

First, the bitch's snarling head emerged. Then her body, paws clawing and scraping at the earth. Her jaws snapped viciously at the end of the rod as Willig stepped on it to hold it in place, then reached for his pick. He carefully moved his spread-out hands toward the bitch, held fast at the end of the rod. Waving his left hand to divert her attention, he brought the hammer end of the pick down hard behind her head, cracking the base of the skull. She flopped on her side. Willig stomped hard in her short ribs, crushing her heart.

He used the burr end on the pups, easily pulling out five, one after the other, from the hole and killing them with quick blows to the head. Feeling no more with his rod, he crawled four feet into the den to make sure. All was silent. Willig eased himself out of the hole, then caved in its mouth with his shovel.

He scalped the bitch with his pocket knife, grabbing an ear and sliding the blade in next to it, skinning in an oval around the skull. He scalped the five pups, too, in this way. The scalps were proof he had taken the den. Willig examined the dead bitch's teeth. She was young, and it was probably her first litter. He figured the dog coyote was young, too. Older experienced coyotes wouldn't come directly into the den the way the one he had shot at had. Instead, they would start to circle when they got close, then come in warily, downwind, to pick up any strange scent there might be.

Willig picked up the dead bitch and heaved her behind a bush, then picked up the pups by the napes of their necks, tossing them beside their mother. Their skins were worth nothing to him, so small and young, and the bitch's was splotchy and still shedding at denning time. When furs were prime, thick for the winter, there was a market for them, especially coyotes and bobcats. A government trapper would skin the freshly killed coyote, casing the hide out from the tail to over the nose. The hide would be put on stretcher boards while still soft to be cured, dried, and tagged with the trapper's name and the area and date the skin was taken, then sold to fur buyers at auction, the proceeds going to the government.

Now, magpies and crows would have a feast on these carcasses after they discovered them in the bush.

It was kill or be killed in the wilds. Now baby lambs would live that would have been killed by coyotes.

THIRTEEN
▲ ▲ ▲
Fresh Tracks

OWLS had not quite concluded their nightly hunts when Jack Willig finished a quick breakfast and stood outside in the dewy, quiet pre-dawn, saddling Sontag and gathering his gear.

With a practiced and orderly manner, he dropped the tailgate on his pickup, led the horse over and placed his hand on its rump. On cue, Sontag reared up his 1,400 pounds on hind legs, dropped his front hooves into the truck bed and hopped up and in.

Willig clambered up alongside his horse and tied his halter rope to the crossbar brace soldered across the front end of the sidewalls. He had customized the truck to carry the horse through endless miles of range. The four-foot-high sidewalls were pipe running the length of the truck bed, to hold the horse stable in the moving vehicle. Willig snapped in place the chain that ran across the back of the horse's rump above the tailgate. Then he climbed in the cab, started the engine and turned south. He was headed for the Hasletts' sheep camp.

Dawn still hadn't broken as man, horse and truck approached the swinging bridge. Beyond a cocklebur flat, Willig stopped, shifted into compound low gear and crawled slowly up the dirt ramp and onto the span. He stole a glance in the rearview mirror to the bed behind. Sontag knew the drill by now; already, all four legs were splayed out to the sidewalls, readying for the swaying, the creaking of the cables, the rattling of the planks.

The first time Willig had taken Sontag across this bridge, the horse had been so badly spooked he'd had his front hooves on top of the cab before Willig could finally quiet him down. All the trips since then had knocked most of the panic out of the horse, but Willig knew enough not to expect Sontag to feel very good about fighting to stay up. The last thing he wanted was his horse to fall down in the truck; it would be hell to get him up again, thrashing and slipping on the cold metal truck bed.

Now as they crept across the groaning bridge, the only commotion Sontag raised was the stomping of his hooves to keep his balance. But when the truck reached the opposite bank, his master stopped and got out to speak softly to Sontag. The horse's eyes were wild and rolling around, but he didn't whinny. Willig circled the truck, checking that everything was in place. As he returned to the cab, he reached over the front rails and patted Sontag on the neck.

Streaks of sunrise were shooting over the distant hills as Willig turned east at the fork and easily made out the fresh tracks left by the Hasletts' truck. He followed the two thin parallel lines as they wound up onto a plateau that ran east away from the river, and wove through sagebrush and over a cover of button sage and curly grass. Willig saw the change of seasons in the flower buds showing on the ears of the prickly pear cactus. Soon, the waxy, beautiful yellow or crimson flowers would be in full bloom.

Several miles farther, the first ledge of rimrock emerged into view. Willig followed the twin tracks around the north side of the rock to the head of a draw. Here was Lizard Springs. Willow clumps surrounded the spring and grew down to the little creek formed by the flow of water from the holding tanks. On the flat, in a small stand of aspen, the Haslett sheep wagon stood.

Even from several hundred yards away, Willig could tell Hod Hogan was out with the sheep. The herder's horse wasn't there. And anyway, Hod was a sheepherder. He'd be up before dawn. When Willig pulled up and got out, he had no hesitation about stepping up into the wagon. The law of the range said no one goes away hungry or thirsty, and food and coffee were for anyone passing by. But Willig could never forget the bright morning he had showed up at the sheep wagon of a shiftless excuse for a herder whom a rancher had had the misfortune of hiring because of hard times, only to find the drunken fool snoring like an idiot, filthy and reeking from too many months between baths. Maggots crawled in his greasy, fly-blown red beard. Willig had been too disgusted to stay.

But Hod Hogan's sheep wagon was tidy. The coffee pot on the stove was cold, so Willig picked some kindling from the wood box, lifted the stove lid and, leaning over, blew on the coals until they started to glow. Soon he had a brisk fire going. He poured a cup of warmed-over coffee and was standing at the wood pile when Hod rode up on his gray mare.

The herder greeted Willig with a grin and a, "Howdy, Jack." He liked Willig. Everyone pretty much did. Willig was a quiet, silent man who minded his own business and never got drunk or into fights. And he was an excellent trapper. Hogan was glad to have him on his grazing allotment. He'd been around Willig six years now. He knew how good a worker Willig was. He was eager to help him. And he was excited about the work ahead because Two Toes, this killer coyote, had become the talk of the range.

"Old Joe said you'd be showing up about now," Hogan said.

"Yeah," Willig replied. "Couldn't get over any sooner. Been hung up the last few days on a coupla dens."

"Get 'em?"

"Yeah."

Willig told about the dens, including the tough one above Leota Bottoms.

"Either of them Two Toes'?" Hogan asked.

"Damnit no," Willig said. "His sign is scarce. But he's over there, somewhere."

"Old Joe and Young Joe were talking with Ty Bingham," Hogan ventured. "They all think Two Toes could be denned this way. Billy Butts even saw his tracks down by their camp on the river."

Willig's mouth tightened, though he didn't know it.

"Yeah, I heard about it," he said. "But Two Toes wouldn't den this side of the river. He never has, and he's not going to hunt this side, neither. He'd have to bring his kills across the bridge to get back to his den, and he's too smart for that. And he sure as hell ain't swimming that river with a lamb in his mouth."

Hogan chewed on this reasoning for a minute. Then he asked, "How do you explain the fresh tracks near Billy's camp?"

"Damned if I know," the trapper said. "I guess Two Toes could have come over the bridge to investigate when Butts moved his camp down there. But the way Bingham was pissing and moaning about it, you'd have thought Two Toes killed a half a dozen ewes."

Willig's anger began to boil just mentioning the rancher. He changed the subject. "All right, Hod, if you'll show me where the kills were made on your band, we'll see what we can do."

"Let's have a cup of fresh coffee and a bite to eat first." The herder dismounted and tied his horse's reins to a wagon wheel.

Inside, Hogan dug up a leg of cold mutton, then fried potatoes and biscuits. As they ate, he explained that the kills on his herd had started right after he moved to Lizard Springs. The first kill was right on the bed ground, an hour before daylight. His dogs had barked and he had found a dead ewe as the band moved off the bed ground. The other kills were during daylight, on the outer edge of the herd near brush or high grass where coyotes could get in close without warning.

Willig soaked up the information—how the hindquarters had been eaten off each kill; how one had also been opened back of the ribs, with the liver and stomach, lungs and kidneys ripped out.

Willig knew Hogan would be a help to him on the hunt. He had useful information. He knew his stuff.

▲ ▲ ▲

Hogan led the way as the two rode off.

He stopped shortly at the carcass of the dead ewe on the bed ground. Willig didn't even leave his horse to examine it. He could see plain well how the carcass had been pretty well picked by coyotes, crows and magpies, most of the wool and hide ripped off and scattered, with little flesh left in dried splotches on the skeleton. Grayish guts trailed out from the carcass and the dried up paunch, a dirty glassy gray, showed a big wad of green grass in it, slightly scattered by birds.

"The sign here's no good," Willig said. "The sheep coming and going have erased all the coyote tracks."

Hogan nodded.

"Where's the closest kill?" Willig asked.

"Couple miles east of here, at the head of the Breaks."

The herder remembered how he'd been moving the band a mile away when he'd heard magpies and crows whooping it up. He'd ridden over, only to find a dead sheep.

"It was yesterday morning so it must have happened night before last," Hogan said.

The two rode out to the head of the Breaks. This was high ledge country that collected a great deal of snow on its north slopes; when the snow blew down into the canyons and gullies, it made drifts that often lasted into May. The melting snow became small streams running down, flowing north into the White River. Willig followed Hogan past the cedar trees and high sagebrush that spotted the hillsides along the Breaks, then up onto the bench land. The herder stopped at a clump of brush at the edge of a grassy spot. Here was the partially eaten carcass of a big ewe, her bag and tits showing she had already lambed.

Willig saw where her hindquarters had been chewed on only hours before. He handed his reins to Hogan. "Hold these while I check around some," he said, stepping down off Sontag.

The herder watched with close interest as Willig, crouching, carefully looked over the carcass. The trapper noted how the meat had been pulled off, the wool and skin peeled back from the ribs and shoulder. Then he stood and began slowly walking around the kill. He made ever-larger circles, kneeling down at bare dirt spots to check sign and tracks.

He found where the dog coyote that had made the kill had urinated and kicked up the dirt with all four feet. He found a track and followed it for several hundred yards, then picked up another and followed it back to the carcass. Finally, he walked up and took his horse's reins from Hogan.

"We've got a pair of coyotes eating on the ewe," Willig said, matter-of-factly. He climbed into his saddle and turned, leaning his left hand on his horse's hip.

"It's a dog and a bitch. She's had her pups and is just now leaving the den to hunt with the dog. The pups aren't big enough to be out of their den so they're maybe 10 days to two weeks old. She's still nursing them, so they are both just filling their bellies and they're not carrying any food back to the den."

Hogan's eyes widened, but he didn't say anything.

"I think the bitch could be a young one," Willig continued. "Her tracks are small, no scars or rough spots on her pads. There's a perfectly clear set of tracks over there. Could be her first litter."

"Shit," Hogan finally said. "How the hell do you know that?"

Willig acted as if he didn't hear. He was looking east, toward the rimrock ledges. "I have an idea we'll find the den in one of those draws below the rimrock," he said, as if thinking out loud.

Hogan repeated his question. Willig still didn't answer. He turned to face the herder.

"You going to help me locate this den?"

"Sure thing," Hogan said. His boss had told him to help Willig all he could.

"I'll have to head for the herd about 6 o'clock," he said.

But Willig had already started for the rimrock.

▲ ▲ ▲

As they neared the first gully below the ledges, Willig spoke up.

"Hod, you get in the bottom of the draw where it's sandy, and check sign down for about a half a mile. If you see any tracks, make a note of them. If you come across a lot of fresh tracks coming and going, ride up on the bench and sit there till you see me, then wave your hat. I'll be coming up every so often to watch for you. If you see me waving my hat, come on over. It means we've got something."

Willig watched Hogan head down into the draw. Then he rode up the bench, crossed the draw and headed for the next one a mile to the east. Looking south, he saw how the tall hills in the distance with their peaks 1,500 feet higher than this plateau were dotted with cedar stands, giving the hills a dark contrast to these grassy plateaus which dropped lower and lower as they stretched north toward the White River, cut by gullies or draws that grew ever deeper and wider.

Sontag threw his ears forward and looked to his left. Willig reined up. Four-hundred yards off, five antelope had jumped alertly to their feet from their bed ground in the cool shade of a large bunch of tall buck brush. Willig saw the buck, with his black horns and mask on his head and throat, staring intently at the motionless horse and rider. Suddenly, the buck blew his distinctive snort and stomped his right-front foot twice. The four does whirled and headed for the breaks. The buck stomped once more, then followed. Within seconds, they were in a gully, out of sight.

It was more than their beauty that had pricked up the trapper's attention. He had noted that three of the does were heavy with fawns, while the fourth was either barren or an unbred yearling. In a few days, there would be young fawn antelope available to draw the attention of denning coyotes. Maybe, Willig thought, that would take some pressure off the sheep.

He was nearing the draw he had been heading for when he spotted coyote sign. It was in a large sandy spot. Willig reined up and stepped down. He led his horse as he scanned the ground. Fresh tracks made this morning were imprinted in two places in the thin crust. The tracks were heading for the draw.

Willig mounted up and headed straight for the draw. Coyote signs grew more plentiful. Against a dead sagebrush, droppings were piled up, and around its side were the scratchings of a dog coyote that had pissed on the brush then kicked up dirt.

Willig found a little gully he could ride Sontag in to reach the bottom of the draw, whose banks were 12 feet high. He put his heel gently into the horse's flank to let him know they were going down. Sontag snorted his protest, then slid his way to the wash bottom.

Willig sensed the den might be among the boulders above that had fallen out of the rimrock over the centuries. But which way to go in the draw. He stopped a moment to consider, then decided on heading up, working slowly almost to its head. But the tracks and signs grew less and less frequent, and when he was sure the den wasn't in this direction, he turned Sontag and headed back down, working below where he'd ridden in through the gully.

The signs didn't get any better this way, either. Finally, he rode out at a good spot on the east side. He sat on his horse, gazing west to see if he could spot Hogan. But there was no sign. Willig had just decided he would ride north along the edge of the draw to three large cedar trees when he spied the herder in the distance, sitting on his horse. Hogan had emerged from the head of the draw he'd been exploring. Willig raised his hand and pointed north, to signal that he had found nothing and was now going to check on down the draw. The herder waved in recognition and started the same way.

After all his years trapping, Willig had a sense about animal habits. As he neared one of the cedars, which stood alone, he could see it was an old mature tree, with shaggy bark, a trunk four feet in diameter and crowned at its 30 feet of height by heavy dark green needles. Nothing grew around the base of the tree. Willig could tell the cedar had served as shade and bed ground for many years for cattle and sheep, wild horses, antelope and deer.

As he approached, his intuition was confirmed. The ground around the tree was a mixture of dead needles and animal manure two feet deep. Here and there lay white bleached bones from small birds and animals brought in by pack rats that had made a huge stick nest against a boulder near the tree. And next to the pack rat nest were coyote droppings—old and fresh.

Willig believed he was closing in on the trail of the killers. He rode back to the edge of the draw. Its steep walls were about 14 feet deep now, and mostly perpendicular. He looked up and down the draw but saw no spot where he could get his horse down. In the sandy bottom were coyote tracks, clear from where he stood.

Willig rode Sontag to a buffalo berry bush and stepped down. He tied the reins to a large branch, pulled his Winchester out and patted his horse on the rump. "Now, you stay here," he said.

At a point where the bank had caved in from a snow runoff, Willig hopped down into the soft dirt and shuffled his feet to the wash bottom. The coyote tracks were old and new. About 200 yards on, he found new tracks leading down from a slight cave-in in the east bank. There were slender tracks from the bitch and heavier tracks from the dog. They had been made this morning.

Willig scrambled back up the east bank and walked back and mounted Sontag. Rifle across lap, he walked the horse out from the brush and stopped to look west for Hod Hogan. There he was. The herder was farther north, sitting on his horse. Jack waved his Stetson twice over his head. Hogan waved back and rode toward him.

For the first time, Willig was aware of how hot the day had become. It was noon. He had worked up a big sweat. He took his right leg out of the stirrup and hooked it around the saddle horn. He balanced his rifle on his lap and took off his Stetson. With his bandanna, he wiped his forehead and the back of his neck, then the lining inside his hat. A little breeze felt cool and nice against his forehead.

Willig remarked to himself that the drought seemed to be continuing this spring. Every day for more than two weeks had been cloudless, and each day seemed a little warmer than the one before. The range itself was getting pretty parched. Any low spots that would have water puddles were now dried up and crusted over. As he put his Stetson back on his matted hair, his head was suddenly surrounded by a swarm of buffalo gnats. In a moment, there were in his nose, eyes and ears.

"Damnit, git away, black bastards!" he cursed. Willig blinked his eyes to keep them off and fanned his face with his hat. He slapped his right foot back in the stirrup and dug his heels into Sontag's flanks. The horse grunted, hopped then trotted away, his rider still waving his hat madly.

The gnats had been attracted by sweat. As Willig wiped his face with the back of his hand, he realized he was sweating like a hog in the noonday sun. He didn't worry about his hands and face, which were like leather from the weathering of the elements and too tough for the little pinpoints of black to bite through. It was his eyelids and inside his ears and nose that he was concerned about.

Mosquitoes and dummy flies never bothered Willig; but a buffalo gnat getting to his vulnerable areas would leave their little red lumps that would smart like a bee sting for a couple days and then itch for a week.

Willig reined up Sontag, relieved to find he had outrun the gnats. While he waited for Hogan, he made a mental note to rub citronella on his face and neck the next morning before heading out.

He felt of his left eyelid. It burned and stung, already beginning to puff.

FOURTEEN

▲ ▲ ▲

An Answered Plea

TY BINGHAM leaned back in his chair, rubbed his eyes that had been straining at the numbers he'd been working over yet again, then reached back and rubbed his aching neck. He turned his head slowly from side to side. His muscles popped and cricked.

He had been sitting at his desk a very long time. He turned toward the window, blinked his eyes and gazed out at the yard and the hard-packed gravel drive leading up to the ranch house. Teddy, the kid who helped out on weekends, was bringing his saddle horse into the barn to grain it. Bingham remarked that the boy seemed to have grown a foot in the past year. The brown-haired youth was 14 now, a high school freshman, and the peach fuzz was thickening on his face. Teddy's family had a small farm in Dry Fork and Teddy's father did odd jobs around the valley. There were four kids, and Teddy was the oldest. He was a good worker. Bingham liked having him around.

He considered that Teddy learned quickly and was dependable. Too bad he wasn't a few years older. His own kids in college, Bingham really needed someone to work with Billy Butts once the sheep crossed over the west side of Green River. Someone to move the herd along more quickly through Two Toes' territory. The thought flickered in Bingham's mind to give Butts some help himself. Maybe he could ride out with the dogs around the bed grounds from dark to daylight to see if that wouldn't stop some of the coyote losses.

Every time Bingham thought about Two Toes, his breathing quickened and his anger welled up. And the notion of riding around dusk to dawn would light up in his mind like a bulb. But it was a dumb and stupid idea, he knew, the product of being overanxious. When the hell was he supposed to sleep? A sheepman wouldn't ask his herder to attempt such a round-the-clock schedule. Maybe he'd have him get up in the middle of the night and stomp around to make noise, turn on a light to scare any coyotes lurking near the herd. But not circle the sheep all night on top of a hard day.

No, Bingham would just have to ride this one out the way he had for more than a dozen springs, the way his father and grandfather had for decades before him: with hard work and lots of pluck, and maybe a little prayer. That, and the help of the trapper the government had working this territory.

Bingham felt a little ashamed about the way he'd jumped over Jack Willig outside the drugstore in Vernal, and again in front of Osh Portle and Young and Old Joe Haslett at the trading post in Ouray. Deep down, he knew Willig was one of the best predatory animal trappers in Utah. Willig was a hard worker, used to long hours in all kinds of weather, dependable and honest. Bingham also knew Willig had to cover a giant territory that was grazed by a dozen sheep outfits. The trapper was often being tugged this way and that by the sheepmen—each after him at the same time to work their areas, especially in the spring.

Bingham thought about that—about all the sheepmen who were probably after Willig at this very moment to get him to work around their grazing grounds as they headed up the stock driveway—and in a surge of anger, his good reasoning evaporated. Blast it, hadn't he been president of the Utah Wool Growers Association two terms? Wasn't he on the advisory board of the federal Division of Grazing? Wasn't his band getting hit hardest by this damned Two Toes?

The sheepman reached for his telephone. He had threatened to call Willig's boss, and by God he would. Right now.

▲ ▲ ▲

Scott Rasmussen was the Utah district agent for the U.S. Bureau of Biological Survey. The federal government had been forced into predatory animal control in the West immediately after World War I, when an outbreak of the dreaded rabies swept through the wolf, coyote and fox populations on the millions of western acres managed by the government. This was also the land that was providing the range and pasture for the livestock run by ranchers and farmers who used the land for grazing, and so the government had had to react after hundreds of deaths from the hydrophobia were reported—of "wolfer" trappers, herders, cowboys and miners, ranchers and farmers who had been attacked by rabid coyotes and wolves.

By the late 1920s, almost every western state had government trappers working their ranges. Rasmussen, Utah's district agent, was not only knowledgeable and amenable to putting in long hours at Salt Lake City headquarters, but also was good with people. It was an important trait, for it wasn't easy satisfying farmers and ranchers, sheepmen and cattlemen, big game and upland bird hunters. All of them blamed their losses, poor conditions or small head counts on the coyote. Rasmussen had quickly learned not to get caught up in a caller's emotions.

When the phone rang this afternoon in his office, he answered it with his customary greeting.

"Biological Survey."

"Mr. Rasmussen?" The voice on the line had an earnest tone.

"Speaking," the district agent said.

"This is Ty Bingham in Vernal."

"Yes, Ty, what can I do for you?" Rasmussen said. He'd met Bingham several times. He tried to picture his face in his mind.

The voice on the other end began speaking quicker. "We've got to have some help with coyotes out here in the Uintah Basin. Our sheep are moving up the stock trail on the Green River and coyotes are hitting our herds nearly every night."

"Uintah Basin?" said Rasmussen. "That's part of Jack Willig's territory. He's one of our best men. Isn't he there yet?"

"Yes, he is," the sheepman retorted, voice rising. "But he hasn't done much yet, and he hasn't gotten that damn Two Toes, either."

Rasmussen bit his lower lip. He recognized a tirade when he heard one brewing.

"This is the third year for that coyote," the sheepman continued, "and no telling how many sheep he's killed the last two years. I know he cost me a thousand dollars last year."

"Well, Ty," Rasmussen began, "as you know, we are always badly strung out in the spring, what with sheep on the trail, outfits lambing and shearing. And we've got a dozen of your fellow sheepmen from Vernal all in the same boat —"

"I don't give a damn," the sheepman cut in. His words were rough and loud now.

"We've got coyotes denning all the way up the Green River to Jensen, and none of us can stand the losses we took last year. We've got to have some more help. Now I want some help for Willig, and I want it now, Scott. Now."

Rasmussen took a deep breath. He let the phone line go silent a second, then resumed in his same measured tone.

"Now see here, Ty, I don't have any more men. They are all assigned to their own areas, working with their own sheepmen, I can't take one of them off his own sheep range to put on yours. Now listen to me. You've been in this business long enough. You wouldn't like it if I moved Willig off your range and put him, say, over on the Duchesne, would you?"

The brief pause told Rasmussen his wording had done the trick.

"No, I wouldn't," Bingham spluttered. His voice softened. "I'm sorry I yelled at you. But we're about to the end of our rope here. See, it looks like there's more coyotes denned along the Green than ever before, and we're walking right into 'em. Willig can't possibly get the job done alone."

The plaintive appeal of the sheepman's voice triggered a thought in Rasmussen's mind.

"Ty, wait a minute, hold the phone," he said. "I'll be right back."

Three minutes later, Rasmussen returned to the line.

"Ty, we've got a young man we started out last year working on coyote denning. We had him spend three months with three of our best denners in the state. He's about through down in Beaver County. We were going to have him work with Evans in Iron County next, but I'll tell you what. I could send him out to work with Jack Willig until all the herds are off the trail. He should be a good hand."

"Is he an experienced trapper?" Bingham sounded skeptical.

"Not exactly," Rasmussen replied. "But he was a major in biology and game management at Logan, and after this year he'll be training some of our better men in denning. We've only got five men like Jack Willig who are self-taught in the art of finding dens, and it is an art, Ty."

"Damn," snapped Bingham. "That's all we need is some dumb college kid who doesn't know his ass from a hole in the ground out there screwing up Willig's efforts."

Rasmussen's patience had run its course.

"Look, Bingham, I said he would be a help to our trapper, and he's the only man we've got. If you don't want him, fine, I'll send him down to Iron County."

Bingham seethed. "I guess he's better than nothing," he huffed. And with that he hung up the phone.

Rasmussen took the receiver from his ear, looked at it in disbelief, then set it in its rest, shaking his head.

FIFTEEN

▲ ▲ ▲

More Tracks, Another Den

HOD HOGAN rode up to the edge of the bank until he was opposite Jack Willig.

"Find something?"

The trapper immediately put his finger to his lips. In a hushed tone that managed to carry without disturbing the afternoon calm, he said, "We've got our den down this draw and I don't think it's too far away. Back away from the draw and go down three-, four-hundred yards, Hod. Tie your horse, then get in the bottom of the draw and slowly work your way up."

Willig pointed to where he meant.

"Keep quiet and watch for the dog and the bitch. I'll be working down to meet you."

The herder nodded and rode away.

Willig had found a good spot to get down into the draw, which was 10 feet wide. Leading Sontag, he slid down the steep wall to the bottom, the horse stepping carefully behind, and started slowly through the sandy soil where horse and man seldom trod, hidden from the ground above by the dirt banks rising sharply.

Here, in the soft earth, the coyote tracks were plain to see. They grew thicker as Willig worked down, leading his horse by the reins. Up ahead, a little spot darkened the sand. The trapper stooped for a better look. It was dried blood, and the marks in the sand told where the dog coyote had laid a piece of lamb meat to rest his jaws. The blood had to have come from a lamb, Willig knew, because the coyote's tracks were the same ones he'd seen near the herd.

The blood was now completely dry. The kill had been made this morning. Willig slipped his Winchester from its scabbard. With his thumb, he quietly levered a shell into the chamber and let the hammer down carefully. Then he picked up Sontag's reins and started down the draw again.

Presently he came to a set of tracks that were fresher and deeper, all four paw prints close together. Willig looked up the bank, then back to the where the tracks were gouged in the sand. Leading away from the deep marks were the bitch's tracks. They were like words written on a page. The bitch had jumped off the bank into the draw with something in her mouth. She'd left little blood spots where she'd hit the bottom.

Willig started once more down the sandy floor. Rounding a bend, he peered ahead down the wash. There, about 100 yards off, was the den.

The trapper shifted his Winchester to his right hand, gripping his horse's reins in his left. At 25 yards from the opening, he dropped the reins, set his hand on the horse's nose as a stay command, and moved cautiously ahead.

His breathing sounded loud to his sensitive ears. He imagined that his heartbeat was echoing through the draw. When he was almost in front of the den, the bitch, unaware of the intruder in her midst, popped out of the opening.

Hunter and hunted were both startled. The bitch froze at the man's sight; but as he raised the gun to his shoulder, she disappeared back inside. Willig cursed his slowness. But it didn't matter now. He walked up to the den and studied the dirt around it for signs of pups. There were no tracks or droppings; they weren't old enough to get out and move around.

The story was clear. The bitch was getting ready to wean the pups and the blood marks in the draw said that both coyotes had been bringing the first lamb meat to the den for the young to eat. Willig scrutinized the mound left from the dug-out den where the dog and bitch had vomited up meat for the pups. He bellied down on the mound in front of the opening and took his Stetson off, then stuck his head into the hole. Listening closely, he could make out the pups' whimpers.

"Hey-yay!" Willig yelled into the den to frighten the bitch from coming out. Then he backed out, stood and walked back to Sontag. He was loosening his denning tools from the saddle when Hod Hogan rode up.

"By damn, you found it!" the herder exclaimed, face grinning broadly through glistening sweat.

He took his hat off and wiped his forehead with his shirt sleeve. "I've seen all kinds of tracks and figured it was getting close," he said. "I didn't see either one of the coyotes."

Willig untied a folding shovel from the saddle, his back to the herder.

"The bitch is in the den. She was coming out just as I walked up and ducked back in the hole. Take this shovel and see if you can open up the hole some. The bank looks to be solid dirt."

As Hogan cleared out the hole, Willig fit his den tool together, leaving off an end piece. After the herder had the hole cleaned out about three feet, the trapper ran the rod in. At a length of nine feet, he felt it hit the bitch. He pulled the tool out.

"This den ain't too deep. I'll see if I can grab her with my leg hook."

Willig screwed the hook on and shoved it deeply inside, pushing until it hit something, then yanked back on it. He repeated the action six or eight times, until he felt the solid object inside jerk but the hook hold.

"Got her!" he said. He could tell by the tugging motion that he had her by a hind leg.

"Get the pick hammer and hit her in the head as I pull her out of the den," Willig said. "She's gonna be coming out backwards, so for hell's sake, don't let her turn around."

Hogan knelt at the den's mouth. Willig pulled steadily, bracing his feet, hands working up the rod. It was her left hind leg that the hook firmly clamped above the knee joint. First her back legs, then her gray and tan body, were pulled into the sunlight.

As her snarling head appeared, the other man brought the hammer end down hard and sharp in back of her ears.

The bitch's body dropped. Her legs jerked in brief spasms as she kicked four times, and died. Willig disengaged the hook. He dragged her by the legs several yards from the den's mouth. Then he fished in the tool bag, found the cable burr, and replaced the hook.

Hogan dug into the hole some more with the shovel. He could hear the bewildered pups whining and crying inside.

"Hell, Jack, those pups aren't very far back there," he said with enthusiasm. "I think I can almost reach them."

"Wait a minute," Willig said. He walked back to Sontag and pulled a flashlight out of the saddle bag.

The two men crouched in front of the den. Willig shined the flashlight into the blackness. He moved the beam slowly back and forth; red reflections of pairs of eyes were all they could see, plus brief glimpses of the individual furry faces as the light crossed for an instant over each. The pups were six feet inside.

"I can scrape them out with the leg hook," Willig said.

A few minutes later, the five pups were lying dead outside the den. Hogan watched as Willig knelt over the little carcasses.

"Three males and two females," the trapper declared. "They're about 15 to 20 days old. Still sucking, but the bitch was bringing some meat to the den. See where the pups have been licking it?" He pointed to one of the motionless pups, its muzzle bearing a tiny stain of blood.

Willig moved to where he had dragged the bitch. He scrutinized her teeth and bag. "She's probably two years old. Her first litter. Next year she would probably have had six or eight pups. She's pretty thin. Was probably in the den three or four days. This looks like about her second day out, according to her tracks. I'll bet her belly is full."

He opened his pocket knife and slit her open. Hogan watched as Willig pulled out her stomach and then sliced that open with his blade. Red meat came out in his hand.

The herder took his hat off and scratched his head. "I'll be damned," he said sheepishly. "I can't believe it."

"Believe what?"

"I thought you were giving me a string of bullshit. Telling me back there that the bitch was young, her pups weren't out of the den, that she was just starting to hunt with the dog and that they would soon be carrying meat back to the den. You hit it all, right on the nose. Darndest thing I ever saw."

He walked back to his horse, shaking his head.

Willig smiled to himself. When he was done scalping the bitch and pups, he put the scalps in his saddle bag and stepped up and swung onto Sontag.

"Show me the next kill, Hod."

SIXTEEN

Cutting Ewes

IT WAS SUNDOWN. The west banks of Green River cast shadows nearly across the water: dark shapes of old cottonwoods with large crowns, wavy outlines of bluffs. As dusk slowly descended on the Twist Hills, Two Toes jumped out of a small draw.

He stood in the open, perfectly still, keen yellow eyes scanning for anything moving or out of place. His ears cocked forward and his nose raised, sniffing the slight breeze blowing north, upriver.

Every morning for the past several days, the big coyote and his bitch had hunted together. She was weaning the pups and every day they demanded more meat. Their hours were a constant cycle of playing outside the den, sleeping inside and eating, eating, eating. They were four weeks old and had doubled in size.

The dog and his bitch had to hunt long and hard to satisfy the pups. This morning, they had come upon a band of sheep grazing the wide bench land on the west side of the river, below Bow Knot Bend. All day, the herder and his dogs had stayed with the sheep. Two Toes was not afraid of the dogs; he could outrun them. He could outrun a greyhound, if he had to. But the dogs were a nuisance. Finally, he and the bitch left to hunt for rabbits and prairie dogs.

They got one prairie dog that strayed too far from his town of holes, then teamed up on a jackrabbit, taking turns running him ragged in wide circles until he finally gave out. Back at the den, the pups made fast work of their food, growling and fighting over scraps. At sundown, the bitch stayed behind while her mate started for another hunt.

Now in the evening dark, Two Toes could smell the scent of sheep downriver. He could hear their baa'ing as they headed for the bed ground. He remembered how in the late afternoon they had slowly grazed the bench land below where he had hidden and watched. The man on horseback had come off the river bottom and up on the bench with his two dogs. The man and horse had circled the band until they were behind it; then, working with the dogs, they had slowly turned the sheep south and started them back to the bed ground. The dogs had been quick to turn any sheep that strayed the wrong way.

The dogs were Scotch shelties, and the herder was Billy Butts. Ty Bingham had finally moved camp from the cottonwood grove just above the swinging bridge on the east side of Green River. To Billy Butts, it seemed his boss had waited as long as he could, as if he hated to move his sheep to the west side. He understood why: Two Toes. He also knew that if the infamous coyote started picking off his sheep, there would be hell to pay.

The sheep camp they were using now was halfway between the swinging bridge and Bow Knot Bend. It was one they hadn't used for several years. Butts figured his boss was aiming to move the herd upriver pretty fast. As sunset spread dark shadows over the land, the herder and the band were still a half-mile from the bed ground. He put the sheep down into a wide wash and followed it to the river. Here, the west bank of the Green stretched wide and flat, covered with grass and wild clover in the open spaces between towering cottonwoods. No floods or high water had swamped this ground for several years. Willow and greasewood, squaw berry and snow berry and tall white sage grew scattered along the bank.

The sheep were spread wide as they moved south, grazing on the new shoots of sweet grass and clover. They were moving too slow for Butts. The trail was to blame. On one side flowed the river; on the other, a steep cliff rose 30 feet, crowding the bank almost to the rushing water and leaving a narrowing corridor, through which the sheep trickled.

The herder looked behind, at the bottleneck. He moved his horse nice and easy back through the bunched up sheep until he reached the tight point between the cliff and river. He climbed down from the saddle. He and the shelties passed through and got behind the clogged band. With the dogs yapping and nipping the sheep, the band started moving more rapidly through the gap and toward camp. But those far behind still grazed leisurely, unable to hurry forward until those in front had gone through the narrows.

Moving in the pools of shadows deepening along the hills and bank, Two Toes stole quickly and cautiously down from the hills, closer and closer to the river, lured on by the hot musk of sheep. Now, he was hunched behind a squaw berry bush, watching the man and dogs moving the sheep through the spot at the cliff.

The west bank of the river was now almost completely covered in shadow; the final golden rays of the sun were drawing past the very tops of the cottonwoods on the east side. Shadows were creeping up the rimrocks beyond the trees. At the rear of the band, the few remaining sheep were almost at a standstill. When the man and his dogs followed the band through the cliff point and didn't return, Two Toes slowly walked up to the last few sheep waiting to pass through. Dust from the trampling herd hung heavy in the air, fogging visibility, but the baa'ing was constant and loud.

Two Toes saw where a small wash opened up right where the cliff began to narrow down the sheep trail. Moving exactly like a sheep dog, he ran right up to five ewes standing in a bunch at the tail end of the herd. He nipped at their flanks and shoulders and pushed them. As they ran to get away, he turned two in the direction he wanted, easily as the shelties might have. He cut them away from the herd, moving them up the small draw.

As soon as they were out of sight of the river bottom, the coyote trotted up alongside the closest ewe. With his sharp teeth, he seized her neck right behind her ears, clamping down with his jaws. As his canine teeth broke into the base of her brain, she went down baa'ing and kicking. Instantly, she was dead.

Leaving her where she lay, Two Toes darted up the draw for the other ewe, who had stopped to watch the coyote make his kill. Now she turned and ran. In four jumps, he was upon her, grabbing her just as he had her band mate. She went down like the other, dead on her feet before she dropped.

Two dead ewes lay in the draw, outlines motionless as rocks. Two Toes knew he could return to feed. For now, he would eat what he could. He moved to the first, ripped open her belly and expertly pulled out the unborn lamb. He tore meat from its hindquarters, gulping it down in large chunks. When he had eaten his fill, he severed the lamb's soft spine behind the ribs and headed for the den with the front half flopping between his jaws.

Two Toes was on the big bench trotting west, still far from the Twist Hills, when he paused to drop the lamb and rest. He was very tired. It was a moonless night by now, pitch black. No scent carried on the breeze as he looked back down toward the river, sniffing and listening. A coyote howled across the river and a pair of long-eared owls hooted along the banks, readying for their nightly hunt.

Later, Two Toes neared the first ledge of rimrock. He didn't follow his usual, careful pattern of going around well north or south of the den and then walking on the rock and sandstone to the spot above and dropping down to it. Instead, he climbed onto the ledge and trotted straight for it.

At the den, he barked. His bitch came out, followed by the pups. The dog coyote laid the lamb down, vomited up the chunks he had eaten, then went up to his bed ground under the big boulder.

It would be weeks before the dog coyote would up and leave the pups for good, either run off by the bitch nipping at his butt or knowing from his internal clock that he was tired of providing for them and they could take care of themselves, anyway.

He curled up to sleep. Below him, the pups, with much growling and tugging, tore into the meat with their puppy teeth.

▲ ▲ ▲

The following morning, just as it was getting light in the east, Two Toes met the bitch at the den. Together, they headed for the sheep kill in the draw far below. Moving quickly, taking advantage of every low spot and little swell, they reached the river bottom. The stench of wool and fresh sheep droppings still clung to the air, even wiping out the horse and dog smells.

Two Toes led his mate to the dead ewes. The two coyotes filled up on hindquarter meat at the second ewe. Then Two Toes pulled the unborn lamb from her belly to carry back in halves. The pups were playing outside the den, scrapping with each other, when the coyotes arrived.

The next morning, the dog and bitch again returned to the sheep kill at daylight to fill up on mutton.

They did not return a third time. It was a good thing they didn't.

SEVENTEEN

▲ ▲ ▲

Into Two Toes' Country

WHEN Ty Bingham and Billy Butts moved the sheep across the swinging bridge to the west side of Green River, Butts placed Moses, a large 10-year-old black bellwether at the head. Butts valued the old ram almost as much as a trained dog at times like these. It was trying work to get hoofed animals across the swaying span. But once a leader like Moses, with his tinkling bell, started over, the rest would follow, even as the clattering of their hard hooves on the boards raised a fearsome din and the creaking bridge swayed side to side.

As they approached the ramp, Butts got off his horse, tied a rope around Moses' neck, then led both animals onto the bridge. The old bellwether, his black fleece turned mostly tan with age and the fat and bounce long ago worn out of him, had been through the routine so many times he moved forward with what seemed to Butts solemn resignation. Moses didn't look like much, but he was full of the wisdom of years. Butts felt lucky to still have him.

The two shelties came up on each side of the ramp, keeping the line of sheep behind moving ahead. Soon, the herd was stringing out on the bridge in reasonably good shape. With their bawling and baa'ing and crowding in among themselves, some jumping over others, it looked and sounded like sheer bedlam. But it was controlled chaos. A half-hour later, the band was safely on the west side of Green River, and Bingham was pulling the sheep wagon behind his pickup over the bridge.

Butts untied Moses, gazing briefly into the long, ancient face. An old lesson had once again been shown. Wits, not strength, meant survival on the trail. That, and a helping of luck.

Bingham's face was more taut than usual as they set up their new camp at Willow Spring, about eight miles south of Bow Knot Bend. They hadn't used this camp for several years, but Bingham aimed to get the herd up river as fast as possible. When it was close to dark, the rancher left for Vernal, admonishing his herder, "Watch out for Two Toes."

With any good luck, he won't strike right off, Butts thought to himself.

The first three days on the west side of Green River had been good. The feed was plentiful—lots of early grama and curly grass—and the sheep were eating their fill. Now it was night and Butts had bedded down the herd. He was fixing a cold supper of potatoes and mutton when he heard the sheep baa'ing.

He poked his head out of the sheep wagon and saw sheep on the south side of the bed ground start in a panic. The shelties began barking and growling. Butts knew coyotes were bothering the herd. In a moment, he'd grabbed his carbine and was running towards the bed ground, circling around the band on the west side. As he reached the south side in the fast approaching darkness, he saw the forms of three coyotes racing toward the river. One carried a lamb in its mouth.

Butts raised the carbine to his shoulder, hurriedly sighted and fired at the hindmost. He was just trying to run the coyotes off; a shell from a .30./.30 carbine would start dropping after 100 yards. Yet a split-second after he pulled the trigger, a splat from the connecting bullet resounded and the coyote yelped, went down, rolled, rose and continued.

The shelties, barking wildly, chased the coyotes a short distance along the river. When they returned to their master, Butts was standing over a dead ewe that had just given birth. The clear and waxy sack of afterbirth still hung from her rear.

Butts shook his head. One dead ewe and lamb, all in one whack.

A trio of coyotes hunting together was unusual, he knew. They must have been yearlings from the same litter. Butts knew that mated coyotes hunted alone and would fight to kill any coyote that tried to join them. Coyotes might hunt in threes or fours or even packs in winter when food was scarce, but seldom in spring when game was plentiful.

Butts bit his lower lip. He was apprehensive. His luck had just turned sour—very sour. He had just moved to his first camp across the river and already there were losses to coyotes, and they weren't even from Two Toes. A doubt that lingered in the outer reaches of his mind gnawed its way to the fore: if Ty Bingham went down, so could he.

When Butts had headed west after leaving Texas, it had been in part to satisfy his lifelong hankering to get into the Rocky Mountain country. Now, even though he knew he was a fine herder and that the sheepmen out here all knew it and might hire him in a second, the sense of setback, of losing his job, snaked through him like a chill.

He always did the best job he could. But he would have to try a bit harder now.

The first stars were out as he and the dogs got the sheep quieted and bedded down again. Then Butts returned to the south side of the bed ground. He broke off branches of greasewood and sagebrush and built two fires to spook predators stalking the herd in the dark.

He went back to the sheep wagon and finished supper. The coyotes wouldn't be back tonight, he figured.

▲ ▲ ▲

Billy Butts was up before daylight, eating a hearty breakfast of cooked ham and eggs, sourdough biscuits and good hot coffee. Fortified for the work ahead, he fried an extra couple eggs and a large piece of ham and made a big sandwich.

He would stay out with the sheep all day today and bring them in a little early this afternoon. He was taking no chances.

Butts got the herd spread out on the big flat bench where the early grama and curly grass were like a fresh carpet of green, and watched them graze, slow and contented. About noon, the warm day playing out calm and peaceful, he decided to ride down to the river to have his lunch. He started down alongside a draw that ran to the water just above where the cliff closed in and the stock trail narrowed to a small gap. He'd had a little trouble getting the herd through this point two evenings ago. The high ledge ran almost to the river.

As he moved down the draw, Butts was suddenly aware of the chattering magpies. The shrill squawks were coming from above the high ledge by the river. Mixed in were the hoarse cawing of crows.

Butts' face paled. This could only mean one thing. Something big was dead down the draw. A cold sensation ran through him. Something had gone awry. He reflected that neither he nor the dogs had seen or heard any hint of trouble two nights ago, bringing the sheep past this point. But maybe he hadn't been as lucky as he'd thought.

He rode right up on the north bank of the draw before the carrion birds even realized he was there. When they finally spotted him, they flared into the air with a mad rush of wing-flapping and screams. Butts hardly noticed: his eyes were fixed on the scene below. What he saw made him sick to his stomach.

At the bottom of the wash lay the remains of two big ewes.

Butts dismounted, tied the horse reins to a sagebrush and slid down the bank. He walked slowly past the dead ewes to the draw's mouth, where, crouching, he found tracks where a coyote had herded the ewes up the draw and killed them.

Anger and disgust filled Butts. He walked back up the draw 100 yards above the dead ewes. He easily picked up two different-size tracks. They were fresh, very fresh, and plain as day to see. They weren't from yearlings. They were from a dog and a bitch—mates—and there was no question about the dog. His signature was right there: the two middle toes missing on the right-front foot.

Butts spat and kicked at the track with his boot toe. With renewed determination, he returned to the ewes' remains. He saw that the coyotes had carried off the two unborn lambs and also eaten a lot of meat out of both sets of hindquarters. Two Toes and his mate had pups to feed. More bad news.

Lunch forgotten, Butts scrambled back up the bank of the wash to his horse, mounted and headed back to the sheep. The sight of them as they came into view was heartening. The herd was still grazing blissfully up the wide bench. He whistled to his dogs and circled the band to start them grazing back down the bench toward camp. He wasn't about to take them back down the river. Not now.

Within minutes, Butts had most of the sheep turned south except about 30 that were moving out of a low grassy swale toward the main band. He swung his horse over to the little bunch moving slowly up the grade and fell in behind. From the corner of his eye he caught something white remaining in the swale. He rode toward it.

It was a dead ewe, partially eaten in the hindquarters, the blood just starting to harden. Butts didn't even look at the tracks. What coyote could have stolen in during the half-hour he'd been away from the herd, killed a sheep and eaten its fill, but Two Toes?

The herder considered that even the shelties weren't aware the sheep had been attacked. They were on the other side of the herd. He tried to spit again, but his mouth was dry. It tasted of copper.

That night after the sheep were bedded down and he'd eaten supper, Butts went out to the herd with his dogs. He backed up to a big boulder on a high spot above the bed ground, pulled his heavy sheepskin coat up over his shoulders like a blanket and settled down for the night. The dogs would bark and wake him if the sheep were spooked.

He slept fitfully until 4 o'clock. When he woke, stiff from the cold, he stretched, one hand pressed against the small of his back, then picked up his coat and rifle and walked back to the sheep wagon.

He stoked a fire and fried some bacon and put it on the back of the stove while he sliced some cold boiled potatoes in a hot pan with butter. When they were brown and hot, he put them on the bacon plate, fried two eggs and made toast.

He'd just sat down to fill his groaning belly as his boss drove up.

EIGHTEEN

▲ ▲ ▲

Bad Words, Good Shot

JACK WILLIG had returned to camp very late the night before, his shoulders, knees and the small of his back aching with little fires. But like all outdoorsmen, especially trappers, he was tough every inch of his body. He had slept a dreamless sleep and now, an hour before dawn, was awake and alert, stretching and rubbing the stiffness from his sore joints and warming his innards with a steaming cup of bitter black coffee.

Willig reviewed the past couple days. He and Hod Hogan had done a good job on the coyotes hitting Joe Haslett's herd. They'd nabbed 14 pups and two bitches in a pair of dens; and that last den had had nine big pups. They would have caused a mess of trouble, since it took a lot of meat to feed that large a litter of growing coyotes and the two adults hunting for them. Willig was sure that getting that den would stop much of the killing, or at least slow it down.

In all, he'd taken 21 pups and three bitches in four dens since the sheep herds had started north on the stock drive along Green River. But he knew his work would get even more urgent now. The Hasletts would be moving camp, either to the cottonwood grove at the swinging bridge or across it and over on the west side of Green River. Willig knew they wouldn't camp too far north because that would place them too close to Ty Bingham's herd, which was now somewhere between the bridge and Bow Knot Bend.

Willig hadn't seen anything of Bingham's herd the night before as he'd headed for his camp wagon. But he'd caught plenty of sign. The grass was closely cropped from their grazing and the soft ground was all chewed up by their trampling hooves. The strong smell of wool still hung in the air and there were endless piles of marble-sized sheep droppings everywhere.

Willig's wagon was camped southwest of Bow Knot Bend at Badger Spring, smack dab in the center of the stock drive going up to Ashley Valley from Ouray and the swinging bridge. Badger Spring was a quarter-mile west off the river and six miles east of Leota Bottoms. From this camp, Willig could cover a good 20-mile stretch—10 miles to the south and 10 to the north. Most importantly, somewhere within this area was Two Toes and his den of pups.

With Bingham's and Haslett's herds moving west of Green River, coyote losses would grow. Willig prayed he could get to Two Toes before too much killing began. The trapper had toiled so hard the past few days he'd worked up a nagging hunger. Standing in the wagon now, he whipped up some sourdough hot cakes, fried six strips of bacon and sliced two potatoes. It was just daylight as he finished his hearty breakfast. Leaving the dishes to wash after supper, he saddled up Sontag and headed for the river. First order of business was to check in with the sheepherder of the lead band heading up the stock trail: Billy Butts.

As Willig rode south, he checked for coyote sign in each draw and gully. When he topped out on a tall ridge he reined Sontag in and looked around. Back to the north he could see the high cliff that ran right to the river's edge. Panning slowly southward, down the line of green that marked the trees, brush and clover along the river, Willig spotted Butts' sheep wagon: a tiny patch of bright white camped at what would be Willow Spring.

The trapper touched Sontag's flanks with his boot heels and headed down the flat to the spring. As soon as the sheep wagon came into view, with its silver marking on the side of a circle around a "B," so did the blue half-ton pickup with the sideboards that belonged to the rancher, Ty Bingham

Willig's jaw set as he rode up, his arrival hailed by the excited barking of Butts' sheep dogs. He hoped there hadn't been any killing so far on this part of the trail. He reined up at the back of the wagon and stepped down. He was tying Sontag's reins to a rear wheel when Bingham came around the corner of the wagon.

"How about some coffee?"—the normal greeting on the range— was what he expected. Or maybe a, "Had breakfast?" or even, "Hello," would have kept the morning easing along.

But it was Ty Bingham he was faced with.

"Where in the hell have you been?" the sheepman said in a stone-cold voice. "No one's seen you for four or five days."

Willig winced. The anger welled up in his throat like bile. So this was how it was going to be.

"You knew I was over helping Hod and the Hasletts locate some dens," he replied. "They were having some losses. I just got back to my camp last night."

Bingham barely waited for the response. "We've been here four days and we've been hit three times already," he snapped, his voice growing loud and souring up the morning.

"I've lost six ewes and their lambs that I know of, and by damn, you'd better do something about it."

Billy Butts had shown up behind his boss. He spoke up quickly. "How about some coffee, Jack?"

Willig nodded. He walked around Bingham and stepped up into the sheep wagon. He grabbed the pot and a cup and filled it up.

"Tell me about the kills," he said to Butts. "Where were they? What time of day? Did you see some sign? Anything you can, Billy."

Before the herder could answer, Bingham's voice called into the wagon.

"Goddamn it, Willig! You're not going to get Two Toes loafing around."

The rancher stepped up into the wagon and glared. "You spend too damn much time talking," he growled. "It's me that's losing the sheep, not you!"

This was too much for Willig. His hand trembled, and coffee sploshed over the tin cup's side. He set it down hard on the stove.

Breath snorted in his nose like a bull. He pushed past Bingham and stepped down out of the sheep wagon.

The other followed. Standing with his back to the rancher, heart pounding, Willig took in deep breaths, trying to roll back the tide of anger and frustration that had come on like a flash flood. He hadn't been in a fist fight in 20 years—he didn't drink and he didn't get into quarrels—and this ugly sensation felt old and strange.

Bingham tapped him on the shoulder. Willig flinched. The tide again rushed forth. It took every ounce of self-control to keep from immediately turning and smashing the rancher on the chin with a right fist. He could already feel the sweet impact of his knuckles cracking against flesh and bone, the smacking sound it would make and Bingham's head twisting backward as it hit the ground.

Willig locked his teeth and tightened his hand into a ball until it hurt. But as he dug his right heel into the dirt and turned his face and left shoulder toward his man, Billy Butts, who had hopped down from the sheep wagon, stepped quickly in between. He grabbed Willig by the arm.

"Let me give you all the dope on the killings," he said, in a genial tone.

The two walked a few steps off, but then Willig yanked his arm free. He whirled to face the rancher. His face was red and his eyes flashed with ire.

"Bingham, I've taken all the hazing and crap from you I'm going to take. Every time we've run into each other, you've jumped all over me. And I'm sick of it. You've chewed me out in front of other sheepmen and you've tried to embarrass me by insinuating that I'm lazy and don't know what the hell I'm doing.

"Well, let me tell you something. I work long and hard. I don't drink nor smoke. And by God, I know my business. And I'll tell you something else. You say one more word to me—one word—you can take your sheep and stick them up your ass. I won't set another foot in your camp if it costs me my job."

Bingham looked stunned. The trapper walked up and stuck his nose inches from the rancher's face. He could feel Willig's hot breath against his cheeks as the trapper glared into his eyes and said, slowly for emphasis, "Do—you—savvy?"

Without waiting for an answer, Willig wheeled, untied his horse's reins, stepped up into the saddle and started to ride off. A moment later he reined up. He turned and called back.

"Billy, I'm camped at Badger Spring. If you have any information for me, you're welcome to come over. I'll not be coming back here." And with that, he touched his heel to Sontag and rode north up the bench.

Bingham's face burned red as a beet. He spun toward his sheepherder.

"That sonofabitch, what the hell is the matter with him? He can't talk to me that way."

Butts' stony expression made it clear where his sympathy lay. "He already has, boss."

Bingham wore a look of pained amazement. He turned away, gazing toward where Willig had ridden off.

"You've been riding him hard all spring," Billy Butts said, breaking the silence.

"Too hard, boss."

Bingham muttered under his breath. He climbed into his pickup truck. He headed back down the road, toward Ouray.

▲   ▲   ▲

Jack Willig cut Sontag back toward the river. A mile on, he stepped down to read the sheep signs.

Hoofprints from the wide-flung herd cut up almost every inch of soft earth, and the grass was cropped close to the ground. The trapper could see where the sheep had grazed upriver then come back. The tracks looked two or three days old.

Back in the saddle, he dropped Sontag off the bench down to the river bottom. Here the herd had moved straight south with out grazing. Probably headed back for the bed ground, he figured.

Willig continued up the river bottom. It was still morning and he might as well check the country out. He hadn't been through this way since fall. Up ahead was the spot where the bench land rose sharply as it got to the river, dropping off steeply to the bank. Willig worked his horse slowly toward the cliff's lower end. Squinting down below, it was clear to his eyes where the heavy sheep tracks squeezed through between the cliff and the river's edge.

Willig picked up the tracks from Billy Butts' horse. He saw how Butts had been on foot, leading his horse with the dogs, no doubt to get the last few sheep through the narrow spot at the south end of the point. At the north end of the cliff, the river bottom widened. Here, a good-sized draw opened up to the water. Willig headed Sontag over. As he did so, he was suddenly aware of a chorus of crows and magpies making an awful racket up the draw. The trapper's curiosity perked up. He started up.

Soon, he spotted a horse track that was fairly fresh. It led down near the mouth of the draw then turned and ran back up. They were the hoofprints from Billy Butts' horse. Willig knew he was close to one of the kills that Bingham had referred to. He stepped down and tied Sontag to a large squaw bush, then pulled his rifle out of its scabbard and silently levered in a shell. Senses honed for a hunt, he took stock of the breeze and found that what there was of it was blowing down the draw. He was downwind of it.

Willig worked his way up the draw, keeping to its bottom, moving quietly and easy. Just ahead, the south bank had caved in and several sagebrush hung down by stringy clumps, held only by the big ropes of tap roots still clinging to the soil. Willig stole up to the dangling bush and peeked around, using it as cover.

About 100 yards farther on, a large coyote was feeding on a sheep carcass. It was smart, feeding on the downhill side of the sheep while keeping its noise pointed up the draw to catch any scent that might waft downwind. The coyote would rip off a piece of meat, then chew on it, never abandoning caution that would send it into flight in a moment.

Willig's heartbeat quickened and sweat moistened his palms. A few yards beyond the coyote lay the carcass of another sheep. The coyote had scared off the carrion birds feeding on these kills. Now, three crows were stalking along the edge of the south bank, 50 yards up the draw, cawing their wrath and dismay at being run off their meal. Three or four long-tailed magpies sailed back and forth above, dark forms screeching.

Willig slipped off the safety and was calmly putting the rifle to his shoulder when he gasped. My God, he realized, that coyote is Two Toes!

Heart pounding, the veins on his temple throbbing, Willig lowered the gun and drew in deep breaths. *I've got him!* his mind screamed. *I've got him!*

The target ahead shifted as Willig raised the rifle once more. The coyote's attention had been diverted by the ruckus from the magpies and crows. Not once had he looked back down the draw, but now he backed away from chewing on the ewe. The animal's posture told Willig he had eaten his fill. The crows knew it, too. The black birds flew up in a flush of wing-flapping, cawing louder than ever. The big coyote turned and started up the draw.

Quickly, Willig threw the rifle to his shoulder, brought the coyote into his rear sights and squeezed the trigger. There was a short yelp. The coyote rolled twice, jumped up, and hobbled on three legs around a corner in the draw. The birds shrieked and flew for the cottonwoods on the river.

Willig felt the world spin. Here he was, a veteran hunter who had downed all kinds of wild game and predators—and now he couldn't catch his breath. His calm and cool had escaped him. He was as thrilled and nervous as a kid.

Willig rose shakily to his feet and stood without moving for several minutes, letting his pulse slow. He knew he had his coyote. His .30/.30 bullet had hit it right in the shoulder. It wouldn't go far.

Willig lowered his gun, pumped another shell into the chamber and shoved the safety on. He walked slowly towards the sheep carcass. There were all kinds of sign marking up the ground: some horse tracks, but mostly coyote. He was about 10 feet from the dead ewe when he spotted a clear coyote track.

Bending over, he saw it was missing two middle toes.

Willig gulped and let out a yell. Clutching his rifle in one hand, he began running up the draw as fast as he could, following the fresher tracks of the coyote he'd shot. He'd killed Two Toes, by God. His trouble was over. He'd deal presently with Bingham, waving a right-front paw in his face.

Willig rounded the bend in the wash. Right there lay the coyote, dead, flat on its side in the sand. Willig jabbed at the body with the muzzle of his gun, turning it on its back. He laid down the rifle and grabbed the right-front foot, holding it up and preparing for the moment of triumph.

Just as quickly, he dropped the paw. He flopped down on his knees, stunned. He blinked his eyes as if dreaming. Then he felt like laughing hysterically.

In an afterthought, he seized the left front foot. All the toes were there, too.

NINETEEN

Territory Fight

TWO TOES and his mate were out hunting very early. The growing pups were now devouring food with ravenous hunger then whining for more. It seemed the more meat they were brought, the greater their appetites grew.

It was not yet daylight as the two coyotes headed south along the Leota Bottoms. Two Toes' highly honed hunting instincts had led him to pass up a fourth foray to the draw where he'd killed the two ewes. Now he and the bitch were headed for the Indian ranches on the Duchesne River.

They were after fresh kills. But the smell of a cow's carcass made Two Toes lift his nose and stop. It was an old one he had known about for some time. It lay in a clearing among the grease-wood and rabbit brush. He left the bitch and swung off to check it out. As he neared the carcass, a fresh scent carried to his nose and caused the hackles to raise on his back. It was the smell of coyote urine. Indeed, a wet spot on the cow's skull showed where a dog had just pissed on it. Nearby, the dirt was kicked up.

Curious, feeling his terrain invaded, Two Toes nosed up to the skull. He was sniffing the wet spot when his mate started yelping. Then he heard her wail in pain.

Where she was standing alone, a big strange dog coyote had appeared from nowhere and run her down. He'd grabbed her by the back and thrown her to the ground. She'd rolled over, jumped to her feet and run, only to be grabbed by the neck and thrown down again. Now she was on her back, her tail between her legs. The dog coyote stood over her, growling.

He spun as Two Toes burst through the brush at a dead run. There was a rough collision. Two Toes hit the stranger at full speed, knocking him flat. Before he could get up, Two Toes had him by the neck and was sinking his fangs in deep.

Howling in anguish, the strange coyote tore loose and gained his feet. Head bent sideways, he slashed at Two Toes, missing his throat by inches. For an instant this left him off balance: Two Toes darted in and found a target for his teeth. He snapped high at his foe's left front leg, caught hold and clamped his jaws down tight.

A coyote who senses he is about to win will try to get the other off its feet. Two Toes sunk in all four feet and gave his head a mighty sideways jerk, throwing the big coyote onto his back. That was what he was after. Two Toes let go the leg and grabbed the stranger by the throat. Straddling him, snarling and growling, he tightened his grip on the skin, sinking his teeth in deeper and deeper, tasting the blood.

In panic and terror, the fallen coyote flailed upward with his hind feet. With a desperate thrust, he kicked Two Toes loose. He jumped to his feet, blood dripping from his neck, and bolted into the brush. Two Toes did not follow. He stood, staring at the spot in the brush where his adversary had disappeared. From the corner of his eye he saw his mate come to him, tail between legs. She licked around his muzzle.

Stiff-legged and sore, Two Toes trotted back toward the river. She followed, her tail still down. They crossed a wash and headed up on the north bank. Two Toes lay down to lick his belly where the strange coyote's toenails had scratched deep. The bitch lay on her belly and crawled up to him again, licking his throat and muzzle. When he licked her in return, she jumped to her feet and bounced around him, making soft yelps.

Two Toes finally stood. He looked down the long flat bench to Green River, then started trotting east, toward it.

His mate trotted behind, her tail now up. They were hunting once more.

TWENTY

▲ ▲ ▲

Bingham's Scheme

T Y BINGHAM drove away from the sheep camp, Jack Willig's words still ringing in his ears. *I won't set another foot in your camp if it costs me my job.*

Bingham was a powerful sheepman. He was used to running the roost. It had been a very long time since he'd been dressed down like that, by anyone. The rebuke stung bad.

Bingham had never seen Willig lose his temper like that. He couldn't believe it. And then, as he thought some more, he couldn't believe he had been dumb enough to let it happen. Not now. Not when everything was so critical, when there was zero margin for error and he needed every break he could get to make that extra 10 percent on his lamb crop.

It all seemed a cruel, absurd development. But Bingham clung to disbelief. It couldn't be that Willig would not stop at his sheep camp. How would the trapper know what was happening to Bingham's herd? Billy Butts would have to go to Willig's camp to update him, and that would mean leaving the sheep unattended for a couple hours—at the least.

But reality slowly asserted itself in Bingham's mind, crowding out all doubt about Willig's intentions. The trapper had been ready to punch him when he'd stuck his nose right in Bingham's face. And to top it all, his own sheepherder had sided against him, saying he'd been riding Willig too hard.

Bingham gripped the steering wheel until his knuckles were white. He was breathing hard. He was mad.

"Damn it, he's paid to kill coyotes," he said aloud. "And by God, he better get started fast."

Outside the Ouray Trading Post, he killed the engine and stepped up onto the porch. Before entering, he took off his hat, pulled out his bandanna and wiped dust and sweat from his face and forehead. The trading post was the radio and newspaper in this area. All the sheepmen passed through. A herder who hadn't been by for three weeks would stop in and say where he was headed. It was the way information traveled on the range, from one herder to another, from one rider to the one that followed, from one pickup to the next.

Bingham figured he had a week until the next herder crossed the river with his band. But now, via the post, he was to learn different.

As he entered the cool dark of the store, Osh Portle called out, "Hello, Ty."

"How goes it, Osh? Anything new?"

"Yeah," the storekeep replied. "Some more sheep are crossing the river. Buckwalter is crossing about now, and Sundstrom's herd will cross tomorrow."

"Damn," Bingham said, perking up at the unexpected news. "They'll be right on our heels. I guess I'd better tell Billy Butts to move north tomorrow."

He quickly drained a Hire's root beer then moved out into the sunlight with new urgency.

As he headed back again for his sheep camp over the rough road going up the stock driveway, Bingham's mind locked on Two Toes. Like a wagon-trainer trekking west 80 years before through Indian land, Bingham's senses tingled with the intuition he was now in enemy territory. The sheep kills plaguing his band would continue, he knew.

Deep down, he realized it was too big a job for one man to fend the coyotes off. As good a trapper as Jack Willig was, Bingham knew he couldn't cover all the country he was assigned. With renewed remorse, the rancher reflected again on the fateful words the trapper had spoken earlier that morning. He would not be

back to Billy Butts' camp. Butts would have to leave the herd and ride to Willig's camp to report any losses.

The wheels turning in Bingham's mind suddenly spun. He remembered his call to Scott Rasmussen, the Biological Survey's district agent in Salt Lake. Rasmussen had promised to send out a new man to help Willig, hadn't he? Well, where in the hell was this new man? Now is when he was needed.

Bingham resolved to phone up Rasmussen as soon as he got back into Vernal. As he pulled into the sheep camp, he saw Billy Butts moving the band along the grassy bench land about two miles out. The herder, having seen the dust trail from his boss's pickup, was heading back to camp. When he rode up, Bingham had his Levi's jacket with the blanket lining off and was swinging the single-bit ax with easy, accurate motions, chopping up the cottonwood limbs dragged into camp at the end of a lariat tied to his saddle.

The wood was stacked up near the wagon for the next sheep outfit using the camp. Like leaving some food in a cabin when you left. It was a rule of the range. Bingham sunk the ax blade in the chopping stump and turned to face his herder.

"Anything wrong?" Butts asked as he swung down from his horse.

"Buckwalter is moving his herd across the river right now," Bingham said. "Sundstrom's herd will cross tomorrow and Chance's is right behind."

Butts shook his head. "We'll have to move north tomorrow or we'll be mixing some herds for sure."

"That's the last thing we need—spending two or three days separating mixed herds," Bingham said, with more force than necessary. "We'll have to move north in the morning. Hasletts will be on the move and I'd just as soon stay ahead of them and get first shot at the spring grass."

Billy Butts shot his boss a funny look. It faded in an instant, but Bingham noted it just the same.

"The next water on the trail is Badger Spring," Butts said. Lowering his voice, he added, "That's where Willig is camped."

Bingham's eyes flashed. "I don't give a damn whether he's there or not. We'll camp there for a couple days and then move up to the Ute Seeps."

The rancher's indignation was in full flame now. Butts could see how his boss's back had gotten up at the mere mention of Willig's name.

"We need more trappers," Bingham said, stalking toward his jacket on a log. "We've only got three other men besides Willig out here and they're spread too thin. Rawson is working the stock driveway on the Colorado line south of Blue Mountain. Keeper is south, between Wall Canyon and the Duchesne, and Walkup is over between Myton and LaPoint.

"Now, there's something you should know, Billy Butts," Bingham said, pulling his jacket on. "The trapper's boss man, Rasmussen, said he'd send a man to help Willig." Bingham fastened the buttons and hunched his shoulders forward. "Damn it, that extra man should be here now when we need him."

The sheepman got in his pickup and turned the engine over. It backfired, kicked again and started up noisily. He stepped on the pedal, racing the engine, then released the brake.

"I'll be back here at daylight," he called out over the din. Then he drove off in the direction he'd come.

Standing next to the sheep wagon as the quiet of the camp engulfed him, Billy Butts stood expressionless. Then he shook his head. If his boss weren't so hot-headed, they'd be camping at Badger Spring alongside Willig now. Butts liked to have the trapper's wagon close by. Willig was a good hand and coyote losses had always been fewer with him around. Every time Butts had lost sheep to coyotes in the past, Willig had been right on them the next day and usually got the killer within a few days, either with his traps or rifle.

The sheepherder knew if anyone was going to put an end to Two Toes' killing, it was going to be Trapper Jack. Anyone could stumble upon the famous coyote and kill him, but Willig was the one tracking him now and he had an eye out for him. Butts knew his boss realized this, too. And yet, Ty Bingham could be too dad-blasted headstrong for his own damn good.

Butts didn't know what would happen tomorrow when they moved their wagon to Badger Spring. But there was nothing he could do. When it came down to it, he was just the hired hand. But he knew for damn sure that Willig would keep his promise. He would take no more guff off Bingham. Which meant anything could happen.

As Billy Butts was thinking all this out, Ty Bingham, driving back toward Ouray, was contemplating another notion:

If they moved camp in the morning to Badger Spring, where Willig was, the trapper would have to talk to Billy Butts. That meant Billy could keep Willig informed of any sheep losses or any sign of Two Toes. It would mean a lot more protection and help.

At this idea, Bingham felt cheered for the first time that morning. Now his practical side began plotting in earnest. The more he thought, the more hopeful he grew.

Willig would be gone from his wagon at daybreak. Sure he would, he always hit the saddle at dawn when he was denning. Bingham and Billy Butts would be breaking camp about that time. That meant they wouldn't be getting to Badger Spring before 8 or 9 o'clock. And that would be long after Willig was gone. So there was no chance Bingham would get into it again with the trapper when they set up next to his wagon. What's more, he would be long gone by the time Willig returned at night.

Damn, Bingham thought, camping next to Willig would surely help cut the losses. And if Two Toes were denning near Badger Spring, chances were a lot better that Willig would find the den. Who knew, maybe his assistant would show up, too, and this crisis would be over and done for good.

Bingham turned his truck off the stock driveway and headed towards Haslett's camp on the Green River. Up ahead, he could see no smoke from the wagon chimney and no horse tied to the wagon. Hod Hogan was out with the sheep.

Standing outside the wagon, Bingham undid a flap on the left breast pocket of his Pendleton shirt and tugged out his dog-eared notebook. He flipped past scrawled notes and telephone numbers and checks tucked into pages until he found a clean sheet. He penciled a short note to Hogan: "We've moved up to Badger today." He added the date.

The sheepman folded the note once and slid it into a crack in the door.

TWENTY-ONE

▲ ▲ ▲

On the Trail Again

J ACK WILLIG finally rode Sontag out of the wash, leaving behind the coyote he'd shot at the remains of the ewes. He had calmed down considerably; now he coolly mulled over what had transpired, fitting together all the information like a puzzle.

He was sure that Two Toes had killed the two ewes. After all, there had been plenty of sign. Two Toes and his mate probably had fed at least twice on the sheep, and since so much meat was missing from the hindquarters, they were feeding pups. Big ones.

The coyote he'd just shot was a big dog hunting alone. His mate was probably in the den, nursing much younger pups. That meant there was another coyote den in the area, in addition to Two Toes'. There would be plenty of trouble for the sheep herds passing through this country, if Willig didn't get to the dens quick.

He considered turning back and going up the draw from where he had killed the coyote. There would be good fresh tracks up that way, from both pairs of denning coyotes. With this new plan firmed up for the day, Willig swung Sontag around. As he did so, he saw a faint line of dust on the big flat bench land to the south and west, some two miles distant.

Willig shaded his eyes with a hand. He could make out a band of sheep moving slowly southward, and among them, the gray horse that belonged to Hod Hogan. Hogan had already spotted Willig. He was waving his Stetson back and forth in the air. Willig sat still in the saddle, watching Hogan begin riding toward him.

He seemed in a hurry. Willig moved Sontag ahead at a slow trot. At 100 yards distance, Hogan called out, "I found a fresh kill."

"It was Two Toes," Hogan said as he swung up to Willig's side. "I was moving the sheep north just this side of that sagebrush line up that bench. Two Toes killed a big lamby ewe right at the edge of the sagebrush. I didn't even see or hear nothing."

The large man cussed and swiped with a beefy open hand at a swarm of buffalo gnats casting a dark pall around his head. He took off his Stetson and fanned them away violently. The swarm dispersed, he continued.

"We fed north about an hour. Then I turned them around to feed back towards camp. As we passed along that line of high sagebrush, I seen a couple magpies flush up."

He'd thought that was suspicious and had ridden over. That's where he'd found the dead ewe. "Two Toes must have killed her as we went by going north," Hogan summed up.

Willig looked skeptical. "How do you know it was Two Toes?"

"Hells bells!" Hogan said, "his tracks were all over the place. He had another coyote with him."

At this, Willig felt a jolt of excitement.

"Did they eat a lot of meat?" Willig asked.

"I'll say," Hogan said. "They cleaned up one hindquarter and part of the other one. She was just starting to lamb and they didn't even touch it."

Willig could barely contain himself. He touched his heels to Sontag's flanks. "Let's take a look," he said, and was off at a fast trot. Hogan spurred his horse to catch up.

"Did you keep the sheep and dogs away?" Willig called back over his shoulder.

"Yep," the big-framed herder replied, trying to keep pace. "The dogs were moving behind the sheep and I herded them past the ewe before I went back and didn't even get off my horse. The ground was soft. Them tracks were plain as day."

At the edge of the sagebrush, they reined up. Willig peered closely at the dead ewe. Reluctantly, Hogan said, already knowing the answer, "Do you need any help, Jack?"

"No thanks," the trapper said, still staring fixedly at the sheep remains. "I'd rather check it out myself."

Hogan swung his horse around. "I'll get back to my sheep," he said. "Stop at camp if you're close by."

As he said this, the trapper was already off his horse and tying the reins to a bush. He moved directly to the carcass.

It was all as Hogan had said. The ewe was well eaten on in her hindquarters. She had probably gone to the brush to drop her lamb and that's where Two Toes and his bitch were hiding. Her final muscular spasms as she died had forced the lamb's head out. The coyotes hadn't even touched it. They were feeding big hungry pups. The lamb's head was still now, eyes shut, choked half-born. Its circulation had quit when its mother died on the other end of the umbilical cord; and it had had no chance to breathe the air of the outside world because of the afterbirth covering its face.

Willig moved carefully around the kill. He found the tracks coming in toward the carcass. They were coming from the south. He retraced them as they led back and forth. Back at the kill, he found where their tracks went after they'd fed on the ewe. They led more or less in a straight line, as do predators that have filled their bellies and were heading directly home.

Willig walked these tracks for 200 yards or so and stopped. They seemed to be heading steadily south. And here he'd figured their den was north. A red-tailed hawk circled overhead. For a brief moment, Willig stared at the blue sky with a pang of envy. That hawk knew where Two Toes was at this moment. If only the trapper could soar, too. But though he lacked wings, he had something almost as good: a human brain. It would be enough to get him started on the trail.

Willig walked back to Sontag, untied him and mounted up. He rode back and quickly picked up the coyote tracks. He followed the trail for several hundred yards, then stopped and looked back at the spot where the dead sheep was. It marked one point on the straight line. Looking south again, Willig used a bare spot on the bank of the big wash he was heading for as a guide to continue on the line. Moving at a trot now, he hurried toward the spot a quarter-mile away. Reaching it, he dismounted, dropped the horse's reins and started looking for tracks on the ground. They would be there. Somewhere. They had to be.

But Willig could find no markings in the earth. He walked slowly down the north bank of the wash. Yes: there were Two Toes' distinct tracks where he had crossed the wash with his mate.

Willig climbed down into the wash and found where the pair had gone up the south bank. Wishing he could move as easily as a coyote, he scrambled up the bank, hunched over a minute, then followed the tracks a short distance. He stopped again to look back to the bare spot, and then way back to the sagebrush where the dead ewe lay. It all fell into a straight line.

Two Toes and his mate were headed directly for his den. It was sure as shooting. A grimace of confidence and determination creased the corners of Willig's mouth. He gazed off south again where the imaginary line would lead him. It was headed for the hills above the Indian ranches. And here he had been so sure Two Toes was denned west of Bow Knot Bend, toward the Twist Hills. But now he had tracked him and his bitch for a couple miles—at least—and the trail led in a straight line south of him. It led to where the den was, by God.

Willig glanced at the sun. It was at 6 o'clock in the sky. Late afternoon had come already. He had done good work this day. He would make it back to this very spot early tomorrow morning. Everything would be fresh and undisturbed at first light—no sheep or dogs or anything to ruin the tracks that lay in the sand of the wash almost as clear as footprints in snow.

Willig was elated as he headed for Hod Hogan's camp. He arrived just as the herder was bringing the sheep to the bed ground. Willig helped him move the band in, telling about the day's big find. He would be back on the trail at the crack of dawn, he said. He had a glint in his eyes.

"Why don't you get your wagon and bring it back here?" Hogan said. "You'll be a couple hours closer. You can be back here before dark and I'll wait supper for you."

"Great idea!" Willig said. "By damn, I'll just do that."

He and Sontag headed back for Badger Spring. All Willig had to do was gather a little gear, hop Sontag into his pickup, hook the camp wagon to his truck and get back to Hod's camp. That would put him camped close to where he should find Two Toes' den.

Morning couldn't come soon enough.

TWENTY-TWO

▲ ▲ ▲

The Trail Turns Cold

THE PRE-DAWN AIR filled with the rich smells of sizzling bacon and hot coffee as Hod Hogan cooked breakfast in his sheep wagon. Jack Willig loved the aromas. He considered it had been a great idea to move his wagon to Hogan's camp. Even with all his years of experience, it could get lonesome on the range. He'd been out three weeks now.

As Hogan poured him another cup of coffee, Willig filled him in on his finds from the day before, when he'd tracked Two Toes and his bitch straight south from the latest sheep kills. "I still can't quite figure it," Willig was saying. "The kills at the cliff and the coyote tracks weren't the best signs, but they seemed to indicate that Two Toes' den was toward the Twist Hills. I couldn't believe that Two Toes and his mate headed straight south for the Indian ranches, but yesterday the tracking was good enough that I could follow them three or four miles. And they went straight south after they filled up on that ewe.

"And now that big dog coyote I shot messed things up. He was hunting alone, so his bitch must be in the den, nursing. He was eating enough for the both of them. His den is up there somewhere, too."

"Jack, there is sure as hell more than one den out there," Hogan offered. "Too many sheep being killed too fast, even for Two Toes."

"You're right," Willig agreed. "I think there's at least two or three dens, and if the mate of the dog I shot had her pups, then she'll really be after anything she can get without him to feed her and the pups. "Anyway, I'm heading back south right after break-fast."

Hogan refilled the trapper's tin cup. "I'll fix you something to eat," he said. "I know I won't see you till late today."

As Willig drained his cup and rose to leave, Hogan handed him a cold mutton sandwich wrapped in wax paper.

"If I don't get things sorted out, it'll be dark when I get back," Willig said.

"Fine," Hogan said. "I'll keep supper warm."

Willig saddled Sontag, stowed his rifle and gear on the saddle and slipped the sandwich into his saddle bag. He mounted and turned his horse around.

"Thanks for breakfast," he said. Touching his boots to Sontag's flanks, he rode off into the gray start of morning.

Willig rode southwest for some time, to the bench where he'd left Two Toes' tracks the night before. He followed his own horse tracks and finally came to where he'd left off. There, he stepped down from the saddle and walked back and forth for a few minutes, leading Sontag, searching for Two Toes' tracks. Then he spotted them. Shortly thereafter, he found both Two Toes' and the bitch's tracks, heading south.

The ground was good for tracking. Willig, on foot leading Sontag, covered a good distance. Once, he located where the coyotes had rested, each dropping a big chunk of meat. He was positive they were headed for their den. Looking behind toward where he'd come, Willig could still see the bare spot he'd used for a mark. Looking north the other way, he could barely make out the sagebrush line on the bench where the dead ewes lay. The two points—the bare spot to the south and the sagebrush on the bench—told him he was still on a straight line for the low hills that crowded in just north of the Indian ranches.

Willig left the tracks now and rode straight for the hills. Soon he was at their base and cutting across for sign. On one ridge, he picked up Two Toes' track in soft dirt. It was several days old, and headed south toward the ranches. Willig rode farther west, up into the hills, and picked up another track moving north.

But after several hours crisscrossing for at least two miles, he was sure no den lay there. Willig rode east, along the first big bench north of the ranches. Again, he picked up little sign. Once, he saw a good print of Two Toes' telltale right-front foot, but that was all.

He was beginning to feel frustrated. He rode farther southeast now. Skirting a patch of greasewood, Willig glimpsed an old cow carcass. Immediately, he turned Sontag. There was enough coyote in Willig to know that such a remnant was irresistible as a pissing post.

Sure enough, the tracks leading up showed him many coyotes had been stopping at the carcass for a long time. Turds and scratch marks were all over the ground. Willig slowly circled the carcass, and quickly spotted fresh tracks from Two Toes and his mate. He dismounted and tied Sontag's reins to a greasewood.

Searching the ground, Willig found where the coyote had pissed on the carcass and scratched heavily. Then, suddenly, the tracks disappeared. Willig, bent over, scratched his head and straightened up. He moved to the greasewoods and there more tracks showed up, but distanced apart. Two Toes had been running. A bit farther on, a clear spot of earth revealed all kinds of tracks. The ground was dug up. Balls of coyote fur lay in several places.

Willig bit his lower lip and mulled it over. It was obvious Two Toes and another dog coyote had had one hell of a fight. The strange dog's tracks broke for the brush, while Two Toes and his bitch headed northeast. Crouching, the trapper picked up a grayish clump of shedding fur that had been torn out of one of the coyote's sides. He wound it around his finger tips. A piece of Two Toes?

"Wish I had the rest of his hide," Willig whispered to himself.

Spots of blood flecked the earth near one ball of fur, but after further scrutiny, the trapper saw no tracks contained blood, and no sequence of their movements were interrupted to suggest a leg had been injured. He wasn't surprised. Neither of the coyotes had been badly wounded. It was their nature that in a fight, the moment one realizes the other has the upper hand, it turns and bolts. Safety and good sense always overrules pride in the species. It was a key to their survival.

It was now past sundown. Willig had burned up a long hard day. He was confused and disappointed. Beyond the fight spot he'd found where Two Toes and his mate had crossed a deep draw and gone up on the north bank, then laid down. There was a little fresh coyote fur there. But that was all.

Riding back to camp, Willig swallowed the hard truth that he hadn't found anything to lead him to believe there was a den anywhere in this entire area. He still harbored a nagging feeling that Two Toes' den lay between Bow Knot Bend and the Twist Hills. Yet here he was—following yesterday's tracks, and they had shown the coyotes to be hunting northeastward. The night before, they had made a kill, eaten a lot of meat and were carrying more in their jaws, yet had been heading south. None of it added up. It just didn't fit together.

Willig was still puzzling this out when he arrived in camp. Hogan was in his wagon, the yellow brightness from his Coleman lantern shining out the opened top of the Dutch door. "Just in time," the sheepherder called out. "Soup's on."

Willig stripped Sontag of saddle and bridle, blanket and gear. He wiped down the horse's sweaty neck and sides with a gunnysack, then filled an old beat-up bucket halfway with oats and set it on the ground. As Sontag nosed up to it, Willig carried the gear over to his wagon and hung it up.

Over dinner, Hogan listened silently to Willig's account of his day's work. He noted the furrow in the trapper's brow that showed how perplexed he was—a complete change from the optimism the night before. After Willig finished up, the sheepherder let the silence sit a minute. Then he asked, "Well, where do you think the den is?"

"I'll be double-damned if I know," Willig replied slowly. "Except it sure as hell isn't where I've been."

He set his knife and fork down with a motion of finality, and looked away, past the double doors, into space. "There's something crazy that I don't know," he said, a distant look in his eyes.

He turned back to Hogan. "Listen, I've got to go to town to-night," he said. "I need groceries, clean clothes and a bath. If you'll water and grain Sontag in the morning, I'd appreciate it."

"Sure," Hogan said. "Don't worry about a thing, Jack."

Inside his pickup, Willig figured not worrying was the best he could do. He lifted a sleeve and sniffed an armpit. It was sour. He hadn't had anything but a wash-basin bath using a cloth and bucket for the past three weeks. He was out of clean underwear.

He rubbed his scrubby face. He'd get a haircut and shave, too, while he was back in Vernal.

TWENTY-THREE

Willig Gets Some Help

BRETT GALE, Junior Biological Aide with the U.S. Biologi cal Survey, was two hours into his three-hour drive from Salt Lake City. In the beginning, he'd passed a number of stock trucks, refrigerated trucks and oil tankers along two-lane Highway 40, plus a smattering of farmers in pickups and a few passenger Fords or Buicks; but the past hour there'd been almost no traffic to interrupt his thoughts. His pickup towing a horse trailer was making good time on the 175-mile trip to Vernal.

Earlier that morning, he'd met with his boss, Scott Rasmussen, and been told about the calls from Ty Bingham. Rasmussen related how the rancher had ranted and raved about a coyote he called, "Two Toes," how this wily critter was killing sheep on the stock trail three years running and how this year the losses were going to ruin him.

"Bingham demanded more help from government trappers," Rasmussen had said. He explained how the Ashley Valley sheepmen were now on the trail to the Uintah Basin after wintering in the high desert between White River and the Book Cliff Mountains. This Two Toes was supposed to be killing sheep on the trail up the west side of the Green River, and Bingham was claiming the coyote had already killed a large number of ewes heavy with lamb.

"Bingham complained pretty strongly about Jack Willig, who as you know is one of our best," Rasmussen said. "He said Willig's covering too much country and not getting the job done. He demanded at least one more trapper. That's where you come in."

Over his 18 months training with three different denners, Brett Gale had met many a sheepman. When the trappers weren't way out in the wilderness, they kept in constant contact with the herders and sheepmen, exchanging information. From this, Gale had gotten the flavor of their breed. They depended on the trappers to get coyotes, so it was understandable when one of them filled you up with bull, overstating losses to press his case and get the trappers over to work his range.

"What kind of sheepman is Bingham?" Gale asked. "Do you think he's exaggerating?"

"No," Rasmussen replied. "I think the coyotes *are* hitting him pretty hard. He gets excited when he talks about this Two Toes coyote. But I will say he's probably blaming all his kills on him. I've met Bingham at Wool Growers meetings. He seems to me to be a good sheepman. He's been active in the association. He was president a few years ago. His father was raising sheep in the 1880s. I think he's on the Grazing Advisory Board now."

Gale knew what his boss was driving at. This Bingham couldn't be shrugged off. No wonder he'd been pulled off his denning schedule now to go to the Uintah Basin instead of Iron County. This was all about politics and public relations.

On the other hand, maybe this Two Toes really was a special case. Either way, it stood a chance of being interesting.

"What do you suggest?" Gale asked.

"I'd suggest you maybe call on Bingham once you get out there," Rasmussen said. "Let him know you're getting together with Jack Willig and you'll do your best to stop the killing. Spend at least a week out there. Good luck."

Gale's directions were to stop at Jack Willig's place in Vernal, hook up with the trapper and then call the office and give Rasmussen an update before the two headed for the Green River. Gale checked his watch. It was about half-past 11. He hadn't even stopped for a cup of coffee at the Junction Cafe.

He was driving around the north end of Strawberry Lake now. No boats were on the lake. Fishing season wouldn't open until spawning was finished. The big rainbows would now be going up the feeder creeks to spawn. The Utah Fish and Game Department biologists would be stripping the roe from the hens. Each year they took several million eggs from Strawberry Lake for the state's hatcheries. Gale was glad to be out trapping instead.

He shifted gears as his truck started the slow climb to Avintaquin Plateau. Soon, spread out before him almost as far as the eye could see, stood dark, endless forests of pinion pine. To the north was the only real break in the sea of trees—the red ledges cut by the Duchesne River several thousands years before, and rising like steps toward the High Uintah Mountains that were still capped by snow. The mid-morning sun reflected off the 12,000-foot peaks like a mirror, making the mantles of white glisten like ice.

Gale's spell of admiration was jarred suddenly and violently. A big doe mule deer had jumped out of the high rye grass and crossed the road in front of the truck. Gale swung the pickup sharply to the left to miss the deer, and as he swerved back to stay on the road, his horse stomped heavily in the trailer behind, swaying it and the truck.

"Holy shit!" Gale exclaimed.

He eased on the brake and slowly stopped the truck, then jumped out to see if his horse was down. The animal was still on his feet, but he was mad. He snorted and reared his head up and down against the halter rope and rolled his big eyes wildly at Gale, while pawing his front feet on the trailer floor as if warning his master not to do that move again.

Gale carefully stepped up on the trailer tongue and spoke softly to the horse, whose name was Socks. Gale's 7-year-old daughter, Susie, had named the horse after her daddy had first brought him home—a pretty dark bay yearling with both hind feet white. "Look, Daddy, he's got white socks on!" she'd said.

All was right with Socks now, but he was still upset at the sudden swerving. Gale patted him and stepped down from the trailer.

Close call, he thought. Highway 40 was a major east-west route, but you never knew when cattle or sheep or horses or dogs might pop up along the road, and even deer could bolt across it when you were out on the range. A big animal could cause a bad accident.

Gale crossed the Avintaquin Plateau and dropped down to the Strawberry River. He pulled up at Jake's, a little cafe in the town of Duchesne, and had a cup of coffee. He arrived in Vernal in mid-afternoon and drove straight out to the fairgrounds in the southeast part of town. The fairgrounds consisted of a typical racetrack surrounded by a wood fence with a shorter fence around the infield. A grandstand with a slanted roof stood on one side. Corrals were at opposite ends, and the stalls were always empty except during a fair or a rodeo. Gale pulled up in front of a stall, dropped the tailgate and backed Socks out. He walked the horse for five minutes, getting his legs back underneath him. Like all horses, Socks would get ornery and scared whenever he felt out of balance—just a bundle of nerves. Even though he was pretty used to the trailer, the ride had been a long one. But after five minutes, his nostrils no longer flared and his eyes gazed gently.

Gale tied Socks' halter to the manger in the stall, put hay he'd brought along in the trough and filled the tub between the two stalls with water. Patting the horse on the neck, he removed the halter. Then he closed and locked the stall gate, tossed the halter in his pickup, jumped in the cab and headed out to find where Jack Willig lived.

The worker at the Conoco station came out to the pump spitting tobacco juice over a shoulder of his bib overalls. He gave Gale directions. Ten minutes later, Gale pulled up in front of a small, tidy-looking white house back off the Maeser Road northwest of town. The house had black trim and a green, well-watered lawn lined with flowers stretched to the sidewalk, behind a low fence. Alongside, a dirt driveway ran back from the street about 15 feet past the house to a small one-car garage that was also painted white.

Gale climbed out of his truck and went through the front yard gate, carefully closing it behind. The porch was screened in. Gale walked up two stone steps, pulled the screen door open and walked across the porch to the front door. He knocked. A short time later, a face peaked through the little window and then a gray-haired lady wearing a calico apron opened the door. She gave Gale a quick, pleasant smile as she wiped her wet hands on the apron. "Yes?" she asked. She seemed to be in a hurry.

Gale introduced himself and inquired whether Jack Willig was home.

"Oh, I'm Mrs. Willig," the woman said. "I've been expecting you. Mr. Rasmussen's letter said you should be here today. Excuse me, please, I'm right in the middle of washing."

She left. Gale heard her turn off the washing machine. Presently, she returned.

"Will you come in?" she asked, no longer hurried. "Excuse me for leaving you standing there."

"No thanks, ma'm," Gale said, politely. "Do you expect Jack?"

"Yes, I think he will be in tonight. Where will you be?"

"I'll get a room at the Dinosaur Auto Court," Gale said. Having lived in Vernal before, working out of a Civilian Conservation Corps camp, he knew the town well. "I'll be over at the Stockman's Cafe until then, having supper, so please ask Jack to stop by when he gets in."

Gale was having a cup of coffee and finishing a piece of apple pie when Jack Willig came through the front door. Gale watched the six-foot-tall, slender man move in, looking over the tables. He was wearing fresh-washed Levi's, a dark brown flannel shirt open at the collar and a green silk kerchief tied around his neck. His Stetson had seen a lot of weather. It was wrinkled some, and the hat band had sweat stains all around it. Willig, too, had seen some years and lots of sun and wind, Gale could tell. His face was deeply tanned with crow's-feet wrinkles spidering from his eyes. He was also a little stoop-shouldered and walked with the small steps of a man who had spent half a lifetime on a horse.

They made eye contact. Willig approached and spoke first.

"You Brett Gale?"

"That's me," Gale said, standing and extending his hand.

Willig's hand was callused, like rawhide, and hard and firm.

"Just finishing," Gale said. "Have a cup of coffee?"

"Yeah. I'll have one with you."

Willig sat down. The cafe was half-empty. It was a stop on the route that the Burlington bus took out of Salt Lake, and when the bus unloaded, the stools and booths filled up and the jukebox got plenty of use. Passengers took the bus from Vernal to Craig, Colorado, 120 miles away, but some traveled as far as from San Francisco to Denver. At present, "Chattanooga Choo-Choo" was playing, which sounded good to Gale's ears, but did nothing for Willig. Gale resisted tapping his fingers on the table.

The waitress, a cute schoolgirl with bobbed black hair, put a cup of coffee down in front of Willig. He looked down at it, stirred it with his spoon, then looked up at Gale. The young man's appearance and manner reassured him. Something about him said he was one of the bunch. Maybe he wasn't just some smart-ass college kid. Besides, Rasmussen had written that Gale had put in a lot of months learning, denning and trapping in the Biological Survey.

"What's the plan?" Willig asked.

To Gale, the trapper's tone sounded non-committal, but he could sense the door was open to acceptance. "Ty Bingham has called the boss several times," he began. "He's complaining about the coyote losses ever since his herd hit Green River. I guess the losses have been pretty heavy. Some of the other herds have been hit, too, and now Bingham wants more trappers and, of course, there aren't any available."

Willig's face remained expressionless.

"So Rasmussen said he'd send me out to help you, especially for den hunting," Gale continued. "I was supposed to go down to Iron County to work with Abe Evans, but the boss is curious about this coyote, Two Toes."

Gale paused. "So," he said, "have you located his den?"

A pained look flitted across Willig's face. Gale saw he had touched a sore spot.

Willig ignored the question and asked one of his own. "You ever do any coyote denning?"

"Yes," Gale said. He told how he'd spent the previous spring denning with Jake Judd in Tooele County, with Evans in Iron County and with Jose Walls in Beaver County.

"This spring I denned with Jake again, until Rasmussen sent me out here."

Willig could see that Rasmussen must have something special for this young fellow. Judd, Evans and Walls took almost as many dens each spring as he did. "How come he's going to so much effort to make a denner out of you?" he asked.

Gale detected a little sarcasm, but shrugged it off. "The director in Washington has started a pretty intensive study on coyote dens," he said. "Utah is one of the states in the study, and Rasmussen happened to assign the project to me."

Willig's interested perked up. He was all ears as Gale explained the program.

"We'll write up a report on every den we take. We'll locate it on a large map and fill in all the details: what kind of country the den's in, soil types, elevation, ground cover, type and depth, sex of pups, how many, how old, what they're feeding on—a real complete report. And all dens taken in Utah will go onto a big state map marked by colored pins. It's a five-year program, and the results should tell us something about coyotes and their denning habits."

Willig stared at Gale. Then he shook his head.

"I'll be damned," he said. He allowed a small smile to crease his lips. "I always thought we should compare notes on coyote denning. I've been digging out coyote dens since I was a kid. Cleaned out the same dens year after year. I know that bitches den in the same area."

He paused, then looked at Gale and leaned forward. His face was grim.

"I've taken Two Toes' den the last two years, but I can't get that two-toed sonofabitch."

Willig's voice tightened and his face reddened before he spoke again. "I'd give a month's wage to get him. He's making my life pure hell."

He sat back. Gale was surprised by this confession. "Tell me about him," he said.

For nearly an hour, Willig gave Gale a detailed history of Two Toes—how he got his name, how the coyote had eluded Willig's traps, how he would spring a trap, turn it over and crap on it. He described how Two Toes would recognize Willig's best blind sets and his new scent sets. He told of his tireless tracking, and his frustration.

He finished up with Two Toes' latest kills on Bingham's and Haslett's lambing herds and his run-ins with Bingham. And then, having unburdened himself, Willig was embarrassed.

He had spilled his guts to a total stranger. Talking about his problems was something he never did. But he had studied Gale and liked what he saw. Somehow, he knew that Gale understood exactly what he was going through. Besides, he felt a lot better getting his feelings off his chest.

The two men stood. "I'll meet you at the fairgrounds in the morning," Willig said. "What time?"

"How about daylight?" Gale said.

"Fine," Willig said, inwardly pleased with the answer. The kid seemed all right.

Willig walked out of the cafe and drove home. Gale headed for the Auto Court.

TWENTY-FOUR

▲ ▲ ▲

Moving the Pups

T HE FIRST GRAY STREAK OF DAWN lit a narrow band above the Deadman Bench hills east of Bow Knot Bend, and slowly climbed westward.

Rising from his bed in the shelter of the large boulder above the den, Two Toes shook himself violently, so hard his hind feet almost came off the ground. Near him, the bitch also rose and shook her matted coat. Between her shedding and being mauled by the pups, balls of fur hung at her sides. The nursing pups had pulled almost all the hair off her belly, making her milk bags and tits look large and swollen.

The night before, she had joined the dog coyote under the boulder's cover. The pups were now too big to coddle. Their playing and fighting whenever she lay near made it impossible for her to sleep or rest; and so she had abandoned the den to her brood and joined her mate outside.

The pups had at first tried to follow to her new bed ground, but she and the big dog coyote had growled and nipped at them. Finally they had gotten the message. Now all it took was a growl and the pups would back off and not try to follow.

The bitch walked over to Two Toes and licked his muzzle. He raised his nose to the breeze, sniffing for scent, and strained his ears forward to hear any sound. A moment later, he turned and nuzzled the bitch at the shoulder, then trotted down the ledge. She followed behind. The coyotes trailed down the bench toward the river. Once, the bitch broke off to check a patch of sagebrush for rabbits. Two Toes waited until she finished, then started again down the bench. He was heading for the draw where he'd killed the two ewes several days before. The bitch, sensing he was not hunting, trotted up alongside.

It was getting lighter. The first rays of sun topping the Deadman Bench hills would soon strike the peaks of the Twist Hills. Two Toes stopped several times to watch and listen and sniff the wind. The only disturbance in the calm was a pair of high-flying ravens, cawing to each other as they winged from their night perch on the river. As the two coyotes neared the Green River, Two Toes turned north for the draw. Then, abruptly, he stopped. The chattering of magpies carried up on a small breeze coming from the north. He sniffed and immediately detected the distinctive odor of new meat.

Cautiously, moving then stopping to listen, smell and search their surroundings, the dog and bitch coyotes reached the south bank of the draw. Their sudden appearance startled and alarmed the magpies feeding on the two sheep carcasses. They flared into the air and flapped down the draw, screaming raucously.

Two Toes and his mate continued down the south bank below the kill to get downwind, and jumped into the wash's bottom. Instantly, Two Toes picked up the smell of Willig and his horse and the hair raised on his back. Sniffing the ground, he followed his nose to the hanging sagebrush where, unknown to him, the trapper had shot the coyote. Smelling everything now, the cautious dog coyote moved forward a little ways, stopped and lifted his head until he was satisfied no danger lurked, then continued his wary tracking. In this manner, he followed the man's tracks past the sheep carcasses. And then the coyote smell was strong.

Around the bend, Two Toes saw the dead coyote lying on the sandy bottom. He stopped, still as the carcass, and the bitch beside him also froze. When satisfied there were no others, Two Toes approached the body of the coyote and carefully smelled all around it. Willig's scent rose powerfully in the boot tracks. The dead coyote had not even been touched.

The bitch whined and nudged Toe Toes with her nose, then began to run up the draw. She paused and looked back. Puzzled,

he watched her. She whined again, louder, then turned and trotted up the draw. At a cave-in on the north bank, she climbed out
of the draw and turned once more to look back. Two Toes was
following now. She whined again, then turned at a trot and started
back for the den.

Nearing the first sandstone ledges, the bitch crossed the draw
to the south side and moved onto the ledges she and her mate
had come down earlier that morning. The coyotes followed the
ledges around to the head of the draw where their den was, and
dropped down into the wash. At the mouth of the den, the bitch
barked sharply. The pups, having retreated into the recesses at
the sound of animals approaching, now came tumbling out at
their mother's low bark, falling over each other to get at her. She
growled and they stood still. Then she moved to the smallest of
the litter, grabbed it by the back of its neck and trotted up the
draw, stopping briefly to look back at Two Toes. He stood for a
second, watching, then seized a second pup by its nape and followed.

The rest of the pups sat outside the den, confused. But when
the bitch dropped the one she was carrying, ran back and growled,
they immediately crawled into the den, out of sight. She picked
up her load again. Leading the way, she and Two Toes carried the
pups up the draw 200 yards then climbed out, up onto the low
sandstone ledges.

They trotted north. The pups made no whimper, dangling by
the loose skin at the back of their necks, accepting anything the
mother would do, and when the adult coyotes stopped several
times to rest their jaws, the pups sat on the ground, waiting without
a move.

About a half-mile from the den, the bitch dropped off the ledge
at the head of a long narrow bench that ran toward the river. She
trotted down the bench a quarter-mile, then turned and suddenly dropped off the bench into a draw. Two Toes was right
behind.

The bitch went up the draw a short distance to a hole in the
south bank. It was one she had cleaned out about the same time

she had dug out the den she had used to birth her litter. She crawled into this unused den, still gripping the pup in her teeth, and laid it down at the back. She emerged, picked up the pup Two Toes had carried, then went back in, setting it beside the first pup. As she backed out, she issued a low warning growl to the pups. Then she gave a sharp bark at Two Toes and, without looking back, climbed the bank and headed back to retrieve the rest of the brood.

Back at the first den, the bitch called the pups out. Once more, she and Two Toes picked up a pup by the back of the neck. Again, the bitch growled at the remaining pups, and back in the hole they went. The two pups in the new den were curled up and sleeping when the second pair arrived. Later, by the fourth and final trip to the old den, the long shadows from the Twist Hills were traveling east down the bench toward the river. The last pup, the biggest of the litter, was outside the den whining as the two parent coyotes approached. Seeing the bitch, he ran for her, yelping his delight. She growled, grabbed and shook him. He fell silent.

Two Toes watched the bitch, pup in mouth, head for the new den. Then he turned and trotted down the wash.

He was heading for the bed ground of Billy Butts' herd.

TWENTY-FIVE

▲ ▲ ▲

Bingham's Scheme
Blows Up

TY BINGHAM'S narrow face looked almost gaunt. His brow furrowed, creasing a deep vertical line above the bridge of his nose and two long, upside-down U-shaped lines over that. He was deep in thought.

He'd left Vernal before daylight, wanting to get to Willow Spring early to move Billy Butts' sheep wagon up to Badger Spring. He wanted to get camp set up while Willig was out denning, and be gone before Willig returned. He didn't want another run-in.

Bingham was a bit ashamed of how he'd talked to the trapper. Deep down, he knew he had been unreasonable and that he'd ridden Willig too hard. Jack Willig was the best coyote trapper Bingham had ever seen and he was also hard-working, honest as the day is long, and utterly dependable. He wasn't like a lot of trappers, who were a tough bunch—drinking, swearing, hard-living men who played as rough as they worked and never let their job interfere with a good time.

Bingham recalled how many times trappers had gone to town and went on a bender for days. They were as bad as some of the herders—only more rugged. Bingham had often stopped at a trapper's camp and been able to tell by the cold stove and dusty water bucket that he'd been gone for days. But Jack Willig wasn't one of that lot.

No, Willig was unusually clean and decent. Here Bingham had had one of the best trappers in the whole damn state working his range, doing his best, and the sheepman had gone and alienated him. Bingham wasn't one to apologize. Ranchers weren't that way. But he sure as hell would let his actions speak loudly from now on. He'd go out of his way to treat Willig the way the man deserved.

Bingham's sheep would be in Two Toes' territory now for at least two weeks, and he badly needed the trapper's help to keep his losses down. God knew they were bad enough with Willig working his range; what would they add up to if Willig stayed away, trapping and denning someplace else? Bingham's brow pinched harder at that thought. Then it released. He was giving himself a headache. He reminded himself of his plan. That gave him comfort.

Moving his camp up to Badger Spring where Willig was camped would work out fine. Willig and Billy Butts got along good. Each knew the other was a top hand at his work. They respected each other.

Bingham would let his sheepherder do all the talking with Willig. He'd do his best to not be in camp when Willig was around. Butts could tend camp in the middle of the day when Willig would be out hunting dens. He'd make sure to let Billy Butts know the exact day he'd return from Vernal, and he'd come to camp around noon. Butts would hang close to camp with the sheep on the preset day so he wouldn't have to leave them out alone too long. Bingham would bring the herder's supplies and mail and then he'd leave immediately for the return trip, making sure he wouldn't bump into Willig.

Bingham sighed. "This will work," he said, thinking ahead. "It's got to. I just can't afford many more losses—of *any* kind—especially to coyotes."

Bingham made a mental note to remind Butts to watch the herd real close and not leave the sheep alone unless it was absolutely necessary. He'd emphasize watching for lamby ewes and making sure all the new lambs were mothered up. If the ewes were young, wild and spooky when dropping their lambs, Butts would have to tie them to a brush so they'd have to let the lamb start sucking.

OK, Bingham thought. *I've got some luck now. Jack Willig's at Badger Spring and now Billy Butts is going to have some help during this dangerous time.* It was a good idea.

Bingham drove past the Ouray Trading Post without stopping. Buckwalter's truck was parked in front. Must be moving his herd up the west side of the Green by now, Bingham thought.

Going up the stock trail road, the sheepman came to the tracks that cut off down to Hod Hogan's camp on the river. Fresh tire tracks plowed the ground. Bingham figured the Hasletts were in camp. There wasn't any fear of rustlers. It wasn't worth the risk to steal a pickup load of sheep. A smart rustler would need a big stock truck with a double deck, and it would make all kinds of noise trying to move up a stock driveway at night. Might as well put a big sign on it reading, "I'm stealing sheep."

Bingham thought about checking in with the Hasletts on his way back to Vernal. He drove on up to his camp wagon at Willow Spring. As he stepped out of the cab, he could see Billy Butts already riding toward him. The sheep were scattered out on the bench, feeding northward toward Badger Spring.

Bingham checked over the sheep wagon. Butts had everything secured for moving. The rancher got back in the pickup and backed it up, and was hooking up the wagon tongue when the herder rode up.

"The sheep are moving good," Butts said. "We should be at Badger around 3 o'clock."

Bingham was stooped over, hooking the wagon tongue to the pickup. Three o'clock would mean that Willig would still be out tracking or denning.

"I'm going to leave for Vernal as soon as I set your wagon," he said. "I'll park it next to Willig's."

Inwardly, he considered that even if Willig was near camp when they showed up, the sight of Bingham's pickup would probably stop him from coming in.

Bingham rose and faced his herder with a solemn look. "Remember, Jack Willig said he'd talk with you. So you keep him posted on any coyote trouble. I'll be back in three days, and I'll come at noon."

Bingham did not need to emphasize "noon." Butts understood. He nodded. "When Jack's on a coyote den he's gone at daylight and sometimes doesn't get in till way after dark," the herder said.

"OK," Bingham said.

As he climbed into the cab, Butts called after him.

"Hey. Did you see anybody coming in?"

"No," Bingham said, "Why?"

"I heard a truck go south about 9:30 last night. Somebody was out late."

Bingham started the pickup and pulled out.

"I'll stop at Hod's camp on the way out and see what he knows."

He slowly turned the sheep wagon around and then, as it fell into place behind the truck, started up the road for Badger Spring. The load he was tugging felt substantial, as if confirming the solidity of his plan.

Soon he caught up with the herd. He slowed way down. Sheep were scattered out on both sides of the road, well spread out. Bingham stopped the pickup to look them over. They seemed in good shape. There didn't see to be one ewe that wasn't well-rounded in the belly.

In front of him, out about 100 yards, stood four ewes with lambs. There didn't seem to be any dries in this herd. It was just like Bingham had hoped: a big lamb crop with lots of twins. It would make him a real good year. He sure as hell needed it now.

He remembered how Billy Butts had said that the bucks bred the ewes this year about as fast as he'd ever seen them work. One thing Bingham made sure of was that his rams were all young and registered with good rambouillet blood lines. He knew that care in the quality and condition of his sheep paid off. Here all around him was the evidence.

In his rearview mirror, Bingham saw Butts riding up. The herder came up along the driver's side. "I'll part the herd for you," he said. He moved up in front of the pickup and began riding in a slow zigzag while yelling, "Hi! Git, git! Move, move!"

Butts slapped a coiled lariat against his leg with loud cracks and the sheep parted, creating a lane for the pickup and sheep wagon to inch through. In 15 minutes, Bingham was free. He waved at Butts and headed on up the stock trail.

There were several draws to cross and one of them was pretty steep down the south slope. Bingham slowed the truck to a crawl as he rattled down. He was worried about the sheep wagon, but knew he'd make it if he took it easy. When he reached the sandy bottom, he was surprised to see fresh tire tracks. He set the brake and climbed out for a better look. Walking, he followed the tracks across the wash to where they started down on the north side.

There were two sets of tracks left by a pickup pulling a trailer. The back end of the trailer had dug into the road fairly deep as it came off the steep hill to the wash bottom. Who could have been up the stock trail coming back down going south? Bingham wondered.

He pulled the camp wagon slowly across the wash and shifted into low gear as he started up the steep north slope so the pickup wouldn't scrape or high-center, the transmission hitting bottom and bouncing. He eased out on the bench with no trouble and shifted into second, headed for Badger Spring.

Badger Spring flowed from a little pocket under a ledge of rock where the long bench dropped down to Green River. The road to the spring turned off the stock trail and ran toward the water. Where the bench ended above the river bottom stood a little grove of cottonwoods, where the spring flowed to the river. There was a flat level spot of ground there above the spring that was perfect to park sheep wagons. Badger Spring had been used for a sheep camp for more than 50 years, both for herds going south to the winter range in November and coming back north again in March and April to the lambing and summer range.

Bingham had a lot of fond memories of this little speck of beauty in the harsh environment of rock ledges and long bench-like plateaus bordered by the deep washes cut by cloud bursts and snow runoff. As a boy, he'd visited the spring twice a year with his father. He always loved the fresh bright green of the cottonwood leaves in the spring and even more the pure gold leaves in the fall, standing out like a beacon of light amid the drab hues of sagebrush, the dried grasses, the faded browns and grays of greasewood and rabbit brush, squaw berry and buffalo brush. The place was spiritual for Bingham. It filled him with a sense of eternity, of time stretching into the past and into the future.

His mind was dwelling on memories of years past as he headed toward the campsite. All was peaceful as he pulled onto the flat ground . . .

Suddenly, like a bolt of lightning, he did a double-take and blinked his eyes.

There was no sheep wagon.

Bingham drove quickly, too fast, to the campsite and ground to a halt. He jumped out of the pickup, looking wildly around.

Jack Willig's camp wagon was nowhere in sight. Badger Spring was empty.

TWENTY-SIX

▲ ▲ ▲

The Hungry Young

TWO TOES trotted straight down the bench, headed for the bed ground of Billy Butts' herd.

He was cutting across the bottom of a draw northwest of Willow Spring when he stopped to sniff the breeze and caught the smell of a strange coyote. The smell was coming up the draw he was in. He walked forward, senses on high alert. As he came to a sharp curve, the puppy smell in the breeze told him he was nearing a strange den. He rounded the curve, expecting an attack at any moment.

There, in the south bank of the draw, was the den. A bitch coyote stood in front of the hole. She snarled and made a run at Two Toes. He jumped and hit her with his shoulder, knocking her over. Immediately, he was straddling her with a light throat hold, keeping her pinned on her back, tail between legs.

Two Toes held her tight and growled. When she whined, he let go and jumped back. She stood, facing him, tail still between legs, Two Toes did not move, watching her carefully. When she realized he was not going to attack, she scurried into the den.

Two Toes sniffed around the opening. The pups had been playing outside only the past few days and weren't as old as his litter. He recognized the smell of the bitch's mate. It was the dog coyote that had been lying dead near the two sheep carcasses in the draw by the river. Little meat and a few bones were strewn around the den opening. Two Toes found some rabbit and prairie dog fur, but little else. With her mate dead, the bitch was hard-pressed to feed her pups.

Two Toes trotted down the wash, then up on the bench to the north. It was near sundown and the shadows were passing down the east side of the Twist Hills. Four ravens flying north up the river to roost cawed back and forth as they passed overhead. One dipped down on straightened wings to check out the coyote, then climbed back up the sky, voicing his discovery to the rest.

Two Toes moved north across the bench, scouted the wash and continued onto the next flat bench to the draw by the river. As he crossed it and went up the north bank, he halted and lifted his nose into a breeze blowing upriver. His raised ears detected the faint baa'ing of sheep.

Billy Butts was moving his herd to the bed ground just west of Badger Spring. Shadows had formed on the cottonwoods along the river, and Butts was bedding the herd down so he could get to his sheep wagon before dark. He had to get water, cut wood and otherwise square away the new campsite.

The bed ground was a humped high spot just west of where the bench dropped down to the river bed. North of the bed ground, a large wash came down from the high hills. Butts had most of the sheep well bunched on the ground. The two shelties were moving the tail end of the herd at a nice slow walk toward the spot. Several of the bellwethers were standing, moving little but enough for the bells around their necks to clang and let the herd know that this was the bed ground.

In a patch of sagebrush north and west of the bed ground, Two Toes lay on his belly, watching closely. The breeze came directly into his face, carrying the smells of the man, his horse and dogs and the sheep. The shelties had no such advantage; the coyote's scent was upwind to the north, away from them.

Butts turned his horse and called his dogs. He headed for his wagon, leaving the few remaining sheep to move onto the bed ground by themselves. The entire river basin—even the hills on Deadman Bench, east of the river—was now cast in shadows.

Toe Twos flattened himself and did not move. Five ewes, one with a new lamb, were trying to pick a bed down spot not 100 yards in front of him. The rest were bedding down over a large area on the other side. After a minute, the big coyote stood. Quietly and slowly, he walked around the ewes and lamb, circling until he was between them and the other sheep. He stopped and listened, watching the camp closely.

Hollow whacks echoed out over the bed ground. The man was splitting wood.

The coyote walked slowly toward the ewes and lamb, herding them carefully toward the draw. The lamb stopped to watch the coyote, too young to recognize danger. Its mother bleated to it and nudged it toward the other ewes. Bouncing friskily, it followed them down into the draw.

Huddled now in the draw's bottom, the sheep watched the coyote. Two Toes walked up to the closest, grabbed her by the neck at the base of the skull and with one powerful bite, bit into her spinal cord. She dropped to her side, kicking her last. One after another, the big dog coyote killed the rest of the ewes. Each new victim would circle nervously then stand facing the enemy as he made his kill. The last standing was the mother of the lamb. Her lamb, thinking this to be some kind of game, hopped and jumped toward the coyote. He grabbed it by its head and killed it with one bite, it bleating as it died. At this, the frantic ewe rushed at the coyote. She stomped her front feet, trying to scare him away.

She died just as the others. Two Toes ripped large pieces of wool and skin off a hindquarter, then filled his stomach with the fresh warm meat. His meal done, he tore off a large chunk and headed for the den, the meat clamped in his jaws.

Several minutes after he'd disappeared into the dusk, another coyote raised up out of the brush 100 yards down the wash. It was the lone bitch. She had followed Two Toes to the kill. She had been downwind from the big dog coyote, but her scent had mixed with the smell of sheep and hadn't given her away.

She, too, filled up on the still warm meat of a ewe. Then, in the gathering darkness, she headed for her hungry pups.

TWENTY-SEVEN

▲ ▲ ▲

The Sheepman's Story

BRETT GALE looked at his watch. It was just 8 p.m. He was checked into the Auto Court, but knew he couldn't settle down until he took care of business. He looked up Ty Bingham's number in the directory.

It was Mrs. Bingham who answered. "He's just driving up the driveway," she said of her husband. "If you'll hold a minute, I'll tell him you're calling."

Minutes passed. Then Gale heard the receiver being picked up. A flat voice said, "This is Bingham."

"We've been expecting you," the sheepman said, after Gale introduced himself. "What are your plans? We need help and we need it right now."

Gale said he'd be glad to come out to Bingham's place and go over it all. In fact, he'd be glad to come out right now.

"No, I'm coming into town," Bingham said. "Where are you?"

"The Dinosaur Auto Court, in No. 9."

"I'll be right there," the sheepman barked into the phone, and hung up.

Gale sat on the bed and smiled ruefully. It was obvious some fur was going to fly. But he wasn't going to allow himself to get worked up over it. He'd be cool, calm and tactful. He recalled Rasmussen's last words to him, "Get both sides of the story." That he would do.

He was reading an article by Hemingway on pheasant-hunting in Idaho when there was a knock. A slender, clean-shaven man entered as soon as Gale opened the door. "I'm Ty Bingham," he said.

"Brett Gale."

They shook hands. Bingham's grip was firm, with callused palms. He took the chair at the small desk. He acted like he owned the place, like he was used to having his way.

Gale sat on the bed facing him.

"We've got some real problems," Bingham said, starting right in. His clear blue eyes fixed on Gale's. "Some real big problems. And by damn, something has to be done about it. And I mean now."

Gale made a quick read of the sheepman. Here was a working man who knew his business, he thought. Bingham was wearing Levi's and a clean shirt, but his boots showed plenty of good wear. His face was well-tanned from the outdoors, and this morning's whiskers were showing gray tips against the brown of his skin. Those tough palms from the handshake showed he worked hard himself. Gale knew he probably demanded the same from everyone else concerned with his operation.

"That's what I'm here for, to see if we can help you Uintah Basin sheepmen cut your losses to coyotes," Gale said.

"All of us are taking losses," Bingham continued. "But I happen to be the first herd up the stock driveway and the coyotes are raising hell. I'm getting hit almost every night."

Bingham caught the sound of his own voice rising, and, still chastened from his recent-past experience with Jack Willig, consciously lowered it. He added, "Hasletts, Chance and Buckwalter are all right behind me and they are having coyote losses, too."

He eyed Gale rather coldly for a moment. Then he asked, "What is your plan? I asked Rasmussen for another experienced trapper. He said he didn't have an extra man to spare."

He looked appraisingly at Gale. "How long you been with Rasmussen's outfit?"

"Two years," Gale said, inwardly surprised that much time had gone by. Up to then he hadn't much considered the amount of experience he'd accrued. But he also saw the sheepman was unimpressed.

"Damn it to hell, we need an experienced man," Bingham shot, his face suddenly dark with anger. "Willig's been trapping all his life and he can't stop the killing. In three years he can't even catch that damned Two Toes."

He rose from his chair as if to leave, but stopped at the door. He turned and walked back to the chair, but didn't sit. For a full minute, Bingham just stared at Gale, as if weighing his next words. Finally, he spoke. His voice was tinged with a plaintive tone. Most of all, it was choked with frustration.

"That goddamn Willig, you can't tell him anything, you can't even talk to him. I don't know what he's doing. We had words at my camp the other day and he tells me he won't come to my camp or talk to me again. Just got on his horse and rode off."

He paused, struggling for words.

"The sonofabitch said if we had any trouble, Billy Butts—that's my herder—could talk to him anytime. But he won't talk to me, see."

Gale raised his hand and stopped him.

"Willig's record says he's one of the best coyote men in the state, especially at denning," he said in a quiet, yet firm, voice. "Are you saying he's not on the job? That he's goofing off somewhere? That he's spending too much time in town?"

Bingham's face flushed. He stared at the floor.

"No, I'm not saying that. I just think he, well, he's—."

Gale waited patiently.

"I just think he's got it in for me for some reason."

Bingham's face reddened even more. He had expected a more indignant accusation from himself. Maybe he had wanted Gale to defend Willig against all charges, instead of playing arbiter, so Bingham could press his attack as the wronged party. But instead of coming across as the victim, here he was the one sounding guilty.

"Why do you say that?" Gale asked.

Bingham looked up from the floor. "Damn him," he stammered. "He pulled out and left us."

"What do you mean he pulled out and left you?"

"Damn him," Bingham snapped again. "He was camped at Badger Spring. When we moved to Badger Spring, he was gone. He'd moved camp at night. Knew we were coming. He moved back to Haslett's camp just to stay away from us. I'm telling you, now we're right in Two Toes' territory and we're the only bunch of sheep within miles. We're going to get murdered and that damn Willig goes and works someplace else. You've got to get rid of him, by damn."

Now it was Gale who spoke coldly.

"Mr. Bingham, it sounds like you're expecting Jack Willig to spend all his time protecting your herd. He has a dozen sheepmen to help with coyote losses. You're just one of them. It doesn't seem to me you're helping Willig at all, yet you expect all kinds of results from him. And now you accuse him of running out on you when it's obvious you were going to camp next to him so you could get him to work your range."

Bingham was struck speechless. This young guy had him all figured out. He had played his hand and lost.

With a hurt look in his eyes, he swallowed. He found his voice, but struggled for words. "What kind of help will you be?" he finally lashed out. "You don't know a damn thing about denning coyotes."

Gale remained unruffled.

"Mr. Bingham, I was sent out here to try and help. I've spent two years with three of the top men in the state. In that time, we took 31 dens. I've learned all they could teach me, and I aim to spend all the time I can when I'm out here with Jack Willig doing my best, and that includes getting Two Toes."

Bingham started to speak, but Gale interrupted.

"You say Willig pulled up in the night and moved camp so he could stay away from you. You may be interested to know that on that day he got a good lead on Two Toes. Hasletts' herder had a fresh kill and the coyotes left good sign. That's why Willig moved camp next to Haslett. It gave him two more hours a day for tracking Two Toes, instead of the extra miles each night riding from your camp at Badger Spring."

Gale paused, noting the surprise in Bingham's eyes. He'd succeeded in putting the sheepman in his place. Now he had to keep him there.

"Jack Willig, in the last 10 days, has taken four dens of pups and killed three of the adult coyotes. So, do you call that not doing anything?"

Bingham was silent. He looked away.

Gale had had to do this, no question about it. He'd had to let this sheepman know that his bluster wasn't going to get him anywhere. Now they understood each other.

"We're leaving at daylight to go to Willig's camp," Gale said. "We'll do the best we can. You can catch us there for at least the next week."

Bingham slowly straightened and stepped to the door. He fingered a button on his shirt.

"Well, I hope to hell you can do something," he growled, with little fire, and left, banging the door.

▲ ▲ ▲

TWENTY-EIGHT

Strategy Session

B RETT GALE tossed his suitcase in his pickup and drove out to the fairgrounds. He hooked up his trailer and was loading his horse when Jack Willig pulled in.

The trapper scrutinized the trailer as Gale was closing the tailgate. "Looks like a good horse trailer," he said. "Does it balance well?"

"You bet," Gale said. "It pulls nicely at 60 miles an hour. The axle's the same width as the truck, so it tracks well on the rough road."

"Good," Willig said, "because the trail up the stock driveway is pretty rocky. I see you have good clearance so you won't be high-centering."

"What about groceries?" Gale asked.

"I picked them up last night, enough for both of us."

"Keep track," Gale said, "so I can pay my share when we split up."

Before climbing in his truck, Willig gave directions.

"We take Highway 40 south till we cross Halfway Hollow, then we take the truck road southeast to Ouray. We'll stop at the trading post."

The sun was up as the two trucks climbed the hill out of Ashley Valley. Irrigated alfalfa fields and grass pastures sparkled like seas of emeralds. Horses and cattle were feeding in the fields. A small buck pasture close to the road was full of rambouillet rams on good feed, getting readied for breeding time. Gale gazed at the dirty white-colored sheep that stood nearly 3 feet tall. Their big curled horns reminded him of wild Rocky Mountain rams.

Once over the hill out of the fertile valley and headed southwest through Asphalt Ridge Hills, the terrain changed dramatically. Now the hills were rough. Here and there were ledges and gullies. The flats were covered with grasses and brush, mostly sage and rabbit brush with scattered patches of prickly pear cactus. The ledges and bluffs showed red, gray and yellow clay strata—contrasting vividly with the dark green of the cedar trees scattered throughout the higher hills on the north slopes.

Gale was eager. He couldn't wait to go after dens in this wild and beautiful country. The rugged range always filled him with a sense of freedom. After a dozen miles of hilly, winding pavement on the two lanes of Highway 40, long plateaus or benches stretched out for miles going south and east toward the Duchesne and Green rivers. Low brush and grasses covered the benches, good feed for sheep and cattle grazing in early spring.

Just past Halfway Hollow, Willig's truck left the highway and took the dirt and gravel road. A simple white sign pointing south read, "Ouray—Book Cliffs." Gale dropped about a quarter-mile behind Willig's pickup because of the heavy dust piled up in the desert roads from the hot dry weather. On the skyline to the northeast, he could see the Twist Hills. Soon after, going over a high ridge, he spotted the green strip of cottonwoods that ran along the Green River and, to the south, the Duchesne River.

Pelican Lake lay dry and empty. The ghostlike farms of the Leota Bottoms were grim reminders of the devastation and human misery dealt by the double-blow of drought and depression. Not a living thing stirred before Gale's view, except when a couple jackrabbits popped out of their tumbleweed cover alongside the road. The road pulled up on a long, wide bench land that stretched for several miles to the south. Gale saw the Green River coming in from the left and the Duchesne River coming in from the right. They would meet just below the trading post at Ouray, a good seven miles off.

Willig's truck was at the head of the cloud of dust, a mile in front now. Occasionally, Gale could see the pickup glisten in the sun at the front end of the line of swirling brown that stretched nearly back to his own truck. With no breeze to break it up, the dust hung right over the road. It would not settle for several minutes after the pickups kicked it up.

There was a cover of dust in front of the trading post as Gale pulled up alongside Willig's caked pickup. Inside, the store was dark and cool. Osiah Portle was handing a bottle of Coke to Willig when Gale walked in. The trapper turned and squinted.

"Brett Gale, meet Osh Portle," Willig said. The two strangers shook hands.

"Brett's going to hunt dens with me for a few days," Willig said. "Maybe we can catch up with Two Toes."

"Hope so," the storekeep replied. "Coyotes seem to be hitting pretty hard this year. By the way, Jack, those dens you got for Hasletts seemed to stop the killing out that way. Haven't heard of any losses since."

Willig's face bore a wry expression. "At least I did one thing right," he said.

Outside the trading post, Willig called Gale over. They stood by Willig's pickup. "This weather isn't helping us a damn bit tracking coyotes," Willig said.

"You're right," Gale said. "Tracks are tough to find on hard pan and if you do get some fresh ones, it only takes a small breeze to wipe them out."

Willig pointed down the road toward the Green River.

"There's a band of sheep at the cottonwoods on the east side of the bridge, and another bunch heading north up the west side," he said. "That's Chance's herd. Buckwalter's herd has already crossed."

Willig paused. The wry look he'd worn in the store returned. "Osh says neither outfit has had any coyote killings. I've already cleaned out two dens east of the cottonwoods when Haslett's sheep were there and the first two dens I got were around the

Leota Bottoms west of where Hod Hogan's camp is. We'll pull up there. That's where my wagon is."

Several miles up the dusty road, Willig turned off toward the river. Shortly after, Gale, still trailing a good distance behind, made out two sheep wagons camped in a little grove of old cottonwoods. He parked next to Willig's truck.

"We'll unload here and get a bit of lunch," Willig said. "You can water your horse at the river and there's grain in that barrel over there. My horse is hobbled and he'll be somewhere along the river close by."

Gale put the tailgate down. He untied his horse and backed him out. Socks tossed his head and snorted, letting Gale know he was glad to leave the trailer.

The two men watered and grained their horses, then fixed sandwiches and a pot of fresh coffee. They sat in Willig's sheep wagon. Willig felt good to have this new man along.

He still didn't know if this Brett Gale would be worth his salt once they started denning, but nothing so far had led him to think otherwise. He was also tickled to have a partner, instead of being the only punching bag for the likes of Ty Bingham. Now there were two to take the heat.

Willig decided it was time to bring his new helper up to date. He needed to fill in Gale on all the information he had. Two men could find a den twice as fast, or even faster, than one man, provided each knew his stuff. Willig was hoping Gale knew his stuff.

"I know Two Toes' den is not down near the Indian ranches or the Leota Bottoms," Willig said. "I feel it in my bones. I got a den on the Leota Bottoms about 10 days ago and never did see any sign of Two Toes. "From my tracking, I found where he and his bitch made a kill. They loaded up on meat and went straight south for two or three miles. The tracking was good and their sign was easy to follow. They got to an old cow carcass and that's where Two Toes had a fight with another coyote. Fur and hair all over the place.

"Now it looks to me like he and the bitch went north to make the kill and then right back down the same trail to the cow carcass with their sheep meat. The best I could tell was after that, they went north again. I followed a little ways and then it got dark on me."

He stopped and scratched his head. Willig's confusion and consternation were obvious to Gale. Willig realized this. But he didn't mind. There was a calming presence to this kid. Besides, it felt good to have someone to listen to him, someone he could get all this off his chest to.

"Damn it, I don't know which way to turn," Willig said. "Whatever I do will be wrong. If Bingham has any more losses, he'll be all over me like baby shit on a blanket."

Gale didn't dare laugh or smile. Willig was dead serious. So, he spoke up.

"Everything else aside," Gale began. "Forget Bingham, Two Toes, sheep, coyotes. What is the first move you should make?"

Willig looked at Gale without seeing him. His mind was busy sorting out everything, trying to decide the next step. Slowly, his expression changed from bewilderment to clarity, and then to certainty. It seemed to Gale as if minutes went by. And then, when Willig began talking, he did so as if thinking out loud.

"I've found Two Toes' tracks from the river west—from Badger Spring south to Willow Spring and Hod's camp on the river. OK. We know he's made kills, along with other coyotes, on Bingham's and Haslett's herds. One of the first things I did was check from the Twist Hills south and east and found no sign. There's lots of sandstone ledges in there, and I could have missed something."

Willig nodded slowly to himself.

"Then that damn Bingham started on me and I guess I let him panic me into trying to check everything out at once to find Two Toes' den, and I wound up getting nothing done and not thinking straight."

He paused. Gale spoke up again.

"You're thinking straight now. What's our next move?"

Willig was quick to answer. "Our next move is checking with Hod and Billy Butts before we do anything else. Who knows what's happened in the last couple or three days? Let's jump in my pickup and check in with those two. We can do that and still get back before dark."

"Let's go," Gale said.

TWENTY-NINE

▲ ▲ ▲

Buzzard's Find

BILLY BUTTS was lost in thought. His pocket knife shaved curls off a stick he'd taken from the wood box. The shavings fell on top of newspaper crumpled up in the stove.

He stuck three sticks on top and put a match to the paper, then opened the draft in the stove pipe and reset the lid. Soon, a fire was blazing away. The colors and warmth gave a hearth-like feel in the wagon.

Butts stared for a minute at the water bucket heating on the stove. Evidently it was Jack Willig's truck that had gone south in the dark two nights ago. Willig had left Badger Spring, and now Butts was all alone at the campsite. He hadn't seen Ty Bingham since his boss had moved Butts' wagon up from Willow Spring to Badger Spring, only to discover Willig was no longer camped there. Bingham had turned around and gone south. Butts hadn't seen hide or hair of the trapper since, either.

He wondered where Willig had gone. Herders like to be alone; they're used to it. They know their work and they are happy with it. Sometimes a fire in the stove is company enough. But truth be known, Butts had rather been looking forward to camping next to Willig. Sometimes, after you haven't spoken to anyone for two-three weeks, you crave a body to talk to. And Butts and Willig had always gotten along. They knew their business. They respected each other.

Butts wondered where Willig was camped now. The trapper had said he wouldn't talk to Bingham again. Butts knew he meant it. His boss had pushed Willig too far. But Butts felt sure that

Willig hadn't left Bingham's range. He was too good a man to run from a job. And anyway, Butts knew how badly Willig wanted to get Two Toes. He was too proud to let one coyote whip him. He was around here somewhere.

Butts set a fresh pot of cold water on the stove and emptied a handful of coffee into it. He put the lid on the pot and wiped the remaining grounds from his hand on his pants. Standing in the open door, he saw it was just light enough to see the cotton-woods along the river and the red rock ledges up on the east side. It was quiet and cool, with only a small breeze blowing.

The herder sipped hot bitter coffee, feeling it warm and waken him. With a flip of his wrist, he tossed what was left out the wagon then stepped to the ground. He gazed west. The sun wouldn't touch the skyline of the Twist Hills for another 15 or 20 minutes.

The sheep had bedded down on the bench west of camp, about a quarter-mile away. The dogs had already left their sleeping spot under the wagon and were out watching the herd. Yesterday, Butts had put the sheep up on the bench lands northwest of Bad-ger for the first time. There was good feed there. He'd go north again today, a little farther west of the river. He hadn't had any coyotes bothering the sheep for two or three nights. For that he was grateful.

As he was saddling his horse, Butts heard the coo-cooing of mourning doves. The calls sounded plaintive. The soft, blue-gray birds with their tiny, orangy-pink beaks were somewhere in the cottonwoods. Other early risers were joining the morning's progress. Magpies and crows were winging from their roosts on the river, shrill cries marking the straight lines of their flights. To the south and east came the howl of a coyote, answered by an-other farther off. The pair were already on their morning hunt.

Butts rode west along the draw, then up to the north bank and out onto the bench. Sheep bells were clanging ahead. The herd had started to rise and move out to graze. The shelties sat still, watching the sheep, but as soon as Butts came out of the wash the older dog spotted his master. He watched closely for any signal as man and rider came toward the herd. Butts rode up near the dogs and sat still in the saddle, observing the sheep.

The bellwethers were in the lead, heading west up the bench, just where Butts wanted them. When one of the bellwethers turned north with a number of sheep starting to follow, he spoke to the dogs. "OK, move 'em west, slow and easy," he said, waving his left hand to the west. Immediately, the shelties trotted toward the herd.

The older dog went around the outside of the wayward bellwether and turned him back toward the main herd. The younger dog trotted slowly back and forth at the rear, keeping the sheep going west. No barking, running or nipping heels, just quietly steering the band in the right direction to graze. Butts saw the herd moving just right and whistled. The dogs stopped and looked back. He waved his hand for them to come in.

"Good dogs," he said, as they trotted up and stopped, looking up intelligently. They wagged their bobbed tails and fell in beside the horse as Butts moved out.

By late morning. the sheep had grazed slowly west on the wide bench land. Butts had turned the herd about a mile-and-a-half off the river and west of where they'd grazed yesterday. Now they were on the next bench north. The feed was good and the sheep were hardly moving, cropping grass much more slowly than when they'd started. Butts reined up on a little high spot. He hooked his right leg over the saddle horn and watched, taking it easy. The herd had slowed almost to a stop. They were full. One after another, they lay down, too full and content to continue.

Butts dropped the reins and stepped down from the saddle. He would take a nap, too. He lay down and pulled his hat over his face. He folded his arms behind his head and closed his eyes. The sun felt warm on his chest. The last things he remembered before dropping off were both dogs lying down close by, and the clinking of the horse's bit as the animal fed on the grass away.

▲ ▲ ▲

Butts woke with a start. He pulled the hat off his face and sat up. From the sun's position in the sky, he figured he'd been asleep an hour.

Half the sheep were on their feet, beginning to graze again. The dogs were still lying down, but watching his every move. The horse was still cropping grass, about 300 yards away.

Butts sat up and put his hat on. He looked around. All was quiet. He was walking to the horse when he spotted two birds soaring way high in the sky upriver.

They were circling slow in big wide sweeps. Butts stopped and squinted and shaded his eyes to look closer. They weren't hawks; no, they were too large. The big birds rode the thermal updrafts of the breeze, deep wings spread and motionless, an effortless soaring that was beautiful to behold. The slight north wind was carrying them gradually south toward Butts, who stood beside his horse, a look of admiration on his face.

When the birds were 400 yards north, Butts could finally make their outlines clearly. They tilted their wings and banked slowly, making their wide circles, 500 feet up in the sky. They were all dark in color, except for the wings. The back trailing edge of their broad wing feathers showed light gray that ran clear across the wing, while the rest of the wings were dark, like their bodies.

It was the distinctive silhouette of the turkey buzzard.

The buzzards suddenly stopped gliding and swooped down for a close look at the ground. Their bare red heads raised as they flared up, circled shortly, then came down again, out of Butts' sight. He waited for them to reappear. He stood at the spot where they'd left his vision, then saw them climbing for altitude farther downriver.

Curious now, Butts climbed into the saddle and sat watching the birds. They were high up again, rounding back to where they'd dropped out of sight before. They described a long, lazy arc, then abruptly dove down out of sight again. A moment later, Butts

saw a group of magpies light up from the point where the buzzards had plunged.

No doubt about it, he thought. Something was dead over there. Butts got the sheep started back toward camp. He ordered the dogs to stay, then headed for the buzzards at a trot. They were about where he'd turned the sheep around the day before to head for camp. Butts had a bad sinking feeling in the pit of his stomach.

He galloped across the bench to the next big draw north. Soon he could see magpies walking along the south edge of the draw, scolding the intruders with their boisterous calls. He rode right toward the magpies, which screeched as they rushed into the air. At the edge of the draw, the turkey buzzards, disturbed from their feast, flared up from the draw's bottom right in front of his horse, wings flapping wildly.

The horse spooked, almost tossing Butts. He clamped his thighs and legs and balanced himself as the horse twisted its neck and reared up and turned away. Butts quieted the animal with soothing sounds and strokes, then stepped down onto the ground. Leading it by the reins, he walked to the draw's edge. Looking down, he caught his breath. Then he cursed out loud.

Dead in the bottom of the wash lay five ewes and a young lamb, spaced out within 40 feet of each other.

Butts dropped the reins and scrambled down to the bottom. Taking care not to step on the coyote tracks, he approached the dead sheep. All had been bitten at the back of the head. There had been no mad stampeding, no fuss. They'd been carefully herded up the draw to this slaughter. Two of the carcasses were ripped open, their hindquarters heavily eaten on by coyotes. Their eyes had been pecked out by the magpies and crows, which had also been picking at the raw meat of the hind legs.

The coyote tracks were fresh and plain in the soil. At least two coyotes had been at the kill, Butts saw. Two Toes' right-front paw was clearly imprinted in the sandy bottom. The smaller, narrower footprints were probably from his bitch.

Butts' heart pounded. His breaths came short and quick. He scrambled up the bank for his horse. As he rode back to the herd, his mind raced. Where was Willig camped? How could he find him? Here was a break. Here was a real break.

But as the herder rode forth, he realized he couldn't leave his sheep to go hunting for the trapper. Nor did he even know when his boss would be back. With a regretful grin, he wished Willig were camped alongside his wagon right now. Instead, he'd have to wait a day to see if Willig showed up. If not, then Butts would ride in the evening after bedding the sheep down, to find Willig's camp.

Butts put a heel in his horse's flank. He started for the band of sheep at a fast trot.

THIRTY

▲ ▲ ▲

Two Toes Kills Again

J
ACK WILLIG eased the pickup down the steep south slope of the draw on the stock driveway and then crawled slowly up the north side. He braked to a halt on the first high spot on the bench.

He turned to Brett Gale. "There's a pair of field glasses in the jockey box."

It was getting on 4 o'clock. The government trapper and the man assigned to help him were tracking down Hod Hogan. They wanted to get the latest information from the sheepherder on what the coyotes were up to.

Gale handed the binoculars to Willig, then got out of the pickup and walked west, searching for sign on the ground. About a hundred yards off, he hit fresh sheep tracks, leading northwest. Willig, who had been glassing the bench to the west, lowered the binocs as Gale returned.

"See anything?"

"Yeah, the tracks look like this morning's, and they're headed west up the bench."

"I didn't spot anything," Willig said. "But the plateau northwest of us is behind that low hill out there. He could be there and we couldn't see him from here. Get in and we'll go that way."

In the middle of the bench where it was flattest, Willig turned west off the driveway trail and picked his way through the brush and rocks. On a high spot of the low ridge, he got out and raised the glasses.

"Isn't that a low line of dust way out there about 11 o'clock?" Gale said.

"Uh-huh," Willig said. "They're grazing south. I can see Hod's gray mare."

They navigated the bumpy, brushy terrain toward the herd until they reached a gully in the sandstone that was too steep for the truck.

Willig stood outside the truck, glassing the distance. "Hod's coming this way."

The two men leaned against the pickup, watching the gray horse and its rider work toward them.

"Hod Hogan's a good herder," Willig said. "He helped me find those two dens across the river when he was camped at Lizard Springs. Coyotes started killing as soon as they moved the herd there. But Hasletts didn't have any more losses until they moved across the river to this side. In fact, it was one of Hod's ewes that Two Toes and his mate killed and went straight south with the meat. I still haven't figured that one out, but I'd bet my last dollar their den isn't down that way."

Willig didn't say anything more for a minute. He watched the herder on the mare dipping and rising on the terrain, drawing nearer. Then he said, "That damn Two Toes could be doing anything except what a normal coyote would do." His voice trailed off.

Gale glanced at Willig. He could see his mind was a long ways away, trying to make sense out of the past week to 10 days, sorting out all the different happenings, wrestling vainly for a solution or even a clue. He was one puzzled trapper.

Hod Hogan rode up to the pickup and stepped down from his horse. "Howdy Jack, I knew it was you when I spotted the pickup."

The large man looked over at the stranger.

"Meet Brett Gale," Willig said. "He's going to spend some time with me to see if we can stop some of the coyote killing. Any more kills?"

"None that I've come across since that ewe over along that sagebrush line that I showed you."

"Hear of anybody else having losses?"

"Nope. Haven't seen anybody to talk to. Funny thing, though, the day after you moved back to my camp, I was over close to the stock trail with the sheep when Ty Bingham went by in his pickup like a bat out of hell. I waved but he wouldn't even look in my direction. Must have had some kind of bug up his ass."

Willig's lips tightened. "Seen anything of his herd or Billy Butts?"

"Nope. I saw dust from his herd quite a ways north yesterday. I saw a coyote late yesterday going west up the bench north of me, too. Looked like it had something in its mouth. I couldn't tell what it was 'cause it was close to a half-mile away. It seemed small, though, like a bitch. Too small to be Two Toes."

Gale marveled at how the trapper and the herder were calling the coyote by name.

"You don't know whether Billy's herd has had any losses or not?" Willig asked.

"I haven't seen Billy and Bingham hasn't been back since he sailed past me the other day."

"All right," Willig said. "We'll go on up to Billy's camp and see what's going on. Should be back around dark or after. Brett's pickup is next to my wagon. We fed and watered the horses and they're hobbled."

"I just butchered a wether last night," Hogan said. "I'll have mutton chops and potatoes and onions waiting when you get back."

As they drove north on the stock trail, Willig described to Gale the lay of the land west of Badger Spring. There were long plateaus and more benches—all cut by washes and gullies running east to the river, and growing deeper as they went along.

North of Badger Spring was the big horseshoe-shaped bend in the Green River called Bow Knot Bend. At the end of the bend, as the river turned south again, were the Ute Seeps, the next campsite north of Badger. If Ty Bingham wasn't there now, it would be his next move, Willig said.

They drove toward the escarpment that had been cut several million years before, each set of sandstone ledges raising each subsequent bench 50 to 100 feet higher than the previous one. The sandstone was laid in striated strata, each layer its own color ranging from red to yellow to blue to gray. The ledges were stunning to behold from a distance. And above and below each series of enormous stone steps, stands of dark-green cedars full of purple berries spotted the ledges and cliffs. Scattered across the heads of benches were buffalo and squaw berry, sage and rabbit brush, shadscale and low prickly pear cactus.

What beautiful country, Gale thought. No wonder it was the home of the Ute and Uncompaghre Indians. There were still ample deer and antelope, wild horses, sagehen and rabbits roaming the areas close to water and feed. A wild and rugged paradise.

"White man hasn't ruined it yet," Willig said, as if reading Gale's thoughts. "It's just about like it was before he got here. The Indians have been here several hundred years, and yet about 20 miles northeast of here, they're uncovering dinosaur skeletons that have been there for 13 million."

"Makes you feel like a speck of dust, doesn't it?" Gale said.

▲ ▲ ▲

"Badger Spring is just ahead," Willig said. "It doesn't look like Billy's in camp yet, but it's a little early. He usually beds down his sheep just before dark."

They drove past the road that led down to the campsite. Gale could see the sheep wagon sitting by the cottonwoods. Soon, they came to a wide wash and inched down and up the steep road.

"I can hear the sheep bells," Willig said.

When they'd pulled out on the top of the next bench, the two could see the herd about a half-mile north and west of the stock trail. Willig drove opposite the herd, then turned the truck around and parked.

The sheep were crossing a bare flat on the bench, the back half of the herd hidden by dust. The two men got out of the truck and watched the sheep approach. The breeze was blowing the dust they were kicking up south and east, and soon a wave hit the pickup, warm and gritty. When the herd had almost entirely passed, Willig and Gale heard dogs bark and then the two shelties and their master on horseback suddenly appeared out of the dust.

Billy Butts rode immediately over, brown as the earth. He stepped down, dropped the reins and pulled his bandanna from his pocket. He wiped his eyes.

"Seems like that damn dust gets worse every year," he said. He turned and spat and worked his mouth around. He looked up and smiled.

"I'm sure glad to see you, Jack," he said.

"Meet Brett Gale," Willig said. "He's with our outfit and he's going to be denning with me for a few days."

Butts nodded at Gale.

"Had some trouble, Billy?" Willig asked.

"I'll say," the herder said. He paused and wiped his eyes again.

"Two Toes killed five ewes and a lamb, last evening, I reckon. He cut them out of the tail end of the herd as I was heading them for the bed ground. Got them down in a wash, out of sight, and killed them all right there."

Willig's and Gale's eyes met.

"I was moving the herd west of where they grazed yesterday, along about noon," Butts continued. "I was watching two turkey buzzards soaring north of me towards the river. They lit in a wash and when I rode over there, sure enough, there were five ewes and one lamb, dead, down in the bottom."

Butts grinned, looking at Willig. "No, Jack, I didn't mess up the sign. It was Two Toes and another coyote, small tracks, maybe his bitch."

Willig felt excitement surge through his body. At last, maybe a real break. Maybe the big coyote had made a mistake or gotten careless. He prayed that was the case.

Willig looked west and realized the sun was already behind the Twist Hills. "How far is it to the kill, Billy?"

The herder pondered a moment.

"It would take about one-half an hour to get there, too late tonight unless you want to go. I'd have to get the herd bedded down first and I don't want to leave them that long. No sir. That's why I'm staying behind the herd with my dogs now. That damn Two Toes knew he could cut those ewes out last night. The dogs and I didn't stand a chance of hearing or seeing a coyote, not with all the dust and the baa'ing."

Butts' face grew hopeful. "I'll get the sheep bedded down and meet you at camp," he said.

"No," Willig replied. "We'll get back to our camp. We're at Willow Spring with Hod. We'll be back here just before daylight."

"See you then," Butts said. He touched his horse in the ribs and rode off.

Back in the truck, Willig pursed his lips. Gale was afraid to interrupt his thoughts. Finally, he said, "Looks like maybe a lucky break."

"God, I hope so," Willig said.

He was quiet for a spell more, staring through the windshield as he drove, then said, "If Two Toes feeds on those sheep again tonight, it gives us two sets of tracks to work on. Even if we don't locate the den, it will sure as hell narrow down the country we have to work on."

"What do you make of all the dead sheep Butts talked about?" Gale asked.

Willig shook his head. "I can't figure Two Toes killing five sheep and a lamb. He usually kills only enough for one or two feedings. He must be feeding a large litter of pups, and big ones, fully weaned."

"Do you suppose he would make several trips to the five ewes? If he did, we should be able to track him to his den."

Willig looked at Gale.

"We should be so lucky," he said. "With that damn coyote, we'll be lucky if he makes one more trip. But who knows?" Then, quietly, he added, "We're overdue for some kind of break."

It was getting dark. Gale could see the light from Billy Butts' sheep wagon off toward the river.

Willig turned on the headlights and drove slowly down the stock trail road.

THIRTY-ONE

▲ ▲ ▲

Another Den
of Hungry Pups

TWO TOES' eyes glowed in the night. His irises were yellow horizontal slits surrounding the enlarged black pupils, and there was a red tinge to the eyes, reflecting light, as do the eyes of all animals stalking at night

But there was no moon out tonight. The big coyote was trotting rapidly through the pitch black toward his den, covering the distance almost as fast as if by daylight. He crossed the first bench to the north, dropped down and ran across the deep draw that led to the second bench.

He stopped once more, putting down the large piece of meat he was carrying, resting his jaws. He listened raptly, then sniffed the air in each direction. He neither smelled nor heard anything to alarm him. Night hawks cried shrilly as they hunted in the stillness, and long-eared owls hooted back and forth from the cottonwoods on the river, a prelude to their nightly foray, when they would glide silently over the benches and fly down the draws, preying on mice and kangaroo rats.

Two Toes picked up the chunk of meat and started once more toward the new den. He worked his way up the bench, and after a mile trotted over to the draw along the north side and headed west. Presently, he set the meat down again and walked to the top of the bank on the south side of the draw. With the sheep meat in his mouth, he couldn't pick up the scent of the den. He raised his nose into a slight breeze coming down the draw and that worked. It carried on it the smell of the bitch and pups. The den was up the draw, close by.

The bitch was curled up on the bank above the den. The pups were asleep inside. The two adult coyotes dropped down to the den. Two Toes laid the meat down and began vomiting up stringy chunks already broken down by stomach juices. The bitch barked, calling the pups out to their feast.

Heads appeared at the entrance and bodies tumbled forth, the pups wolfing the meat down and growling at each other at the same time.

The stars packed the wide-open heavens, beautiful sparkling flecks of white, a diamond sky of endless constellations. Had Two Toes been aware of or interested in such things, he would have gloried at the inevitable shooting star. But sleep was the only thing of importance to him. The bitch had bedded down again above the den. Two Toes went to a high spot nearby and scratched out a shallow bed under a large sagebrush. It gave him a clear view all the way to the river.

Below, outside the den, the pups cleaned up all the meat, then one by one slunk back inside. Soon they were curled up in a pile, asleep.

Not long after, Two Toes and the bitch were also asleep.

▲ ▲ ▲

Two Toes' red tongue twisted up over his nose as he yawned and stretched full length in the still blackish night. Even the crows, magpies and owls were silent now. The dog coyote shook himself in a movement that began at his head and chest, and by the time the shaking reached his tail his rear feet were bouncing off the ground.

First light wouldn't come for an hour. Two Toes trotted straight for the river, staying further north than any path he'd followed yet. He was heading for the dead ewes and lamb.

Nearing the river, he dropped down into the draw on the north side of the bench and followed it until it opened up on the west bank. At the river's edge, he lapped a long drink from the cold water.

Two Toes reached the gully where he'd killed the six sheep, bent his head and sniffed the ground, then the air. The faintest of smells of man and horse lingered. With keen senses, Two Toes picked up where Billy Butts had scrambled down the south bank and stood looking at the carcasses. It was a ghostly trace of a scent, days' old.

Two Toes came up to the dead ewes. Another smell—from the lone bitch whose tracks were in the soil—wafted in the wash. Two Toes sniffed around. Tiny carrion beetles crawled over the opened-up hindquarter of a ewe. Two Toes found a ewe that had not been fed upon and ripped wool and hide off the upper haunch. Moving his head sideways, he grabbed at the meat and backed away, tearing out hunks that he swallowed whole until his belly was full. Then he chewed and gnawed off a large piece to carry back.

It was the smell of the lone bitch that deterred him from heading back to his mate's den. Instead of getting up on the bench to the north and heading northwest, he went up on the south bench and headed due west. He was curious. He would check out the other den.

The first gray streak of dawn was creeping up the skyline above the hills of Deadman Bench. Crows were cawing back and forth from their cottonwood roosts, readying to assemble their flock before feeding. Two Toes jumped into the wash below the lone bitch's den and walked. The pups were still in the hole. He dropped the meat and stared inside just as a young pup, hearing the coyote and smelling the fresh meat, came out yipping at the top of his voice, the rest right behind.

Two Toes growled savagely. He grabbed the foremost pup by its back and threw him at the others rushing up. The pup howled and ran whimpering into the den. A second growl sent the rest quickly disappearing after him. As fierce as his snappings were, they were no cause for deathly fright. Male coyotes rarely kill the young of their species—unlike bobcats, mountain lions and bears, the last which even slay their own offspring.

The bitch was nowhere around. Two Toes grabbed the meat and went up on the north bank. He looked around carefully. No sign of her. He headed northwest for his new den.

Down by the river, at the wash, the lone bitch coyote cautiously approached the sheep kills. She'd been 100 yards away when she'd smelled Two Toes eating the ewe. She'd stayed back, downwind, lying next to a small sagebrush, the red reflections from her eyes out of sight of the big coyote. And after he'd appeared on the bank above the kill, and then left, she'd waited some more.

Now she ate her fill of meat. It was barely light as she finished. She picked up a large piece in her jaws and headed straight for her den.

THIRTY-TWO

▲ ▲ ▲

The Hunt Gets Hotter

D AYLIGHT was at least two hours away, yet Jack Willig was wide awake. He had slept fitfully and when he had slept, the slumber was full of wild dreams.

In one, he had Two Toes cornered in a box canyon, along with several other creatures: an antelope, a lame hawk, two beavers and a porcupine. He grabbed for his gun but, ridiculously, the scabbard was empty. And then when he reached in again, he'd gripped the gun and pulled it out. Turning back, Two Toes had disappeared, leaving only the odd menagerie staring at him.

But it was another dream—the last and most intense—that jolted him awake. It was still fresh and real in his mind, hysterical as it was. Willig had set a trap near an old deer kill. Two Toes' tracks had been all around—much larger than normal; oversized, monstrous tracks, belonging to no creature he'd seen. Yet Willig had shrugged and accepted the tracks. The crazy dream made no provision for logic.

He baited the trap with his new deer scent, which for some reason smelled like whiskey and gasoline and even his own urine. It seemed perfect, and he was sure he would get his coyote. He retired to his sheep wagon, which was parked yards away, around the corner of a bank. When he heard the trap chain rattle, he was around the corner in a flash. There, he stopped cold.

The trap had disappeared. Then there was a clamp on his leg, which became a burning sensation. Willig's ankle was being crushed. He looked down. He'd stepped in the trap—which was now a bear trap. Its enormous jaws held him tight, biting into his flesh, yet strangely, he felt no pain.

Held firm, unable to pry the jaws free with his hands, Willig panicked. He heard footsteps approach. "Hey!" he shouted. "I'm caught!"

Into the clearing stepped a man, walking backward so that Willig couldn't see his face. Slowly, the man turned. It was Ty Bingham. He was smiling, but upon recognizing Willig, turned red in anger.

Arms akimbo, he glowered. "What the hell're you doin'?!" he growled. "I thought you'd be out after that sonofabitch coyote that's cost me the last two lambing seasons."

Willig found he had lost his voice. He couldn't speak. He made loud mumbling noises and pointed madly at his foot. But the rancher refused to even look down. Then there was a rustling behind.

Into the clearing trotted an enormous coyote, which Willig knew without a doubt was Two Toes. It wagged its tail like a dog, tongue lolling and face seeming to laugh. Willig couldn't believe his eyes when Bingham reached down and patted the coyote on its head. "Go get 'im!" he commanded.

Two Toes started forward toward the helpless Willig. Then he gasped: the rancher's pointing hand was a coyote paw, missing its second and third fingers.

"You talkin' to me Jack?"

Brett Gale sat up, resting on elbows. Willig realized he'd been talking in his sleep. Sweating and embarrassed, he mumbled, "I must've been dreaming. Sorry I woke you."

But Willig couldn't sleep any more. His mind was too fired up. He stared up at the canvas cover of the sheep wagon. Soon, his dark thoughts brightened. *I'll get that sonofabitch this time. If he and his bitch make more than one trip to that kill in the wash. I'd have to be blind to not be able to work with all that fresh sign.*

The thought of new tracks excited Willig. He rolled out of bed in his longjohns and bare feet and quietly left the wagon to relieve himself. The ground was frosty cold. The stars still winked in the inky sky. He felt happy to be up this early. Happy, and ready.

Back inside, Willig lit the Coleman lantern. It hissed and popped into a yellowish flame above a bluish bulb. He whittled wood shavings and stuffed them with crumpled paper into the stove and fired it up. The wagon warmed.

Gale sat up and stretched, blinking and yawning. A moment later, he was getting dressed. He grabbed the water bucket and headed for the river. He grained the horses while Willig cooked breakfast.

"What's the plan?" Gale asked as they ate.

"We'll head for the five dead ewes," Willig said. "We want to be out on those tracks as soon as we can see good enough, and that isn't going to be long. We've got about an hour or a little better to daylight."

Gale could see Willig had plotted it out. The trapper was not confused anymore. He was raring to go. Gale hoped to help any way he could.

"We save an hour if we go to Billy's camp in our rigs," Willig continued. "You put your horse in your trailer and I'll jump Sontag into my pickup. We won't stop to do any dishes."

The men hurriedly cleaned their plates and gulped down the last of the coffee. As Gale was loading Socks into the trailer, Willig closed the sheep wagon doors and loaded Sontag into his truck. Soon they were picking their way up the trail road by headlight.

Billy Butts was just finishing his own morning meal when the pickups pulled up. He poked his head out the sheep wagon's door.

"Come in, I'll pour you a cup of coffee."

"Haven't got time," Willig answered. "We want to hit those dead ewes about daylight."

He and Gale saddled the horses and mounted up. Billy Butts stood outside in his boots. "We'll probably be gone all day," Willig said. "Keep the herd south so you don't mess up our sign."

"I planned on going south today," Butts said. "Tomorrow, too, if you need it. Wait a minute and I'll make you a sandwich."

But the trapper was already putting a heel in Sontag's flanks. He called over his shoulder, "We haven't got time."

The men rode in silence, Willig in the lead, toward where Butts had said the sheep kill was. Gale watched the trapper bobbing in his saddle several yards in front, all quiet determination. It was just getting light enough to see when they crossed the second bench to the north. Gale wondered how the day would turn out. It seemed full of promise.

Butts had said the sheep kill was between a quarter- to a half-mile up from the river. They were coming now to the gully about a quarter-mile up. Gale followed Willig up the draw westward along the south bank. With abrupt surprise, a pair of turkey buzzards flared out of the draw 150 yards ahead.

"There's our sheep kill," Gale said.

Both men reined up. Willig nodded his head, watching the vultures pump their three-foot-long wings, grabbing for air. He had hated these buzzards ever since the time when he was trapping for the sheepmen in Sevier County. He'd just gotten married. The sheepmen were paying him $5 a coyote bounty and Willig got to keep the furs when they were prime in September and October. It seemed like a promising deal, but the damn buzzards used to beat him to the dead coyotes before he could ever skin them. The vultures were after the livers and guts. By the time he'd get to a coyote caught in a trap, it would be pecked full of holes in the flanks. The furs would be worthless.

"God, I hate those birds," Willig muttered.

"How do you figure?" Gale asked. To him, the birds looked as graceful as eagles in the gray light. They had the same hooked beak, almost the same wing formation with the six-foot span, and soared beautifully, one of the prettiest damn things he'd seen. In broad daylight, though, one would be able to see the buzzards' ugly red bald heads, and the wings that were gray, instead of dark like the eagle's.

"Those goddamned birds cost me a lot of money when I needed it most," Willig said.

The men sat side by side in their saddles, watching the big birds wheeling 200 yards up in the sky.

Gale spoke up. "They're a pretty good target right now."

Willig scowled. "You couldn't hit one of those birds up there, no way. Hell. You got one of those telescopes on your rifle. You couldn't even find that buzzard, soaring the way he is."

"There's a knack to it, but it's not as hard as it looks," Gale replied, unfazed.

"Bullshit, I'd have to see this one," Willig said.

Gale stepped down off Socks and pulled his Model 54 Winchester 30.06 from the scabbard.

Unbeknownst to Willig, Gale could flip 50-cent pieces into the air, one after another, and hit four out of five with his .22 rifle, and three out of five with a pistol. Any can or bottle would simply be gone. His deadly eye was the product of many years practicing with his .22 on all kinds of rodents and varmints.

But this was no .22 he had with him today. The Winchester was mounted with the long Wollensack 2.5 power telescope sight. Gale mechanically pumped a shell into the chamber as he backed away from the horses. At 20 yards, he threw the gun to his shoulder. He sighted along the outside of the scope's long barrel until he'd picked up a buzzard, then dropped his eye into the scope and put the target in the cross-hairs.

He could see the whole dark form of the bird with the sky behind it. He followed its flight, the cross-hairs locked firmly on its body. The scope was sighted in for 250 yards. Gale knew that every two or three minutes, a soaring bird will bank, stop and start soaring the other way. He tracked the bird until it came to the end of the updraft it was riding. Just before swooping down to pick up another thermal updraft, it poised, dead still.

Gale squeezed the trigger. The buzzard exploded in mid-air. Feathers and what was left floated down.

"I'll be goddamned!" Willig said. "If that isn't something."

As Gale nonchalantly put the rifle back in its scabbard, the trapper said, "I hope you get a shot at Two Toes."

▲   ▲   ▲

Willig crouched over the torn-open ewe lying in the draw. He rubbed the blood between the tips of his thumb and forefinger. It felt fresh and sticky.

He had picked her carcass out right away as he and Gale stood on the bank of the draw, staring down at the carnage. "That one ewe looks like she was fed on this morning," he'd said.

Now, his fingers had proof. "Those coyotes were feeding on her less than an hour ago. That blood hasn't even started to gel."

Gale was scrutinizing the tracks in the soft sandy bottom. His eyes lit up.

"Here's Two Toes' fresh tracks and here's the bitch's tracks on top of one of his," he said, with the matter-of-factness of a veteran trapper. "They were both here at the same time."

Willig was still surveying the ewe carcass. "They've eaten almost a whole hindquarter," he said. "Those must be big pups they're feeding, and a lot of them."

He straightened. "They're both heading up the draw. You lead the horses on the bank and I'll follow the tracks down here."

The men worked slowly along for 20 minutes. Then Willig hollered, "Hold it." Gale came to the edge and looked down. Willig was backtracking. He was trying to find where he'd lost Two Toes' tracks.

Gale had been checking out the bare spots on the edge of the draw and found a clear print of Two Toes' right-front foot. He called down to Willig. "Two Toes came up here and he's heading away from the draw, going southwest."

"The bitch is still going up the draw," Willig answered. "I'll follow her and you stay with Two Toes."

Leading the horses, Gale saw where the big coyote's tracks steadily angled away from the draw. At 200 yards, he stopped and looked back. There was no sign of Willig. The trapper was still tracking the bitch up the wash bottom.

It felt hot for so early in the morning. The sun had been up for at least two hours and there wasn't a cloud in the sky. It seemed like summer, though it was only April. Gale wiped the sweat off his forehead with his shirt sleeve. As he did so, a swarm of buffalo gnats attacked from all directions. They were instantly in his ears and nose and buzzing before his eyes.

Gale swatted at them with his Stetson, fanning them away. Lowering his chin, he moved quickly off with the horses, tugging the reins grasped in one hand and waving madly with his hat in his other. "Damn it!" he said.

The gnats were still on him, biting him on the neck and under his shirt collar. He dropped his hat and swiped his hand across the back of his neck, then picked up the hat and slapped the swarm away again, wildly. He had once thought about rubbing his skin with citronella before going out trapping, but decided it would be fruitless since he'd end up sweating the lotion away, anyhow. As it stood now, it would be a couple of summers before he'd come up with a suitable solution: olive oil, which would stay on his skin yet drown the tiny gnats as they struck. But at this point in time, the only hope he had was to just try and ignore them, and avoid them if he could.

Gale saw that Two Toes' tracks were heading for the next draw south in a fairly straight line. Now and then he'd lose the tracks in rocky or grassy patches, then pick them up again on bare soil. A coyote covered a lot of ground, that was sure. It took a world of patience to keep up. But that, Gale had already learned, was part of the game.

After a time he looked back for Willig. The trapper had come out of the wash and was tracking in the same general direction, some 300 yards back. Willig looked up and waved and started toward Gale. Gale led the horses to him.

"Still have your track?" Willig asked.

"Yes. He's going in a fairly straight line and headed towards that bunch of rocks over the next draw."

"That's the same direction the bitch is headed," Willig said. "Let's ride over there. The den could be there some place."

They mounted up and headed for the draw. When they were close, Willig reined up and turned to Gale.

"Why don't you ride well back from the wash till you're about a quarter of a mile above the rocks, then go to the draw and work down towards me. Stay up on the bank so you can see everything. I'm going straight south and working my way up to meet you. If one of us jumps one of them coyotes, the other might get a shot."

Willig removed his hat and toweled off his forehead with his bandanna. "Damn," he said. "It's going to be a hot one today. And we didn't bring a canteen. Well, that's what we get for being in such a hurry. But maybe it will be worth it."

Just before he reached the draw, Gale dismounted and put a shell in his rifle's chamber. He started leading Socks down the north bank toward Willig. He peered as far down the draw as he could and also checked the sandy bottom below him. Every now and then he could see coyote tracks.

About 150 yards down, a coyote came up the south side of the draw at a dead run, looking back down toward the way he'd come. Gale knew it had seen or heard Willig. He dropped the reins, jumped five steps in front of his horse and knelt putting the rifle to his shoulder. He picked the coyote up in the scope just as it slowed. Gale waited. Sure enough, the coyote stopped and looked back to see what had spooked him.

Gale took the slack out of the trigger, set the cross hairs on his target and squeezed. The gun bucked up. As Gale tried to get the coyote back in the scope, he heard the splat of the bullet hitting the animal in the ribs.

At the crack of the gun, Willig, who had been following the bitch's tracks, scrambled up the south bank. The splat had been music to his ears. Though he knew better, he was praying under his breath that it was Two Toes that had been knocked flat.

Gale was waving him south. Willig went that way. The coyote was lying about 100 yards off. Willig rushed to it, but at 10 yards his hopes faded. He could see the naked belly and the bag and tits standing out dark against the gray fur of the bitch's flanks.

Gale spotted the den as he was walking down the draw toward Willig, leading Socks. It was directly below. He called to

Willig then dropped the reins and slid down the bank. The hole was in the south bank, about three feet up the side. It had been well used. The dirt below was packed hard. Pup signs ran up and down the draw. The vicinity was littered with feathers and bones, wool and the pups' droppings. Gale saw leg bones of a small lamb, stripped clean of meat and sinew. They somehow seemed innocent.

Willig appeared around a bend down the wash, leading his horse. He walked slowly, eyes fixed on the coyote tracks, working them out in his mind. He tied Sontag's reins to a bush.

"Two Toes and the bitch have both been up this draw this morning," he said. "Their tracks are plain and are on top of her morning tracks going down."

Gale set his Stetson on the ground and stuck his head into the den opening. The den appeared shallow.

"I can hear the pups," he said. "They'll be easy to get out."

"Did you see Two Toes' tracks coming down?"

"No," Gale said. "All I could see were just tracks in the bottom of the wash."

Willig handed him the denning tool bag that he'd untied from Sontag's saddle.

"You fish the pups out. I'm going to check up the draws a way."

Gale didn't mind denning. The first one or two when he started training had twinged him with remorse, because they were pups he was conking over the head, and because their short-featured faces triggered his own sympathetic instincts, as the young of all mammals do. But now it was just part of his job. He did it and that was that.

Using the burr head, he pulled out six pups. He was filling in his notebook when Willig returned, a sore look on his face. The trapper sat down heavily on a hump of dirt at the bottom of the wash and removed his hat. He wiped his forehead and scratched the back of his neck.

"Something's wrong here," he finally said. "Plenty of bitch tracks but damn few of Two Toes. He's been here this morning but I can see only one place where meat was vomited up and one place where a fresh piece of meat was put down by the den for pups."

Willig led Gale to the two spots. Both were close to the den.

"From the looks of that ewe's hindquarter, both coyotes loaded up on meat," Willig said. "Where in the hell is the rest of it?"

The sun bore down on the ledges of the Twist Hills. The air felt heavy with heat, and seemed to thicken with gnats. The heat seemed to blur reality.

"Let's each take a side of this wash and follow it up to the ledges and see what we can find," Willig said.

THIRTY-THREE

▲ ▲ ▲
The Sheepman Backs Down

IT WAS BREAKING DAWN. The sun was drawing a thin line of light above the Deadman Bench hills in the east. Ty Bingham was heading down the gravel road toward Ouray, thinking about his meeting with Gale, the new man with the Biological Survey.

Bingham understood how he'd come out as a result of their talk. On the positive side, Gale had let him know they would try to help him out with the coyote losses. On the negative side, Gale had made it clear they would be working with the other sheepmen. He'd also made it clear he believed that Jack Willig was doing everything possible to stop the sheep losses, and especially to nail Two Toes.

Bingham figured that was all he could do now to salvage the situation with Willig, pushing the trapper too far so that he'd moved his camp wagon. There was no point now in talking any further with Scott Rasmussen in Salt Lake. What's done was done. What was going to come, was going to come.

All Bingham could hope for now was that Willig was somehow staying in touch with Billy Butts. If there were any more sheep kills, there had to be a way to contact Willig.

But how?

Bingham's mind was still turning over this problem as he pulled up in front of the trading post. He was on the front porch before he realized it would be a couple hours before Osh opened the store. Muttering to himself, Bingham got back in the pickup and started up the stock trail.

OK, he thought. *If I can just get by for a week—10 days at the most—I'll be headed for Ashley Valley and the home ranch and I'll be off Two Toes' range.*

As he drove past the turnoff to Haslett's camp, Bingham recalled his talk with Old Joe the other day. Haslett had suffered only a few coyote losses. Willig had camped with Hod Hogan and they'd taken two dens right away, and after that the killing had stopped east of the Green. What's more, they'd only had one loss this side of the river, and that had been to Two Toes. They'd found his tracks. Willig was supposed to be working that kill right now.

Bingham was beginning to wonder about the wisdom of his herd being the first one off the winter range every year and headed up the stock driveway. Normally, it paid off to be the first one on the trail. The feed was better and the sheep did fine, much better than the last herds, which found most of the feed gone. But the last couple years, Bingham's sheep were also the first to be hit by coyotes on the trail. They were the only sheep on the trail then, and the coyotes hit them hard. When several herds were strung along the driveway for 20 to 30 miles, the coyote losses were scattered among several outfits, and no one took the brunt of the killing.

"Look what it's doing to me," Bingham said out loud. After all these years in the sheep business—with the accumulated knowledge of three generations—he had discovered what appeared to be a new truth.

As Bingham neared Badger Spring, he saw Billy Butts far away, moving the sheep south and west. He stopped his truck a half-mile away from the sheep.

The herder saw his boss and returned his wave. He promptly rode over. He didn't waste any words after his boss greeted him.

"We had a bad one," Butts said. "We lost five ewes and a lamb three nights ago."

Bingham stared. The wind escaped slowly through his pursed lips. "What happened?" he said finally.

"Two Toes hit the tail end of the herd as we were coming into the bed ground."

Butts described how the coyote must have cut out the ewes as he and his dogs were on either side of the herd, unable to see to the rear because of the heavy choking dust. Bingham barely heard the words. His mind was racing.

"Do you know where Willig is?" he said, interrupting. "We've got to get to him damn quick. Damn that stubborn sonofabitch."

Butts stopped him. "I told Willig about it last night and he said he'd be back. He and Gale were here just before daylight. They're out there now."

Bingham didn't say a word. He looked out toward the Twist Hills. Finally, he asked, "Where was it?"

Butts pointed north at the big draw above camp. "The next bench north of that one, about one-half mile up from the river."

"Let me take your horse, Billy," Bingham said. "I'm going to ride up there and see what the hell they're doing."

He held out his hand for the reins.

"I wouldn't do that if I were you," Butts said.

"Why not?" Bingham snapped. "Those are my dead sheep and I want to make sure they're trying to get that damned Two Toes."

Butts held onto his horse's reins. He did not budge. Bingham couldn't believe it. He glared at his herder.

"If you chase after them, " Butts said, "God knows what will happen, but it won't be good."

Bingham began to tremble with anger. "That sonofabitch can't threaten me and get away with it. "I'll . . ."

"Boss, you go after Willig and you can get yourself another herder." Butts' voice was cold and hard.

Bingham was struck dumb. He looked at his herder. Butts was staring him right in the eye.

Neither man spoke. They just looked at each other. Finally, Bingham said, "Shit . . . Goddamn it."

He stared at Butts some more, then turned and got in his pickup and slammed the door.

He drove off in the direction of Ouray.

THIRTY-FOUR

Finally, Good Tracking

JACK WILLIG AND BRETT GALE were on foot, leading their horses, sorting the tracks carefully, working the area sepa rately. There was a great deal of sign close to the den they'd just cleaned out. They wanted to study them and work them out so they could tell what the coyotes had been doing, and what the dog coyote—the only one they hadn't gotten—was up to now.

When one or the other lost a track, he'd tie his horse to a bush or ground-hitch him while he toiled through the puzzle. Often, Gale or Willig would get 200 to 300 yards from his horse as he pieced together the riddle of the tracks.

Almost a half-mile from the den, Gale hit a big bare spot right in the middle of the bench. The spot measured about 20 acres, with an outcropping of rock and brush in the middle. The clay and sand soil made for excellent tracking. A small prairie dog town had inhabited the bare spot in years past, but the series of holes hadn't been occupied for a long time.

Gale made out all kinds of sign. Once, he found Two Toes' tracks. They were headed north. He also found tracks of another coyote about the same size. Gale figured it was a dog coyote. Soon after, he discovered several of this coyote's tracks, some fairly fresh and others old, preserved in mud.

Gale picked up several of the narrow tracks of the bitch coyote and it seemed like she was running with the strange dog coyote at times, even trotting together toward the den he'd just cleaned out. He scratched his head.

There were more signs around the rock outcropping. One of the large squaw bushes was a pissing post. Coyote scratches were all around, and there were old droppings. Gale also discovered where a badger had recently tried to dig a rabbit out from under one of the large rocks. He leaned up against the rock and took off his hat again. He wiped his forehead with his shirt sleeve.

It was past noon and getting even hotter, without a trickle of a breeze. Gale was truly regretting leaving the sheep wagon without a canteen. His mouth tasted of cotton. He'd had to go an entire day before without anything to drink, but it wasn't very pleasant. He squatted and brushed the soil, and found a smooth pebble. He wiped it against his shirt then put it in his mouth to suck on.

Gale mulled over the sign he'd found: two male coyotes and one bitch. It was plenty confusing, that was for sure. No wonder Willig was frustrated. This was a real puzzle, and no clear solution presented itself. The strange dog coyote seemed to have run with the bitch he'd just shot, yet Gale hadn't seen any really new tracks of the dog. Most of the tracks went north and south. The southbound tracks wandered back and forth, indicating hunting. The northbound tracks all seemed to be headed for the den they'd just taken.

Why were Two Toes' tracks fresh and so close to the den? It had to be Two Toes' den, right? The bitch had to be his mate, right? But then, what was that strange dog coyote doing, laying down so much sign? Could he have a den close by?

Gale headed back for his horse a half-mile away, but circled a little as he did to not back-track himself, so he could check for new sign. Several times, he picked up both the strange dog and the bitch's tracks. Once, he hit Two Toes' track, but it could have been the same one he'd already caught. What really bothered him was that Two Toes' track at the den had been fresh, probably left that morning.

Glancing west, Gale saw Willig on horseback, way up near the head of the bench, close to the first sandstone ledges. Willig was not moving. Gale waved and Willig waved back. He motioned Gale to join him.

It took about 20 minutes to reach Willig. The trapper was sitting on a sandstone rock under an overhang, resting in the shade. Sontag was under the ledge, too, his reins on the ground.

"What'd you see?" Willig asked.

Gale told about the odd mix of signs: the strange dog coyote that seemed to be running with the bitch he'd shot that morning; both tracks going out and coming back to the den. Sign that was both old and fresh.

Willig took it all in without saying a word. When Gale finished, he asked, "Did you find any sign of Two Toes?"

"Yes," Gale said. "But only a couple of old tracks, one going north and one going towards the river."

He paused, then added, "I can't make it out. It seems like the strange dog was hunting with the bitch. I had their tracks together two or three times, both coming to the den. But we found Two Toes' fresh tracks there. One of those dog coyotes would kill the other if they were both trying to claim the bitch, wouldn't they?"

Willig was impressed. The college kid knew more than he thought he would. He'd picked up a lot of savvy about denning. Heck, most trappers wouldn't have figured out this much.

"I've never seen one dog tolerate another around his mate or his den," Willig replied. "Two Toes the other day had one hell of a fight with another dog near the Indian ranches, just because he was messing with his bitch."

He looked at Gale for a few moments, then said, "You've got it figured out about right as far as you go. This bitch you just shot, her mate must have been the dog coyote I shot down near the river. I thought at first I'd nailed Two Toes. Turned out, he was feeding on Two Toes' kill."

Willig stopped to collect his thoughts.

"I think that bitch also fed on Two Toes' kill after he'd filled his belly and left," he continued. "She was feeding those six big pups all by herself that you got out of her den and she was eating on

Billy Butts' five ewes this morning after Two Toes had left. That's why we saw some of her morning tracks on top of Two Toes' tracks. You see, she fed after he left, and then she headed back for her den."

Gale thought it over. The explanation seemed almost made up, but then, it had the ring of truth to it, too.

"Yes," Gale said, "but what the hell is Two Toes' fresh tracks doing at her den and where is Two Toes' bitch?"

Willig grimaced.

"Damn it, I don't know," he said. "I'm only guessing, but I think I'm right. Maybe some of those bitch tracks back at the five dead ewes belonged to Two Toes' mate."

Willig stood. He walked out from the shadow of the ledges and peered at the sun. "Let's see what we can do before it gets dark. We've got a couple of hours left and we might as well make use of it."

Gale was tired. The hot sun had worn him down, and then there was his thirst. The gnat bites felt sore and the sweat running over them stung. But one thing about two men teaming up, one pushed the other. They mounted up and rode out away from the ledges.

Willig pulled up and looked at Gale. "I'm pretty sure Two Toes' den is north of us somewhere, but I want to make damn sure."

"Do we want to go north now?" Gale asked. "It's going to get dark on us fast. It could get too late to shoot. My scope is no good at dusk or even in heavy shadows."

"I don't want to spook Two Toes this late, no way," Willig said. "What's your plan?"

"You follow the ledge south to the head of the next draw," Willig said. "See if you can pick up anything in the ledges, then go down the bottom of that draw all the way to the river. I don't think there is a den there, but you can read sign in the sandy bottom real well."

Gale appreciated the praise. The two of them were operating pretty darn well as a team. What was more important, they had a chance to get Two Toes. They were closing in, maybe. It would be a heck of an accomplishment. He was glad he wasn't working with Abe Evans right now.

Willig was looking down the bench toward the river.

"I'll do the same thing on the first draw north," he said. "If we find nothing, then we can focus on the land north and west of Badger and Ute Seeps. See you at the pickup."

▲ ▲ ▲

Gale reined up at the foot of the sand rock ledges that rose above. He was at the very head of the wash that ran to the river. From his elevation, with everything sloping to the Green, he could follow the line of the wash easily for three or four miles.

He tied Socks to a buffalo berry bush and worked his way back and forth up the ledge. He made out some scattered coyote tracks, but they were few and far between. It was 80 or 90 feet up to the next ledge. Again, the tracks were sparse and scattered, running always along the ledge, going north or south.

The soft sand at the foot of each ledge wouldn't hold a track. Even a soft breeze would drift fine grains into the tracks, wiping out their paw or toe marks. All Gale could see were the indentations in the sand, showing that some animal had passed by. But he knew they were coyote tracks. Jake Judd had showed him the year before how coyotes walk—putting one foot in front of the other, making a straight line.

Gale worked 300 yards or so in each direction, then back down to his horse. He mounted up and started down the wash. When the wash widened to 10 feet, he got off and led Socks down into the wash bottom and toward the river.

Gale walked slowly and carefully, checking out each coyote track as it appeared. He'd tie Socks to a bush and check out the banks to see where the coyote had entered or left, and from which direction. It wasn't very long before he came upon the tracks left by Two Toes and his mate.

They'd come into the wash at a cave-in in the north side and exited on the opposite side. Gale climbed out on the south side but almost immediately lost their tracks. He led Sontag on down the wash. A quarter-mile farther, he picked up a large coyote track that was soon joined by a smaller, narrow track: a dog and his bitch. The tracks didn't go far before they went up the south bank and out onto the bench.

Now tracks were showing up more and more. Some went up and some down the wash, and some crossed from one bank to another. Gale's expectations heightened. He believed he might be coming onto a den. The tracks were fairly fresh. And the comings and goings were increasing.

The wash was now a good 15 feet deep and fairly wide. Gale left Socks again and scrambled up the bank to see where he was. He saw he was less than a half-mile from the river. It was getting on toward dusk. The Twist Hills cast shadows clear to the water and starting up toward Deadman Bench. He dropped back down into the wash and grabbed Socks' reins. They started down toward the river. If there was a den, he wanted to locate it before dark.

The tracks thickened. Gale grew excited. He pulled his rifle from the scabbard and pumped a shell in the chamber. It could be any minute now. The den was here, somewhere.

Rounding a corner, he saw a dark shape lying 20 yards ahead of him. It was a dead coyote.

Gale found footprints of cowboy boots all around it. All of a sudden it dawned on him—here was where the two ewes had been killed by Two Toes several days ago. He wondered briefly why Willig hadn't scalped this dog coyote after shooting it. But he guessed he could figure it out. Willig had been too worked up to stop and do it. He'd been too worked up thinking it was Two Toes' he'd nailed. Gale couldn't blame him.

Gale rounded the next corner in the wash. Several magpies and a crow flared up, frightened and screaming harshly. Not much was left of the two sheep before him: mostly just bones and wool.

Gale felt foolish. Here he'd thought he was coming up on a den.

It was getting almost too dark to see by the time he reached Billy Butts' sheep wagon, greeted by the barking of dogs.

THIRTY-FIVE

▲ ▲ ▲

Closing In

BRETT GALE felt he was somewhere between sleep and wakefulness as he led the horses back to camp and their grain bags, after watering them at the river.

He had been so tuckered out the night before he hadn't even washed his face before tugging off his boots and clothes and crawling into the wagon's double bed, flopping back. A few seconds later, he was out cold. But the washing chill of the pre-dawn outdoors as he moved through it roused him into alertness.

The wagon light split the darkness like a beam. Jack Willig had lighted the Coleman lantern, and through the open wagon door Gale could see the trapper now, busy over the stove. Yet night had nowhere near yielded its presence. It was dead dark, and the sky looked alive. The Big Dipper and the North Star blazed brilliant. Again, Gale marveled at the beauty of this wild country, and felt sorry for the changes the white men had thrust on the Indians as they took it away from them, little by little.

Gale took off the halters, put on the bridles and tied the horses' reins to the rear wagon wheels then stepped around and up onto the wagon tongue.

"Come in, it's ready," Willig said.

Gale slid in on the bench and started in on his bacon and eggs. He was impressed at how Willig was on the ball even at this early hour, with not a hunch to his posture, as if he possessed some animal strength, some pre-civilization sensibility. Up before dawn like the coyote.

Gale didn't much envy Willig's lifestyle. He had no ambition himself to be a trapper all his life. He'd gone to college. Yet he deeply admired the likes of Willig and Jake Judd and the other pure trappers. They were workers. There was no shiftlessness, no quit in them. They were hewn from a different wood.

Gale stabbed at his eggs and filled his mouth, fueling up for the day ahead. He knew it was going to be a long one again. The horses would get lathered up just standing in the hot sun. He'd be soaked with sweat all day long, and his mouth and throat would get so desert-dry he'd be barely able to whisper.

"What's your plan for the day?" he asked Willig.

"I've been thinking it over while I was getting breakfast," the trapper said. "We've never been very far up the draw above the five ewes kill. If we work that draw clear to the head of it, we should see more good sign and we might even find Two Toes' den up there. I have the feeling he's either up in the sandstone ledges or damn close."

Gale filled his coffee cup. His mind came to life as he sipped the bitter black brew. Willig seemed to be onto something.

"At least we know he isn't south of there, and Billy Butts will have fed that area off pretty soon," Gale said. "He can't go south many more days."

"We can't expect Two Toes to feed off that kill again," Willig said. "We were lucky he and the lone bitch hit it night before last. He's too damn smart to hit the same kill twice, let alone three times. He and his bitch have a real job cut out to feed those pups from the looks of things."

Gale sensed what Willig was getting at. It was Two Toes who could be losing the upper hand, who could not have time on his side. What if he and Willig got lucky today? What if they closed in on Two Toes' den? Gale began to suspect they would, and the notion gave him a spurt of energy.

"You fill the canteens," Willig was saying. "It's going to be hot today. We'll be needing some water. I've made a couple of egg sandwiches. I'll stack the dishes and we can get going."

They loaded their horses. Gale led Socks into the trailer, Willig jumped Sontag into the bed of his truck. Soon they were heading for Billy Butts' camp.

Headlights trained ahead, Gale had to fall back a ways behind Willig's truck just to be able to see through the heavy dust choking him in its wake. With the windows rolled up tight, it was already getting warm in his cab. "Going to be a hot one," he muttered.

It was just cracking dawn as the two trucks pulled up to Billy Butts' wagon. The herder had finished his breakfast and was closing the wagon door. "Sorry, I threw the coffee out," he said.

"You're moving the herd south, aren't you?" Willig asked.

"That's right," Butts said. "I'll keep them out of your way. I'll feed down towards Hod's north boundary, then come back further west. I'll have to go north tomorrow, but I'll stick close to the river."

"That'll be fine," Willig said. "We'll work the draw where the five ewes were killed, clear to the ledges. That will take most of the day."

He and Gale mounted up and prepared to ride out. Willig called down, as if with an afterthought: "Did I see Bingham's pickup come in yesterday morning?"

"That's right," Butts replied. "He brought me some supplies."

"Thought so," Willig said, poker-faced. "He didn't stay very long, did he?"

"No, he didn't," Butts said, smiling.

"See you this evening," Willig said.

He and Gale walked their horses side by side, riding north across the bench toward the kill of the five ewes.

"It seems kind of funny to me," Willig said, out of the blue.

"What does?"

"Bingham tending camp yesterday morning. I thought I recognized his pickup when he was close to Billy's camp. The next time I looked that way, damned if he wasn't leaving camp, headed south, and it looked like he was in one hell of a hurry."

The two rode along, lost in thought. Then Willig nodded his head to the north.

"That must be the mate of that turkey buzzard you shot."

Gale caught sight of a big bird soaring high, a hazy distant form in the sky.

"Could be," he replied. "There's some talk that they mate for life. She may hang around for awhile before she gives up. She'll be too darn smart to let me get a shot at her."

Willig nodded, but didn't say a thing.

Gale's thoughts turned to home, to his wife. She would be up by now, serving breakfast to Susie and their toddler son, Bobby. The daughter would be heading to school shortly. Gale thought about how Dottie never complained about the long periods they were apart. It was how it was during this depression. A fellow was tickled to death just to have a job and a good one. He and Dottie had been married five years, and their roles were defined without them talking about it. She was going to take care of the home front while he took care of the income.

Still, Gale was a young husband and he missed the home life, being away so much. He was doubly glad he hadn't married himself to a life of trapping, like Willig, no matter how tough the work and the exhilaration of matching wits with coyotes. He blinked his eyes and rubbed sweat away. It was barely morning but the sun was warming up pretty fast. He pulled his bandanna out of his hind pocket and tied it around his neck. The cloth felt raw on his gnat bites that were still a little sore. He knew when the sweat ran over them they'd burn pretty good.

As they came to the site of the dead ewes, Willig reined up and turned to Gale. "I don't suppose it will do any good, but why don't we do the same thing again?" he said. "I'll wait here while you go 300, 400 yards due west before you ride to the draw. When you get there, wave and wait till I drop down in. Then we'll work towards each other, me in the bottom and you up on the bench."

"I was sort of thinking the same thing," Gale replied. "You can never tell." He touched his heels to Socks' flanks and headed west. He crossed his own tracks left from the day before, and a little farther on, hit Willig's tracks when they'd been heading for the rock pile on the next draw to the south.

Gale back-tracked Willig's tracks to where he'd come up on the bench. He took his Stetson off and waved. Willig waved back and dropped down to the bottom of the gully.

Gale stepped down from the saddle and pulled his 30.06 from its scabbard. He inserted a shell in the chamber and pushed the safety on. Then, rifle slung over shoulder, he led Sontag slowly forward, working his way toward Willig.

He was getting close to the ewes. It was just around the next curve. No sign yet of coyotes; not even any magpies or crows. At the edge of the bank he called down to Willig, who was kneeling over the ground, reading the sign around a carcass.

"Didn't see a thing and no fresh tracks," Gale said.

"Nothing new down here, either," Willig said. "Our tracks from yesterday haven't been touched. We've got all the good we're going to get here."

Gale saw it was just like Willig had predicted. Two Toes wasn't coming back to these kills. It was like a chess match. Now it was their move.

Willig led Sontag up the steep bank on the north side. "Let's work up to the ledges," he said. "I'll check this side and you stay on the south side."

They started up the draw, moving rapidly until they came to the spot where Willig had left the wash the day before to cover the bitch tracks. Here, they slowed and began watching the ground carefully.

At times, they would be right on the wash bank, then following the track or swinging out away from the wash to check out a large bare spot. They would become separated by several hundred yards as they scanned the ground for tracks and sign. Several times, Gale dismounted and walked. He'd glance back to see Willig also afoot, stooped over, following a track. One time, Willig disappeared down to the bottom, then reappeared a couple hundred yards above his horse and had to walk back.

Gale spotted tracks both coming and going to and from somewhere. Once, he picked up Two Toes' track, heading down toward the river. He looked away to find Willig and saw he was about a quarter-mile out from the wash, heading north on foot, cutting a large circle. Then he remounted and turned back toward the wash.

They drew ever nearer to the ledges.

The sun was straight overhead and the air was heating up, warm gusts blowing across Gale's cheeks. He thought of the canteen and took a short drink, the water cool in his mouth but disappearing quickly down his throat. He resisted taking a second.

Willig was sitting in the shade of a sandstone overhang as Gale rode up. The trapper's hat was off and he was wiping his neck and face with his bandanna. His face was flushed light-pink.

"I hit some sign," Willig said. "Most of it was crossing the wash, going both ways. I had some good tracks of Two Toes for a ways. He was headed towards the kill or down to the river. Saw smaller tracks, too, probably his bitch's."

"You looked like you had something interesting when you were circling out quite a ways," Gale said.

"I had a pretty fresh pair of tracks. Two Toes and his bitch. They must have been carrying meat."

Willig pulled his bandanna back out of his hip pocket, looked into it, then twirled it around into a triangle and tied it around his neck.

"Their tracks were going north, in a fairly straight line. They could be pretty fresh," Willig said.

Gale took his canteen off the saddle horn and took a long swallow. The good news merited a reward. He untied his bandanna and swabbed his face and forehead, then tied it back around his neck.

Willig grinned. "Getting a mite warm," he said. He took a pull from his canteen. "It looks like our den could be north of us. Two or three sets of tracks were headed in a straight line."

Willig rose and walked over to Sontag. He pulled two sandwiches wrapped in wax paper out of the saddle bag and handed one to Gale. "Good time to eat these and take five," he said.

From under his shady spot, Gale looked out at the land around him. The heat seemed to be rising in waves in the bright whiteness of the sun. The ground seemed to be empty, abandoned of animal activity. It was quiet, except for the occasional rustling of the horses or the sound of his and Willig's voices.

Gale breathed in the deep stillness. This break would be brief. "Looks like we work the next draw north?" he asked.

"Yes," Willig said. "We'll work north when we leave here to the head of the next draw. I'll lead your horse, if you'll get up in the ledges and see what kind of sign there is up there. I'll check along the base. When you get to the next draw, come on down and pick up your horse. I'll be waiting for you."

Gale considered that all these steps Willig was planning out would have taken a whole extra day to accomplish if the trapper were working on his lonesome. The measure of such extra work was the exhaustion the men felt at the end of the day. It made Gale feel glad to be there. He knew his presence was appreciated.

He finished his sandwich, took a last swig of water and slung the canteen over the saddle horn. He pulled his rifle from the scabbard.

"I hope to hell you get to use that," Willig said.

Gale grinned.

"Me too," he said.

Gale looped the rifle sling over his shoulder and started for the first ledge of rimrock. He climbed slowly, weaving his way back and forth between rocks and brush.

Willig watched the younger man with a critical eye. He would have gotten Two Toes eventually; but thank God this college kid knew what he was doing. Willig wasn't sorry they'd teamed up. He'd expected a raw, inexperienced man who knew very little or nothing about coyotes, sheep or tracking. But this kid had shown he knew more than a little bit about denning coyotes. He was good with a horse and nobody had to tell him what to do. He was a good hard worker and Willig still couldn't believe the shot he'd made on that buzzard.

It also was clear to Willig at this moment that Gale was a hunter. The kid was making no noise or sudden moves as he made his way up the ledges slowly, stopping often to check sign and to catch his breath. That showed experience. No good hunter would get caught, lungs heaving, heart thumping, out of breath when he jumped whatever he was stalking.

That's when you shot and missed, and maybe lost the only shot you'd get.

THIRTY-SIX

▲ ▲ ▲

Empty Den

NO REAL PATTERN presented itself from the sign Jack Willig had seen. Some of the tracks were old, some fairly new. Some went south, some the other way.

But there was enough to justify his growing suspicion that there could be a coyote down this particular draw. What's more, he was soon going to find out.

The trapper sat on his horse, watching Brett Gale work his way down from the rimrock that stood at the head of the next draw. When the younger man reached the bottom ledge, he skirted two cedar trees and reached his horse. He picked up Socks' reins and turned to Willig, face shining with sweat.

"I saw some interesting sign right above here, tracks going up and coming down from the first two ledges, like they were coming or going from this draw."

"See any along the ledges?" Willig asked.

"Uh-huh," Gale said. "There were a few scattered ones. There is too much sandstone for tracking in much of the ledge.

Gale had seen tracks along the inside of the ledges, where there was wind-drifted sand, but the tracks were filled with blow sand. He had also found the delicate, wide tracks of a bobcat, and the spread-out tracks of a badger, which described a sort of broad course, claw marks sinking into the sand.

"I spotted bobcat and badger tracks," Gale said. "I found where a badger had dug out a pack rat nest, and I saw Two Toes' track where he was nosing around. What about you?"

"There was some pretty good sign, like yours," Willig said. "Seems like coyotes have been coming and going from down this wash."

Willig dismounted and threw the left stirrup over the saddle. As soon as he loosened the cinch before tightening it, Sontag started to take in air to fill his belly. Willig slapped him in the ribs.

"All right, you old bastard, swell up your belly and I'll cinch it real tight."

Gale laughed. "They get pretty cute, don't they?"

"The hotter the weather, the looser he likes the saddle cinch," Willig said. "This horse can swell up like a toad."

Gale looked down the wash toward the river. It was a little larger than the first one, and at its upper end, just below them, three forks came together to make the main wash.

A small sandstone outcropping jutted about 300 yards down, where over the years large boulders had sloughed off. Something about the formation of the boulders told Gale it would be a good spot for a den.

"I think we should work this one down, one of us on each side," Willig said. "You work down this side and I'll cut across those other two forks and go down the north side. Let's not get too far apart."

Willig mounted up and rode off. Gale moved Socks slowly along the edge of the south fork. Soon, he picked up a coyote track. He climbed down from the saddle and followed the track's general direction, which was coming his way. He backtracked it, and was pleased to see the tracking get better. The gully started to cut out a stream bed and widen, its sandy bottom immediately yielded the clear footprints of Two Toes.

Gale's pulse began to quicken. A bead of sweat broke on his brow and ran down the bridge of his nose to the tip, dangling, tickling. He thumbed it away. All of a sudden he heard a rattle buzz and froze.

Gale searched with his eyes. The rattle shook again, from the direction of a small sage bush. Gale had never been struck by a rattler, but he'd seen plenty of them. He always carried a sharp knife, and he'd use it to cut an "X" on each fang puncture and then squeeze the blood and venom out as much as possible. If he could reach the bite area, he would suck as much as he could get out with his mouth.

There was silence for a long moment, then a rattle again. Gale spotted the snake, coiled under the sagebrush, in the shade. Its forked tongue flicked back and forth. Gale picked up a large flat rock and slammed it down. As the rattler thrashed its head free, Gale stomped hard, hammering his heel on its head, crushing it into the ground.

As he walked back to Socks, he noted his boot prints had been left deep in the loose soil. The ground shimmered. The heat was like a furnace in the wash. Yesterday's buffalo gnat welts burned under the salty sweat on the back of his neck.

Gale wiped his brow with his forearm. At his horse, he took the canteen from the saddle horn and took a cool sip that became a gulp.

Two Toes' tracks were right there for him still. Gale picked them up going down. The narrower tracks of the bitch ran with them. They were several days old. Gale pulled his rifle out of the scabbard. He needed to find Willig.

The trapper was also on foot, leading his horse down the north gully. Its banks were steep; the wash was deeper than the one Gale was in. All Gale could see was Willig's and Sontag's heads and the saddle horn moving slowly down. The earth near the ledges was mostly sand, and the runoffs of snow melt and spring rains had cut fast and deep through the top soil, deepening and widening the gullies with every storm.

A few minutes later, Willig and his horse disappeared from sight. Gale could barely see out of his own wash. He led Socks up the bank and out on the south side. Working along even more slowly, he picked up more coyote tracks in the wash bottom. He tied Socks to a sagebrush and dropped down again. The wash was about eight feet deep now. It seemed all the tracks in it were of Two Toes and his mate.

Gale reached the fork where the middle wash joined the south. He walked up the middle one a ways, but there weren't too many tracks, so he went back to the fork, climbed up the bank and retrieved Socks. He still could see no sign of Willig.

Gale mounted Socks and started down the south bank. With Willig tracking down the draw, he'd stay up on the bank in case they jumped the coyotes. A short distance farther, the wash Willig was in came into Gale's wash, which had now grown to 10 feet deep and very wide. Coyote tracks led up and down it. Gale stepped down. He was walking along its bank when Socks reared his head.

Gale looked up to see Willig, leading Sontag, coming into the main draw. He knelt as Willig approached and stopped directly below. The trapper's face was drawn tight, lined with grimness. When he spoke, the words came faster than usual.

"I think we've got a den down below us somewhere," he said in a loud whisper that belied anticipation. "I've got a pair of morning tracks going up the draw I just came down—Two Toes and his bitch. You see anything?"

"A fair amount of sign going and coming, but no real fresh tracks," Gale said. "I've been watching but seen nothing moving." He mentioned nothing of the snake. It was already erased from his mind.

"We'll tie up our horses and work down," Willig hissed. "You stay on top and I'll keep going down the bottom. Keep as quiet as possible."

Gale's hands were clammy as he tied Socks to the sagebrush near where Willig was tying Sontag. He wondered if the sweat would hinder his shooting aim. He felt they were closing in now. He knew Willig was as excited as he.

Working along the wash—Willig down in its bottom, he up along its edge—Gale picked up a single track or two here or there, but didn't dare follow them. He kept abreast of Willig. He watched intently for any movement down the wash. The wash curved to the south. Just as Gale reached the turn in the bank, Willig held up his hand. Gale halted and waited. With slow-motion caution, Willig rounded the curve where he could see down the wash, and stopped dead still.

He stood there, a statue, for several minutes. Then he looked back at Gale, a finger pointing down the draw. He waved at Gale to move on down. Gale returned the wave. Gale took his rifle off his shoulder. He slipped the safety off. He moved back several steps from the bank and walked forward very quietly.

Gale's eyes trained on Willig, who was moving down the draw with equal stealth. Suddenly, Willig was standing perfectly still again, not moving an inch. His hand raised and pointed to the wash bottom. Gale eased over to the bank's edge. Just below, he saw the den. Feathers, wool and bones littered the wash. Pieces of hide and pup droppings were everywhere. Gale released a slow breath. He waved back to Willig.

The trapper started immediately toward the den. As Gale dropped down into the wash, Willig was already bent over at the mouth. "The bitch has been in the den this morning at least twice," he said, as Gale came up. "Both sets of tracks have been up and down the wash from above."

Gale stared at the tracks below the den. "They've been up and down the wash here, too, and they're fresh tracks."

Willig listened expressionlessly at the mouth of the den, not budging for two minutes. Finally, he stood and shook his head.

"Goddamnit," he said. "A day late and a dollar short."

Gale's jaw dropped. "The den empty?"

"Yep. They've moved to a new den, at least two or three days ago."

Gale kicked a stone in disgust. "How come the fresh tracks of Two Toes and the bitch, then? You said she's been in the den this morning."

Willig was crouching across the draw from the den, absorbed in a new task. "Look," he said, "they've laid a piece of meat down here. See the bloody spot in the sand?"

Gale peered down with interest. Three blow flies had already found it. They were buzzing around on the dark patch. "No question about that being fresh," he said.

His confusion was too much for him to keep quiet about. "How do you figure this out?"

Willig stood and wiped his glistening face and neck with his bandanna. He took off his hat and toweled his forehead. His hair was matted flat.

"I figure they moved the pups to a new den," he said. "This fresh sign is what threw us off." He nodded his head, looking at the litter and the tracks. "Those are pretty big pups."

Gale's face was askance. Willig could detect his consternation.

"Two Toes made a fresh kill last night, or probably this morning," Willig began. "That was fresh meat he and the bitch laid down. I figure this den is between the new den and this morning's kill, that's how come the fresh tracks are here. With the new den and the going and coming from the fresh kill, the coyotes would pass close by here. The bitch, out of curiosity, would check her old den and that's what she's doing here. Two Toes coming with her."

Gale was impressed. Willig really knew his coyotes. There wasn't anybody as good as this trapper, the way he could gather in their moves and habits. It was just something fantastic. But another thought, dormant until now, flashed. How much longer could they try for Two Toes? How many more near-misses could he afford before he had to leave?

There were only so many days he could justify tracking Two Toes, fascinating as it was. It was on his shoulders to determine when he'd have to cut loose and start denning other ranges. He just couldn't give all of Willig's time and attention to Two Toes, to denning this area of range. If there was any rationale he could use to continue this hunt, it was that his boss, Scott Rasmussen, had told Gale to go out and get the problem solved. His boss sure didn't want to hear any more about it.

"We'd better check with Billy to see if he's had a loss when we get back to our trucks," Gale said.

Willig looked up at the sun. "It's later than I thought," he said. "It will be sundown pretty quick. Let's go back to the horses and head for camp."

After they'd taken care of their horses, graining and watering and wiping them down, Willig cooked supper. The smell of the beans and lamb stew made Gale's mouth water.

"It seems to me we might have zeroed in pretty well on the location of Two Toes' den," he said.

"How do you figure?" Willig said.

Gale knew he was being tested, to see what he knew about denning, how well he'd figured out the signs. Fine. He was up to it.

"We sure as hell know he isn't denned south of the old den we found today," Gale said. "The fact that both coyotes were at the old den, checking it out, indicates they were going and coming from the north. That's the direction their fresh tracks went, as far as I could tell. What do you think?"

Willig smiled. "I think you've got it figured out right."

They ate and cleaned the dishes and got ready for bed. They were dog-tired but neither could wait for morning. As they settled into the double bed Willig said, "We want to be in that next draw before dawn. I'd like to find that den before the coyotes return from their morning hunt."

We better find their den tomorrow, Gale thought. He kept the thought to himself.

THIRTY-SEVEN

Showdown

TWO HOURS before daylight, Jack Willig and Brett Gale were already finishing breakfast. Gale was as eager as Willig to get after the work of the day. After Two Toes. "Let's stack the dishes," Willig was saying. "I want to be in that draw just when it's light enough to see. With those big pups, they've got to hunt every day for enough meat to feed them. If we can be in that draw early enough, before the coyotes come back from their hunt, we might catch them coming in."

He paused, then in a wishful tone, added, "I'd give a month's wages to get you a shot at Two Toes."

They buttoned up the camp wagon, loaded their horses into their rigs and headed for Billy Butts' camp.

Like the previous two mornings, the dust was so heavy on the stock driveway that Gale kept well behind Willig's pickup. His head lights bobbed and wove in the inky blackness as he moved slowly up the road.

Willig was talking to Butts as Gale pulled into camp. He could hear the sheepherder's voice talking with Willig, but not see either man. They were disembodied voices, like spirits in the night. He walked in the direction of their sounds.

"Me and my dogs didn't leave the herd at any time yesterday," Butts was saying. "We didn't see or hear a coyote and the dogs sure didn't raise any fuss."

The herder nodded briefly at Gale as he walked into sight, and continued. "The dust is awful heavy when the sheep aren't feeding, just trailing. That damn Two Toes could have slipped up on the rear of the herd, I suppose, but we were at the back end of the herd all the time, except when we went ahead of the sheep to turn them around to graze back toward camp."

Willig spoke up. "I know they made a kill. The meat they were taking back to the pups was still bloody. Their pups are big so they'll be making kills at least every other day to keep their bellies full, and I can't see them passing up your herd to go twice as far to kill from Hogan's herd. They will kill where the sheep are closest and handiest and they sure as hell will be killing sheep, instead of rabbits or prairie dogs. They're a lot easier to get. You might be real careful when you push your herd through those deep gullies. Two Toes has hit you twice, killing sheep in a gully, where he's out of sight."

The trapper turned to Gale. "Let's get going. I don't want to burn up any daylight before we get to that wash."

As they rode north, Gale could see that Willig was checking the North Star to get his bearings. The horses knew the way and moved along at a fast walk. But each time they came to a deep wash, they stopped and the men would have to dismount and lead them along the edge until they found a good spot to go down and cross.

It was just breaking daylight in the east as the horses pulled up at the third draw—the first one north of the old den. Willig looked back the way they'd come. He could just make out the cottonwoods along the river. Glancing west toward the Twist Hills, he decided they were about halfway up from the river.

He climbed down and walked slowly along the edge of the wash. Gale followed. The trapper found a decent point to get the horses down. In the bottom of the wash, he turned to Gale.

"We'll go up the wash bottom together," he said. "If one of us trailing a horse is on top, he can be seen for a long ways. I don't want to warn Two Toes if I can help it."

They moved side by side up the draw. It was now light enough to read sign pretty easy. Gale hit a good track of the bitch, going up. Within a short distance, Two Toes' track joined hers. The coyote had come down off the south side of the draw.

Gale hissed to Willig and pointed down in front of him. Willig nodded and pointed in front of himself. He had tracks, too.

They worked their way up. Gale's set of tracks left the wash, leading up the north bank. He caught up with Willig, whose tracks were going down the other way. A little beyond them as Willig backtracked, the tracks entered the wash from the north bank.

"These tracks are coming and going from the north," Willig said. "Let's go back down a ways and then cross over to the next draw north. I think that's where our den is."

Willig's tone was matter-of-fact. He was all business. Gale, yet again, wondered at the trapper's sense of intuition, how he followed his hunches to save time and speed up the tracking.

At the first good spot they left the wash and mounted up. The morning had brightened and they rode rapidly over the bench to the next draw and dropped down into it quickly, to avoid detection. As soon as they climbed down from their saddles, they were met by a large swarm of black gnats landing on their faces and necks. The men swung their Stetsons, fanning furiously, and hurried up the draw to escape the cloud. They stopped and swabbed their faces and necks with their bandannas.

"Damn those things!" Gale whispered. "I don't need any more of their bites. I've still got a dozen burning welts from the other day. Hey, don't they bother you, Jack?"

"No," Willig replied, stoic as ever. "After all my years outdoors, my face and neck are about like leather. But I'll tell you what, when they get me under my hat band, they sure raise a hive."

The men separated, starting up the draw on opposite sides. It was a wide wash, 30 feet across in some places, and at least 12 feet deep. No one—no animal except for the winged kind—would be able to see them from above.

Willig was quite surprised to find no tracks. But 300 yards on, the men hit sign: fresh tracks of the bitch. She had been going down the wash and up the south bank onto the bench.

Shortly, the men hit Two Toes' tracks, doing the same thing. Another 100 yards and they'd found several more tracks, coming and going in the wash. Willig stopped still and waved Gale over.

"Aren't we close to the den?" Gale whispered.

"It can't be very far away," Willig whispered back. "While I tie up the horses, get your gun and crawl up the bank and get behind that large sagebrush up on top. Stay behind it and see if you can spot anything to the south and west."

He added, "Don't make any noise."

Gale nodded and pulled his Winchester out of the scabbard. Very quietly, he pumped a shell into the chamber and clicked on the safety. He slung the rifle over a shoulder.

Willig watched as Gale carefully climbed up the bank, lowered himself flat on his belly and crawled up to the sagebrush. All the long hours walking in the searing sun over the past few days melted away at a time like this. Careful to keep his head below the top of the brush, he peered through his rifle scope. He painstakingly scanned the bench plateau, moving his head very slowly from west to east and back. He saw not a thing except a low cloud of dust way to the south: Billy Butts' herd.

Gale could feel the tingling coming on, but it was an old feeling for him. He was used to hunting. When he was a kid, he'd get so excited about shooting a deer or elk he'd shake—get "buck fever"—and miss. Ever since, whenever he felt the excitement well up and threaten to flood him, he'd reflexively take a deep breath and instantly calm down. This was just another dose of it, another round. He was going to jump these coyotes just like jumping a pheasant.

Five minutes ticked past. Then 10. Finally, Gale backed down into the draw. "Nothing moving," he whispered to Willig.

The trapper was inwardly content. He liked the way Gale handled himself. This young man knew what he was doing and how to do it right. The Biological Survey could use 10 more just like him, and they wouldn't have any more coyote trouble like this business with Two Toes. But that was a just pipe dream, he knew. Mediocrity always outnumbered quality.

Willig whispered low as before, a faint hush in the stillness of the wash. "We've got a real break. What breeze we have is coming down the draw. We're downwind from the den. I'll spend an hour or two to try and get a shot at the coyotes. Oftentimes, when I've got cover and the wind is right, I've had coyotes come right to me and I've usually gotten one, sometimes both."

He looked silently at Gale for a moment. Then he removed his bandanna and wiped his forehead, face and neck. "It's getting hot," he said.

"Want me to go up again and watch across the bench?" Gale asked.

"Yes," Willig replied. "Those coyotes can't come to the den without you spotting them. If you don't see anything in 20 to 30 minutes, come back down and come up the wash. I'm going up real quietly. If I can find the den and remain unseen, I'll do the same thing till you come up. You know, most guys when they find a den, rush right to it, and unless the bitch is in the den, they don't have a prayer of getting even one of the pair."

"Makes a lot of sense," Gale said.

He started up the bank for his lookout spot at the sagebrush. Scanning through his rifle scope, he panned from the western ledges east to the river. There wasn't a thing moving. The dust cloud from Butts' sheep was farther south and hung not quite so heavy or high. The herd must have reached the feed ground and were slowly grazing now.

Gale studied the rock ledges at the head of the draw they were following. It seemed that from where he was the day before, the lower ledges broke away from the high draw, then swung back to the north. The top was 400 or 500 feet above the bench, dropping down in a series of ledges, each 80 to 100 feet above the next. A giant's staircase.

Gale marveled at the beautiful ribboned strata of the ledges, shading from red to yellow to blue to gray. The colors were a sight, and the wide ledges were spotted as well with cedar trees and squaw berry and buck brush, all interspersed with sage and rabbit brush. Here and there stood clumps of giant rye grass six feet high, untouched by deer or sheep, their long seed stems waving gently in the breeze. God's country. Even if it was hot as hell today.

Gale saw where up near the head of the draw, many large boulders were scattered down the south side for several hundred yards, each a different size, and sitting in clusters. As he moved his scope slowly along, he caught a movement at the edge of his field of vision. Quickly, he focused in. It was an animal moving toward the draw. It was the bitch coyote.

She was some 300 yards away, on the bench, trotting in from the south. She was moving rapidly, and carrying something in her jaws. Gale tingled all over. Carefully, he turned over and looked back toward the draw. Willig was nowhere in sight. He had an urge to slide back down and warn Willig, but stopped himself. He reasoned that the bitch had been hunting with her mate. Two Toes would be out there somewhere, also. Gale couldn't wait to get a look at him.

He rolled back onto his stomach and focused his scope where he'd seen the bitch. She was gone. She must have reached the draw and dropped down in it to her den.

Twice more, Gale scoped the bench from the ledges to the river. No sign of the big coyote. He must have been ahead of his bitch.

Slowly, Gale slid backward and down the bank, then started up the draw after Willig. He found his tracks immediately. Willig was proceeding carefully. There were no deep heel tracks of a man moving rapidly in cowboy boots; he was practically tiptoeing.

Gale forgot how thirsty he was. He wanted to rendezvous with Willig as quickly as possible and plan their approach on the den. But the wash's curvy contours prevented him from hurrying. Over the centuries, the heavy runoff had carved it this way. The water, seeking the path of least resistance as it spilled forth from the ledges directly above, would be turned left and right by the sandstone layers.

Gale approached each curve silently and cautiously, peeking around each before stepping out and continuing. After he'd passed several such bends, he came to a place where Willig had knelt in the sand. From the way the knee prints shifted back and forth, it seemed apparent the trapper had been there several minutes.

The next curve bent at almost a right angle. Gale eased up to it, and when he finally could see completely around spotted Willig at the next curve beyond, some 80 yards away. His hat was off, lying in the sand behind him. He was squatted down behind a sagebrush that was growing right out of the south wall of the wash, near the bend. Willig's attention was rapt on something ahead.

Gale moved forward, conscious of every breath. His mouth was caked with dust and dryness. His tongue stuck to the wall of his cheek. He hugged the south wall with his back, inching along. Puppy tracks and droppings were spread all over the wash's sandy bottom. And then he could hear them: growling and yipping at each other. They were just around the bend in front of Willig's position.

Willig caught the figure of the approaching Gale out of the corner of his eye. He had great peripheral vision, like an Indian. He never missed an antelope or deer, or a man. He gingerly backed away from his sagebrush cover, and kept down on his knees in the sand as Gale pussy-footed up and knelt beside him.

Willig leaned forward and in a whisper so low it was barely audible, said, "The den is about 50 yards around that bend ahead of us. The pups were right here a few minutes ago, but the bitch barked and they barreled around to the den. That's when I moved up here. I got in behind that sagebrush. It's perfect cover. She's feeding them now."

Gale started to whisper, "You see any sign of Two Toes?" but found he had no voice. He dared not clear his throat. Instead, he pantomimed his message, raising two fingers, pointing to his toes and shrugging his shoulders while mouthing the words.

Willig shook his head. "We've got to make a move on the pups," he hissed. "They are so big, some may get away from us."

Gale nodded.

"I'll get back behind that sagebrush where I can watch," Willig said. "You get a rock and throw it right over the bank behind me. With that sharp curve, it will land in the bottom close to the den. With luck, it will spook the pups towards or into the den. If they start, I'll clap my hands, then run around the corner at them. With luck, we can get all the pups in the den, and maybe the bitch. I'll wave at you when I'm ready."

Willig crawled toward the sagebrush at the bend's corner. Gale leaned his rifle against a rock and, hunched over, rooted around the ground until he found a piece of sandstone bigger than his fist. He picked up his rifle in his other hand and moved in close to the bank right behind Willig.

The trapper was still peeking around the sagebrush. Then, he put his hand behind his back and waved. Gale let fly with the rock as far as he could throw it. Seconds passed, and then Willig jumped to his feet and ran around the bend, slapping his hands loudly.

Gale was right behind. He spotted the den but no pup was in sight. Willig was still clapping like crazy. The two men raced forward to the den entrance then stopped, breathing hard from the sprint and excitement.

Gale was first to get his breath back. He cleared his throat and found his voice. "What happened?" he said.

Willig puffed a minute more. "Your rock hit the north bank about halfway up and rattled down," he said. "The bitch was up the bank. She was gone in nothing flat. When I ran around the corner, two of the pups skedaddled into the hole and the rest followed."

Willig sat down heavily at the mouth of the den. Gale spoke up.

"I never did see Two Toes. He had to be with the bitch, bringing the meat back to the pups. He's out there somewhere. I'll get up on top of the bank and see what I can see."

Willig nodded. In his heart, he knew that, once again, the big dog coyote had probably gotten away. Hope evaporated like a puddle in the desert after a rare mid-summer shower.

Gale lay on his stomach on top of the bank, scoping the flat. Presently, he slid back down. Willig had backed across the draw to the north bank.

"I didn't see anything," Gale said, "but a horse could be in that big boulder pile out there and you wouldn't see it."

"Yeah, I can just see the boulders from here," Willig said. "The bitch probably ducked into them when she flew out of here."

"You want to keep the pups in the den while I go back and bring the horses up? We need the denning tools," Gale said. He didn't add that he could use a drink of water. It went without saying in this blasted oven they were baking in.

"Yes," Willig said. "Them pups are big enough to pop out of that hole any time."

Gale shouldered his Winchester and headed down the wash. Willig sat on the dirt mound in front of the hole.

A half-hour passed before Gale reappeared with the horses, riding Socks and leading Sontag. He tied the horses to a large sagebrush that stood 20 feet down from the hole, well stripped of bark and leaves, as high up as the pups could jump.

Willig untied the saddle bag holding the denning rod and screwed the sections together. Gale crawled halfway into the den, listening for the pups. They didn't make a sound—no whining or whimpering—but he could hear their soft breathing.

He backed out. "They're in there all right."

Willig handed him the denning rod. The burr head was screwed on. It only took 10 minutes to clean out the den. As Gale was sitting on his knees breaking down the den rod, a big swarm of buffalo gnats—attracted by the sweat and blood—flew around his head, especially around his eyes, ears and neck. Their bites felt like a hot wire.

Gale grabbed his hat and swiped violently at them with one hand while wiping his face and neck with the other. He was about to cuss when he looked back for Willig, whom he expected to be scalping the pups. The trapper had left the mouth of the den.

Gale cupped his hand over his eyes and looked around. There was the trapper, backed up against the north bank of the wash, standing frozen as a petrified tree, staring above the south bank.

Gale jumped to his feet. Willig didn't move an inch but Gale could tell he was mouthing something. He eased over.

In a low voice, Willig was muttering, "Jumping Jesus Kee-riste. It's Two Toes—it's Two Toes—it's Two Toes."

Slowly, Gale turned his head. The big coyote was sitting atop a large boulder 150 yards away, ears cocked forward, looking intently at the two men.

Gale's heart leaped into his throat. His legs felt weak as he softly walked back to Socks and eased his rifle from its scabbard. He knew this was all for naught. No coyote would sit there that long. Especially Two Toes.

Gale walked back toward Willig, slipping the safety off. The trapper still hadn't budged. His face was flushed beet-red, as if from holding his breath. Veins stood out on his neck and forehead like swollen blue cords, and the sides of his eyes bulged. Through gritted jaws and teeth, he was mumbling beneath his breath:

"Kill him. Kill him."

Gale resisted making a fast move. He turned slowly and gazed up at the boulders. To his shock, Two Toes hadn't budged. It was a face-off: two mortal adversaries trying to stare the other down. An entire drama unfolding in a matter of seconds.

Gale slowly raised the gun to his shoulder. He dropped his eye along the scope. It was unreal. He couldn't believe the coyote had sat there this long. Through the scope, his eye two inches back of it in preparation for the recoil, Gale could see the coyote's fur, all tan, except for his chest. It was white, the long hairs stirring in the breeze.

Gale was amazed at his inner calm; no rapid heartbeat, no chest heaving from shortness of breath. It was all like a dream. As if everything from the past five days had led up to this moment.

The cross-hairs of the scope held dead still on the coyote's chest. Gale slowly and carefully took the slack out of the trigger, until there was no give. There was perfect pressure.

He squeezed off the shot. It was at that very instant that the sharp pain stung his eyelid.

Gale flinched from the bite of the gnat. The gun roared. It bucked upward from the recoil, knocking his shoulder back. Instantly, he had it back focused on the boulder. But through the scope, the rock was empty.

"You got him, you got him!"

Willig yelled as he ran across the bottom of the wash and scrambled up the bank like a boy. As he raced toward the boulder, he shouted, "You knocked him clear off the rock. You got him, you got him!"

Willig ran around behind the big rock and came to a dead stop. A few seconds later, he was darting madly behind the nearby rocks.

From rock to rock he went.

Gale knew the slap of the 30.06 soft-nosed bullet would have knocked the coyote flat off the boulder. But he'd flinched. It was almost impossible, timingwise, but he'd been stung right at the moment he'd squeezed the trigger off.

He walked behind the rocks and on the downhill side behind the pile. He picked up Two Toes' fresh tracks, dug deep into the soft sandy soil where he'd been running hard.

Gale followed the tracks for 300 feet. There was no sign of a staggering, wounded coyote. No hair, no spots of blood. Just tracks, running hard toward the sandstone ledges to the south.

Gale rubbed the welt on his right eyelid. Heavy and irritated, it was swelling shut. The sun above beat down mercilessly. Sweat ran over Gale's face, making the bite sting that much more.

It was burning hot, hotter than he'd even realized it was. Too hot.

Two Toes was gone. Untouched, unhurt. Gone. It had been a clean miss.

Epilogue

JACK WILLIG searched frantically among the boulders for Two Toes. Later, he just stared as Brett Gale explained about the gnat bite, the flinch, the missed shot. Willig's face was drawn, gaunt, expressionless.

Neither spoke as they scalped the seven big pups. At Billy Butts' camp, Willig said they'd taken Two Toes' den and he believed there would be no more sheep losses. Butts asked about Gale's eye, which was swollen nearly shut.

The next day, Willig moved his camp wagon to Ute Springs. Gale stayed on another week. They took two more dens, getting both bitch coyotes and one of the dogs. Gale did not miss another shot.

When the week was up, he joined up with Abe Evans to den in Iron County. For the rest of his years with the U.S. Biological Survey and its successor, the U.S. Fish & Wildlife Service, and in his varied careers that followed, he never forgot his adventure with Two Toes.

The coyote kills in Uintah Basin did slow down that spring and summer. Several of the sheepmen told Willig what a good job he was doing. But Ty Bingham did not see Willig again. As soon as denning season was over, Willig moved to south-central Utah and trapped for the sheepmen in Sanpete and Sevier counties. They greeted him with open arms. They knew they were getting one of the best trappers in the state.

Bingham moved his sheep into Ashley Valley for the shearing, lambing and docking, and then Billy Butts headed the herd out for the summer range in the Uintah Mountains. Bingham didn't know it then, but his troubles were soon to be over. That December, the United States entered World War II. The government placed a big emphasis on sheep and wool for the war effort, and the campaign against the coyotes escalated. Bingham finally paid off his debts and made his operation solvent and healthy. His family is still sheep ranching, his sons running the outfit.

Billy Butts stayed on another 12 years herding for Bingham. He helped break in his boss's sons in the handling of sheep. One day, when he felt he was getting too old, he left, perhaps back to Texas, and wasn't heard from again. But his name endured in the lore of the Bingham clan and the sheepmen of the Uintah Basin, taking on legendary status and serving as a standard of a good herder. "He sure ain't no Billy Butts" was a phrase used to describe a mediocre herder. "He's almost a Billy Butts" was the highest compliment a herder could receive.

Today, the herds in the Uintah Basin number perhaps 400,000 sheep, instead of the 1 million-plus that roamed the range before and during World War II. Synthetic threads took away much of the demand for wool; yet, in the cyclical nature of the business, wool eventually rebounded. Prices were up again by the time of this writing.

The Uintah Basin still has lots of coyotes, too, including on Bow Knot Bend (now called Horseshoe Bend) on the Green River. Among them are surely Two Toes' descendants.

The summer and fall of 1941, there were many reports of people spotting Two Toes, but none were ever confirmed. An Indian farmer claimed he'd found a good print of the famous right-front paw in the mud of an irrigation ditch along the Duchesne River. The most accepted story was from the herder who worked for Chance. His sheep were heading for the winter range in late October, when there was an early snowfall on Deadman Bench. The herder said he'd found a clear footprint in the fresh snow.

But no one ever collected Bingham's bounty of $100 for the coyote's famous foot. No one ever claimed to have shot or trapped him. Two Toes was never seen again.

GLOSSARY

Basin - An area of desert or semi-desert land containing many arid water courses and surrounded by low mountains and hills.

Bellwether - A castrated ram, usually black, with a bell around its neck, as a lead for the sheep.

Bench land - Dry, mesa-like flats bordered by dry washes or gullies.

Buffalo gnat - A small, black, minute flying insect whose bites are stinging and create sore welts.

Bummer - A lamb that has lost its mother or which the ewe refuses to let suckle.

CCC camps - The Civilian Conservation Corps was made up of young, inexperienced men during the Great Depression. The federal CCC performed conservation work across the United States, building roads, dams, parks and campgrounds and performing reforestation and reseeding on forestry and grazing lands.

Dock - Docking takes place every spring after ewes have finished dropping lambs. All the lambs' tails are bobbed and the males are castrated. Sometimes they are branded or ear-tagged for identification.

Draw - A water course in the desert, dry except for heavy rains or snow run-off.

Greasewood - A sagebrush-like desert shrub, extremely drought-resistant, found in poor soil. Its leaves are inedible.

Ground-hitch - Dropping a horse's reins on the ground. This is done with horses trained to stand still with reins on the ground.

Gully - A small draw.

Jackrabbit - A large hare with very long ears and hind legs, found in the western deserts and dry lands.

Magpie - A black-and-white scavenger bird that feeds mostly on carcasses of animals, and sometimes on chicks and eggs of other birds.

Mesa - High, flat plateaus bordered by desert or canyons.

Prairie dog - Small rodents, 6 to 8 inches long, living in clustered mounds called "towns" in prairie or desert.

Rambouillet - A brand of sheep noted for hardiness and good wool.

Sage hen - A grouse found in flocks in semi-arid country. A game bird that makes for good eating.

Scotch Shelty - A mid-sized, bobtailed collie excellent as a herd dog.

Shadscale - A small, low-growing desert brush that is a high-protein source of food for grazing mammals.

U.S. Biological Survey - A federal government agency in the Department of the Interior.

U.S. Fish & Wildlife Service - The U.S. Biological Survey and the Bureau of Fisheries were combined into this service in the 1940s.

Wash - The same as a draw—drainage in arid country for storm and snow run-off.

Wolfer - An early trapper who hunted wolves for fur and bounty.

THE AUTHOR

▲ ▲ ▲

Preston Hale was born and raised in Boise, Idaho where his father was land commissioner for Idaho. After college he found seasonal work as a foreman in the Civilian Conservation Corps in eastern Utah, which led to a fifteen year career as a trapper, supervisor and biologist for the U.S. Fish and Wildlife Service. In 1938 he married Norma White of Vernal, Utah, and after many moves in three states his family of four came to Reno where he was the agency's assistant supervisor for Nevada. A diehard westerner, he resigned the agency when asked to move to the east, and began a career in commercial real estate.

Through this change in careers Preston Hale became one of Nevada's most successful and prominent citizens, playing an important role in the development of the state in the second half of the 20th century. He has never lost his love for the outdoors and though he no longer hunts, is an avid fly fisherman. An eagle scout himself, he has been active in Reno area scouting along with Little League baseball and other civic activities. He has been a member of the Reno Redevelopment Commission, is a founding member of Western Industrial Nevada, and has served as a director on the boards of Nevada National Bank and Security Pacific Bank. His interest in reading and book collecting led him to the boards of the Friends of the University of Nevada, Reno Library and Friends of the University of Nevada Press. He has received many honors and in 1990 was named a Distinguished Nevadan by the University of Nevada's Board of Regents.

Now 84 and semi-retired, Preston Hale still remains active in his real estate development firm and makes yearly fishing trips to his beloved Utah and Idaho. He began *Two Toes* when friends and colleagues urged him to write about his experiences with this wily coyote. This is his first book.

THE ILLUSTRATOR

▲ ▲ ▲

Pam McAdoo is a ten-year resident of Truckee, California where she lives with her husband and two children. She grew up on farmland outside New York City and studied drawing, painting and sculpture in Florence, Italy before earning a degree in fine arts at Antioch College. She worked as a carpenter for two years in Nepal, ran her own design studios in Bishop, Calif. and Paris, and earned a master's of arts degree in illustration at Syracuse University.

Pam teaches art to students of all ages. She also has danced professionally, been an art docent in public schools, pens a column for the *Sierra Sun* newspaper, and is writing and illustrating two children's books. She has also been active with the Friends of the Truckee Library.

Influenced by the Japanese aesthetic, Pam strives to portray extreme beauty in the simplest forms and images. He currently works in pencil, oils, and watercolor.

COLOPHON

▲ ▲ ▲

Designed and printed by Bob Blesse at the Black Rock Press, University of Nevada, Reno. The typefaces used are Berkeley Old Style, a modern version of Frederic Goudy's University of California Old Style, and Kinesis, an Adobe multiple master font designed by Mark Jamra. This book was designed using Adobe Pagemaker and Photoshop. Printed and bound by Braun Brumfield, Inc. of Ann Arbor, Michigan.

This was our first clothbound trade book and we have learned a great deal along the way.

Special thanks to Pam McAdoo for her outstanding illustrations and great watercolor cover art. Thanks also to Paul Starrs who interrupted a busy schedule to create two wonderful maps.

Special gratitude to the John Ben Snow Trust who gave the Black Rock Press a very generous grant this year, enabling us to produce books such as *Two Toes*.